THE WINEMAKER'S DINNER

Appetizers

Dr. Ivan Rusilko & Everly Drummond

OMNIFIC PUBLISHING
DALLAS

Omnific Publishing
P.O. Box 793871, Dallas, TX 75379
www.omnificpublishing.com

First Omnific eBook edition, July 2012
First Omnific trade paperback edition, July 2012

The characters and events in this book are fictitious.
Any similarity to real persons, living or dead,
is coincidental and not intended by the author.

Library of Congress Cataloguing-in-Publication Data

Rusilko, Dr. Ivan; Drummond, Everly.
  The Winemaker's Dinner: Appetizers / Dr. Ivan Rusilko & Everly Drummond – 1st ed.
  ISBN 978-1-936305-70-4
  1. Contemporary Romance — Fiction. 2. Erotica — Fiction.
  3. Miami — Fiction. 4. Dr. Ivan Rusilko — Fiction. I. Title

10 9 8 7 6 5 4 3 2 1

Cover Design by Micha Stone and Amy Brokaw
Interior Book Design by Coreen Montagna
Photography by John Conroy (JohnConroyPhotography.com)
Cover Model: Dr. Ivan Rusilko and Adrianne Martinez

Printed in the United States of America

Chapter 1

"Something"

A cool breeze caressed Jaden's body, and the scent of butterfly weed and columbine infused the late-summer air around her. Brilliant purple and orange hues colored the evening sky as she stepped onto the makeshift wooden dance floor that served as the centerpiece for this evening's event at the Florida Wine Festival.

Jaden wrapped her sheer, black shawl tightly around her shoulders and over the open back of her slim, red cocktail dress. She surveyed the scene, looking for table number nine and trying her best not to seem lost.

In the garden of the private estate on the edge of the ocean, throngs of guests had started to arrive. An army of waiters and waitresses dressed in blue scurried around like clockwork soldiers carrying silver trays brimming with glasses of wine, while another army, dressed in green and laden with trays of hors d'oeuvres, followed suit.

Tables set with fine bone China and sterling silver surrounded the dance floor, and beyond them were the well-manicured lawns and shrubbery of the opulent estate—the home of a rich philanthropist couple who were thought to hold a large stake in the premier wine of this year's festival, Mollydooker, as well as being connected with some of Florida's most elite.

As the sun slowly sank beneath the horizon, the vibrant purples and oranges of the evening sky faded into muted shades of gray and black. Scanning the crowd once again, Jaden finally recognized a short brunette in a blue dress. *Thank God.*

Tasha was Jaden's roommate, lifelong friend since they were girls together in Colorado, and only ally in the mob of wine enthusiasts clamoring for a glass of this year's premium blend. Tasha waved from where she stood on the other side of the tent. Beginning the voyage to meet her, Jaden pushed through the crowd clustered at the bar. She made her way along the edge of the near-vacant dance floor, mindful of her formfitting dress with every step.

Jaden could feel the eyes of more than one man following her as she sauntered by. She smiled. It had been a while since she'd enjoyed the calloused touch of a man, and Jaden was determined to turn heads this evening. *Just as long as they're not married,* she thought, sneaking a sideways glance and sighing. Most of the prime real estate at this dinner wore telltale wedding bands.

The Winemaker's Dinner was the hottest ticketed event of this year's Florida Wine Festival, and they'd landed it smack in the middle of Labor Day weekend. Celebrity chefs, world-renowned sommeliers, and politicians were among the guests, and it was pure luck that Jaden had managed to be on the guest list as well. Her new boss, Geoff, owner of a prestigious restaurant in Miami Beach, had come down with the flu and insisted his head chef take his place and network in his stead. Coincidentally, the event fell on Jaden's birthday, which was why she'd been adamant that Tasha accompany her. It had been a tradition since their midteens that they spend birthdays together.

A waiter in a crisp white shirt passed by in a blur, and with a quick flick of her hands, Jaden secured two glasses of the red wine before joining Tasha at their table.

"Jesus, it's a stampede out there," Tasha noted, pulling out the chair beside her. "These people are vultures."

"Well-dressed vultures at least," Jaden replied. "Wait until after dinner. I bet that's when the real fun starts."

"Why did you drag me along, anyway? I could be at home on the sofa with a pepperoni pizza, catching up on my TV."

"Yeah, like you'd pass on a chance to drink wine and ogle VIPs," Jaden scoffed. "Besides, it's my birthday. You wouldn't really make me come here by myself, would you?"

"I knew you'd throw that in my face." Tasha's delicate features contorted in mock surprise. Then she smiled as she reached into her purse. She pulled out a small box wrapped in gold foil and placed it on the table in front of her friend. "Happy birthday."

"Tasha, I told you not to buy me anything," Jaden murmured.

Tasha had been keeping close watch on her finances. The Miami real estate market had slowed to a crawl in the last few months, and making enough sales to keep herself afloat was next to impossible right now. Jaden had implemented a no-gifts rule this year — or at least she thought she had.

Tasha had no doubt gone to great lengths to get something for her, and Jaden blushed as she picked up the small package. She peeled back the wrapping paper and crumpled it into a ball, tossing it on the table in front of her. Slowly, she opened the lid of the black satin box. Inside, buried beneath a layer of tissue paper, Jaden found a delicate silver chain with a silver frying pan charm dangling from it.

"It's an anklet," Tasha explained. "I know you're not supposed to wear jewelry to work, but I figured you could get away with this."

"I love it," Jaden said with a smile. Removing the chain from the box, she unclasped it and placed it around her ankle. "It matches my dress."

"It's not much, but — "

Thankfully a waiter chose that exact moment to appear at their table and interrupt the conversation, because Jaden knew precisely what Tasha was going to say: "It's not much, but it's all I could afford right now." She knew her friend was struggling, but there was no need to announce it to the rest of their table, which was beginning to fill up.

Wordlessly, the waiter placed six glasses of wine on the table as a chime began to sound. When he'd finished he retreated into the sea of people now making their way from the bar to their assigned seats.

"I hope they serve dinner soon. I'm starving," Jaden said, changing the subject. She tried to look nonchalant as she scanned the crowded garden.

Her gaze drifted to the bar where a few people still remained, wine glasses in hand, and suddenly she noticed him. Standing beside a small stage at the front of the dance floor was the most stunning man she'd ever seen: tousled brown hair — the color of aged mahogany — brushed the collar of the crisp, white dress shirt that peeked out from the jacket of his perfectly tailored suit. The setting sun cast a luminous glow, streaking his hair with dazzling flecks of gold and bronze. His well-defined jaw bore what looked to be at least a day of stubble, and a pair of deep-set eyes, brilliant and full of life, now stared back at her.

Blushing, Jaden quickly turned to face her dinner companions and felt Tasha watching her. "What?" She shrugged innocently. "He's cute."

"Damn right he is. Go talk to him!" Tasha laughed and passed Jaden another glass of wine.

"Yeah, right," Jaden responded. A guy like that would never give her the time of day.

"Drink up, girl! It's your birthday, and the night is young." Tasha encouraged her with a smile.

Conceding defeat, Jaden sipped from the glass and sat back in her chair, allowing her eyes to once again fall upon the spectacular sight at the opposite end of the tent. She couldn't help but notice how the designer suit hugged his muscular chest. A hundred bucks said his body was even more magnificent than the rest of him, and Jaden found herself imagining what was hidden beneath all those layers of fabric. She wasn't usually forward with men, but if ever one so fine as this approached her, there'd be no holding back. A blush reddened her cheeks and warmth pooled in the bottom of her belly, quickly spreading to her limbs and leaving a trail of fire in its wake. Certain the wine was going to her head, Jaden brushed aside her lustful thoughts and focused on the lively conversation around her.

"Your friend tells us it's your birthday," a stout lady sitting in the chair to Jaden's right announced. A large hat festooned with colorful feathers sat atop a mass of graying curls, and a royal blue evening gown draped her abundant form. The woman looked a bit like a distressed peacock.

Slightly taken aback by the woman's boisterous voice, Jaden stammered her response, "Yes, ma'am. I turn twenty-six today."

"Oh, to be young and carefree. I remember when I was twenty-six…"

Jaden cast a sidelong glance at Tasha and chuckled as the older woman launched into a detailed description of her younger years. Jaden took note of the relieved look on the face of the woman's male companion, her husband most likely. He seemed thankful his wife had someone else to talk to, relieving him for a few moments from the constant chatter.

When the waiter returned, delivering plates of Waldorf salad that resembled miniature works of art, Jaden was once again glad for the interruption. Sensing it was going to be a long dinner—and an even longer evening—she quietly asked him to bring another bottle of wine. With the simple wave of his hand a waitress appeared and refilled Jaden's glass, leaving the bottle for the table to share.

Tasha jabbed Jaden in the arm and pointed to the front of the dance floor where six tables sat apart from the rest, three on either side of the stage. "What's with those tables?"

"That's the VIP section," Jaden said. "And the table on the far left, beside the bar, is the chef's table. Only the bigwigs sit there, and they must pay quite a bit for it. The cost of a *regular* ticket to this event is fifteen-hundred dollars."

"Well, your Mr. Oh So Sexy must have connections or some serious cash," Tasha reported, "because he has one of the best seats in the house."

Jaden snapped to attention and trained her eyes to the spot where Tasha was pointing. Any remote hopes of finding a way to meet this man vanished. The people at those VIP tables were celebrities, politicians, and others with very large bank accounts—far above her social status.

"I wonder what he does for a living," Tasha mused, still intrigued by the group of people sitting at the front of the tent. "He must be an athlete or something, because guys who look like that don't rely on their intelligence, if you know what I mean."

Ignoring her roommate's obsession with celebrities and stereotypes, Jaden picked up her fork and looked for a way in to her salad. She must have lost herself for a moment, trying to figure out what the chef had done, because the next thing she knew Tasha had elbowed her in the arm.

"This is my roommate," Tasha said, a little too enthusiastically, as she introduced the sexy latecomer now standing before them.

"Hmm," Jaden mumbled around a mouthful of apple. She wiped her mouth and tuned back in. Smiling politely, she shook his outstretched hand. "I'm sorry, what was your name?"

"Michael," he replied with a smile. "Michael Cervone. And you are?"

"I'm Jaden Thorne. Pleased to meet you."

"I know that name from somewhere…" After a moment, he asked, "Aren't you the head chef at Bianca in Miami Beach?"

"Yes, I am," Jaden admitted, embarrassed again that Geoff had submitted a press release to the local papers, which resulted in more than a little fanfare.

"I ate there last week. That place is phenomenal. Well done." Michael pulled out a chair and sat down.

Jaden looked at Tasha and noticed the smile plastered across her friend's face, making it obvious she was in awe of the man now sitting with them. And why shouldn't she be? Curly golden-blond hair, which seemed lightened by the sun, hung loosely around his face, and brilliant aqua blue eyes accentuated his handsome features—not to mention the fact that there seemed to be a smoking hot body under his suit.

Jaden's attention might have been piqued if she hadn't already focused on the man at the front of the tent, but she could certainly give her shy roommate a nudge in the right direction.

Jaden dove right in. "So Michael, what do you do for a living?"

"I'm a mortgage specialist."

"Really?" Jaden gushed. "What a coincidence! Tasha is a real estate agent."

The waiter reappeared with another carefully constructed salad and placed it in front of Michael. With a polite bow the server disappeared, only to return a minute later with two more bottles of wine.

Jaden was beginning to feel the effect of the wine she'd already consumed, but even though she was technically here on business, it was also her birthday. Picking up one of the new bottles, she poured three glasses, passed one to Michael, and raised hers in the air. "Here's to a lovely evening with friends, old and new."

"Cheers!" said Michael and Tasha in unison, followed by the clinking of glass on glass.

Jaden sat back in her chair and watched as Michael and Tasha's friendly banter turned to flirting. She smiled, glad Tasha was finally focused on something other than her lack of sales. The main course—grilled tuna beautifully arranged with couscous and fresh vegetables—arrived, and Jaden sighed as a hint of lime and fresh mint danced across her palate with the first bite. She made a mental note to try to mimic this dish at the restaurant. Geoff would no doubt be pleased if she showed up for work on Monday morning with fresh ideas for an amazing entree.

The occasional note drifted through the air as musicians took to the stage and tuned their instruments while the wait staff served dessert: a mango sorbet flower with white chocolate wafers. People began to mingle as they enjoyed the sweetness, and within minutes, the lively sounds of Frank Sinatra filled the tent. By the time the last of the plates were cleared away, the dance floor had filled.

Michael stood and came around to where Tasha sat. Offering her his hand, he asked, "May I have this dance?"

Tasha looked from Michael to Jaden, and then back to Michael with a stunned look on her face. "I'd love to, but it's Jaden's birthday."

Disappointment and embarrassment flashed across his face. Jaden couldn't believe that after spending the past hour flirting with the guy, Tasha was actually turning him down.

"Are you kidding me?" she blurted. "You'd best be getting out on that dance floor."

"It's your birthday, and I'd feel bad leaving you alone," Tasha insisted, but the eager look on her face betrayed the tone of her voice.

"Go have fun. I have all the company I need right here." Jaden picked up a full bottle of wine and dangled it in the air, sloshing a few crimson droplets on the white tablecloth.

Without a backward glance, the couple disappeared into the throngs of people that now crowded the dance floor, their bodies swaying in time to the music. Jaden knew she would regret it in the morning, but she poured herself another glass of wine. Turning in her seat, she faced the dancing and noticed that the VIP tables had been moved out of the way. Where Mr. Oh So Sexy had been just moments ago, a baby grand now sat beside the stage.

Trying to appear casual, Jaden scanned the room, her eyes coming to rest on a group of men just outside the tent. Among them was the man she'd been watching all night. Maybe it was the wine, or perhaps the softness of the moonlight, which cast an iridescent glow around him, but impossibly, he looked even more spectacular than he had earlier in the evening.

A plume of smoke lingered for a moment in the air above them as the men took turns lighting their cigars, but the smoke was soon carried off by the breeze from the ocean, only one hundred yards away. There was something about the way he held his cigar in one hand, his wine in the other, that made him look regal, dashing, like a real Prince Charming.

Jaden took a deep, cleansing breath, throwing caution to the wind and preparing to march over and introduce herself, but as she stood, a woman in a short, black dress, who was dripping with sex appeal, strolled up beside him. She leaned against him as she whispered in his ear. His roaring laughter echoed in the cool night air, and the woman now dangling from his arm was all the deterrent Jaden needed to abandon any intention of introducing herself.

Placing her empty wine glass on the table, Jaden steadied herself with the chair beside her and stood. Dizziness overtook her as the wine rushed to her head, and she grasped the edge of the table for support. When she was certain her lightheadedness had passed, she retrieved her purse from the back of the chair and went in search of the ladies' room.

CHAPTER 2

"The Way You Look Tonight"

A portion of the first floor of the estate was open for the party. A coat check, parlor, and washrooms were accessible to guests, and a group of women now formed a line in the hallway, waiting their turn to use the restroom. The beauty of the gardens and grounds was nothing compared to the grandeur of the house itself. Fine marble covered the floors, majestic frescos adorned the ceilings, and a large spiral staircase ornamented the main foyer of the mansion. Although Jaden had never been to Italy, she suspected that this might be what the interior of the Vatican looked like. Taking her place in line, Jaden awaited her turn.

A few minutes later, she held a clean cloth from the stack on the counter beneath the cold water before placing it against her flushed neck. She sighed as the chill on her heated flesh helped to focus her disjointed thoughts. She was furious with herself for having even considered trying to attract the attention of a guy like *him*. Jaden gave herself a stern look in the mirror and tossed the washcloth into the basket before nearly stumbling out of the bathroom. She steadied herself and returned to the fresh air of the outdoors.

Jaden followed a footpath that led from the mansion and wound through the main garden. Stars shone like tiny diamonds in the inky sky, and the sound of flowing water entranced her. She sought the source of the liquid music and, hidden behind a row of hedges, found an extravagant fountain among a paradise of lush tropical flowers and exotic greenery in the center of a lawn. The sleek contours of the basin glimmered in the moonlight.

Kicking off her heels, Jaden walked across the grass, giggling as the prickly blades tickled her feet. Leaning over to caress the ledge of the enormous fountain, her fingers trailed along the cool, black marble. A light mist floated through the air and covered her skin as she watched the water cascade from a small spout, creating abstract patterns in the pool below.

She peeked over her shoulder to make sure no one was watching before taking a seat on the ledge. The temptation to soak her feet was too powerful to ignore. Balancing herself on the edge, she swung around and submerged them beneath the rippling surface. Cold water splashed against her legs, and she tilted her head back, closing her eyes and listening intently to the cacophony of sounds around her, letting them quiet the cacophony of wine-soaked thoughts still swirling in her mind. Just then a tantalizing scent floated by on the breeze. *Mmmm…*Jaden thought, her mind beginning to work. A hint of cigar and something deliciously male…

"Excuse me, Miss. Are these your shoes?" A deep voice echoed in the night air.

Jaden's eyes whipped open, and she spun around, almost losing her balance and toppling head first into the fountain. Standing just a few yards behind her was Mr. Oh So Sexy, the gorgeous man she'd been eyeing all night — and evidently the source of that amazing smell. "Yes?" she replied with a quavering voice.

"I wouldn't leave these lying around if I were you." Dangling from the tip of his finger were her black Manolo Blahnik slingbacks. With slow, deliberate steps, he sauntered over to join her on the ledge of the fountain.

Jaden's breath hitched in her throat as she became aware of the proximity of their bodies. She could feel the heat radiating from him. It warmed the bare skin of her arm. That scent of man and cologne and fine cigars clung to his jacket and became more and more overwhelming as he approached. Jaden savored every moment of it, inhaling deeply and breathing him in. Goose bumps rose on her forearms with the feeling of a million tiny pinpricks, and she shivered.

Mistaking her excitement for chill, he removed his jacket and wrapped it tightly around her trembling frame. His fingers brushed her bare shoulder as he pulled it around her and fastened two of the buttons.

"Thank you," Jaden whispered.

In the distance, partygoers reveled and danced, but the only sound Jaden heard was the frantic beating of her heart. She gripped the ledge of the fountain, her breathing erratic as the moonlight reflected in his eyes. Up close, his brown eyes looked like smooth chocolate on a hot summer's day. Jaden imagined diving into their cocoa depths.

"Are you still cold?" he asked. Raising his hand to straighten the lapel of his jacket, he brushed aside a loose tendril of jet black hair that had sprung free from her jewel-encrusted clip.

"I'm fine," Jaden replied, but her mind was unable to make sense of what was happening. "Why are you here?"

"I'm here on business. Networking," he answered matter-of-factly.

"That's not what I meant." Jaden shook her head. "Why are you here…now…with me?"

He offered a warm smile and shrugged his broad shoulders. "I saw you wander off in this direction, and when you didn't return, I started to get worried."

"You were watching me?"

"No," he corrected her with a hint of amusement. "I was watching you watch me. There's a difference."

"Oh," was all Jaden could manage. She looked away, embarrassed at having been caught in the act.

Jaden could feel his fingers trace the faint line of her cheekbone, and she turned to see him smile when she shivered in response to his touch.

"A man would have to be blind not to notice when a beautiful woman like you looks his way." He cupped her cheek in the palm of his hand.

Jaden knew she should pull away, demand that he release her, but the desire she felt for this stranger kept her frozen in place. Every instinct in her body screamed at her to run away before she could do or say something she'd regret when the haze of the wine finally lifted. But despite the nagging impulse to flee, she shifted closer to him on the ledge.

She leaned in, her eyes fluttering shut as the pad of his thumb caressed her cheek with smooth, unhurried strokes. Her breathing ceased as she felt his lips gently brush the sensitive skin beneath her ear. His raw, masculine scent once again overwhelmed her, and her body quivered in response.

His hand left her cheek and wound possessively around her back, trailing down the length of her spine and dipping beneath his jacket to trace seam of her panties through the fabric of her dress. He pulled her closer, pressing their bodies tightly together, and placed a line of heated kisses along the nape of her neck.

Suddenly bold, Jaden grabbed a fistful of his hair and pulled his head back. Their eyes locked in a lustful stare. A low, thunderous groan escaped him, and his lips parted as she crushed her mouth to his. The smoky, sweet essence of cigars and cognac still lingered on his lips, and the taste of him flooded her mouth.

He returned the intensity of her kiss, and their caresses grew less and less restrained. His warm hands roamed freely over her body beneath his jacket, and he pressed against her, his tailored pants doing very little to disguise his growing enthusiasm. After a few moments he pulled away, breathing heavily. "Why don't we go somewhere a bit more private?" he suggested, his voice hoarse.

"I…" Jaden tried to think through the haze of lust consuming her. "I don't even know your name."

"Ivan," he said fiercely, still breathing hard.

"I'm sorry, I can't," Jaden whispered, her voice thick with regret. Her mind flashed back to the woman in the slinky black dress who, less than an hour ago, had clung to him like wet towel.

"Why can't you?" Ivan asked, almost pleading. "Is something wrong?"

Jaden slid back on the ledge, determined to put some distance between them. She needed a minute to think, a minute to clear her thoughts before she made any rash decisions. Her body longed for the feel of his hands again, but her mind kept drifting to the woman in the black dress.

"You should go back to the party, Ivan. Your girlfriend is probably waiting for you."

"What girlfriend? What are you talking about?" His confusion was evident.

"The blond woman who couldn't keep her hands off you?"

"Who — the blonde with me earlier?" He laughed. "She's not my girlfriend. She's a business acquaintance."

"That's not what it looked like," Jaden scoffed.

"Are you jealous?" Ivan smiled, looking intrigued.

"Why would I be jealous? I don't even know you," Jaden said indignantly. The jacket around her suddenly felt constricting, and she struggled to free her arms.

"Let me help you." Ivan unfastened the buttons and removed the jacket, laying it neatly across his lap. He looked toward the party in the distance. When he spoke, his voice was soft and sincere. "It's funny how a feeling can take a few seconds or a few years to surface. When I first saw you, I knew there was something there, something I couldn't put my finger on. It drove me wild." He ran a hand through this thick brown hair, smoothing the mess her recent passion had made. "Whether you want to deny it or embrace it, the choice is yours. But I know you felt it too. I could tell when you kissed me." He looked up and smiled.

"Ivan, I —" A roar from the crowd echoed loudly through the garden. Evidently the band had transitioned into the perfect song. Jaden smiled as the familiar tune drifted through the air.

"You like Sinatra?" Ivan asked.

"Maybe," she said playfully, realizing she'd begun to move with the music. "I do love this song." Jaden felt some of the tension in her body begin to dissolve, and she smiled. Ivan was a stranger, but he'd made her feel things that had lain dormant for too long.

"If you love listening to him, you must also love dancing to him," Ivan said with a boyish grin. "You're practically dancing already." He stood and faced her, offering his hand. "May I have this dance?"

Hesitantly, Jaden let him lead her to the center of an impromptu grassy dance floor. Dew coated her feet as their bodies began to sway. Jaden rested her head on his chest and wrapped her arms around his broad neck as the romantic lyrics of Sinatra's "The Way You Look Tonight" began to swirl through the air around them.

They moved slowly across the lawn, and she smiled at him, placing her cheek against his. A low grumble in his throat grew into a vibrating hum. Her smile widened as the gentle purr of his voice transformed into the song's soft, sultry words, and he began to sing in the faintest yet most seductive way.

With her arms firmly around him and a smile on her face, Jaden couldn't help but join his serenade. Their voices melted into a harmonious blend, fueled by unbridled passion. This was one of those moments she knew was destined to remain with her forever—a complete stranger had captured her heart, even if just for one brief song.

Ivan lifted his head and gazed intently into her eyes. Cupping her chin and bringing her mouth to meet his, he whispered against her parted lips, "Come back to my hotel with me."

"Okay," Jaden managed to whisper before his mouth closed over hers.

Their bodies, and their tongues, danced in unison. Jaden trembled, and Ivan's grip on her tightened as she melted into him. His mouth pressed into hers, hard and fast, her lips pliable as she granted him entry.

The song slowed, as did the fierceness of their kiss, but their bodies stayed pressed together. Ivan lifted his head and panted, "Are you ready to go?"

"I have to find my roommate and let her know where I'm going," Jaden explained, suddenly very practical. "Where are you staying?"

"The Windsor Arms."

"Give me five minutes," Jaden replied, her breath coming in short gasps. "I'll meet you back here."

"You're joking, right?" He laughed. "There's no way I'm letting you out of my sight."

"I have to tell Tasha I'm leaving," Jaden insisted. "She'll kill me if I just run off."

"Your friend already knows you won't be accompanying her back to the hotel tonight. Besides, I think she has plans of her own." Ivan turned and pointed to where Tasha and Michael moved swiftly and gracefully across the dance floor together.

"All right," she conceded. "Lead the way."

Jaden followed Ivan across the garden, through the mansion, and down the front steps to a black limousine. She tried to be carefree, but something still nagged at her. Why would Ivan assume Tasha knew of her plans? Digging her cell phone out of her purse, she flipped on the screen. Sure enough, there was one new text message — from Tasha. *Be safe and have fun!* it read. Jaden made a mental note to find out what *that* was all about, but she tucked it away for later.

Her mind at ease, tonight was now all about Ivan and picking up where they'd left off in the garden. Silently, Jaden slid into the backseat of the limo and smiled as Ivan pulled her into his embrace.

Chapter 3

"Sex On Fire"

A shiver ran down Jaden's spine as Ivan brushed aside a stray lock of her hair. Suddenly feeling the need for fresh air, she pressed a small chrome button on the arm of the car door and lowered the window. The fire that consumed her was not something that could be measured in degrees, nor be extinguished by a gentle wind. It was born of passion and pure need, and it threatened to overwhelm her.

"Are you okay?" Ivan asked, inching closer on the seat.

"Why, do I not look okay?" Jaden replied, her already shaky voice cracking on the last syllable.

"You look absolutely stunning. But if I didn't know better, I'd say…" Ivan hesitated and raised his hand to her cheek, lightly trailing his thumb across her cheekbone. "You seem afraid."

Jaden could feel her cheeks flush and was thankful for the darkness inside the car. Shifting uncomfortably on the seat, she murmured, "It's just that it's been a while since…"

"Since you've felt this?" Ivan asked, slowly lowering his hand to trace the V-neckline of her dress. He caressed the silky fabric where it hugged her breasts, and she felt her body quake yet again in response. "Or what about this?" he whispered and pressed his lips to hers, slowly drawing her bottom lip between his.

The taste of wine and salt air filled her mouth as the kiss deepened, growing rougher as Jaden pressed her body against his, demanding that not a sliver of space exist between them. Ivan tasted her lips with his tongue and dove deep into her mouth.

Ivan pulled back, cupping Jaden's cheeks in his hands, and rested his lips tenderly on her forehead, both of them gasping for breath that wouldn't come. His eyes glimmered in the light of passing streetlamps. Tentatively, she placed her hand on his thigh, caressing him lightly with the tips of her fingers and stopping when she felt him tense beneath her touch.

Expeditiously removing her hand from his leg, he warned, "If you so much as touch me, I'm a goner."

Jaden smiled. Having this effect on him was more of a turn-on than she'd ever imagined. She intended to indulge. But her smile was short lived as Ivan once again caught her lips with his and snaked his tongue into her mouth with slow, delicious strokes. *He's trying to drive me insane*, Jaden thought. But then all thoughts vanished from her mind as he laid her down on the backseat. His arousal pressed firmly into her leg, and the leather creaked as he lay on top of her, pinning her against the padded cushion.

Jaden clawed at his clothing, needing to remove all barriers that separated them, needing to feel Ivan's skin against hers, but the sound of tearing fabric caused her to freeze. "Oops," she said with a giggle.

Ivan paused to investigate, and Jaden saw that the stitching on the shoulder of his jacket was torn. But torn fabric seemed the least of his concerns. With no more than a slight shrug, he reached between them and found the hem of her red silk dress. He skated his hand beneath the fabric to explore her thighs. Jaden arched her back, and he moved his fingers that final inch to caress the thin strip of silk between her legs, which was now moist with anticipation.

Jaden froze again as a voice echoed over the speaker.

"Excuse me, Dr. Rusilko. We're here."

Panting like a runner after a 5k, Ivan pressed the intercom button and responded, "Thanks, Drewe." Turning his attention back to Jaden, he smiled. "We're here."

"Thank God," Jaden chuckled. "Any more of that and *I'd* be a goner."

"Me too," Ivan replied breathlessly as he sat up, releasing her.

Dr. Rusilko, huh? Jaden now knew Tasha's assumption was one hundred percent incorrect. It wasn't just his looks that had gotten him where he was. He was a doctor…but of what?

Not waiting for the driver, Ivan flung the car door open and towed Jaden behind him as they rushed toward the hotel hand in hand, giggling and laughing like teenagers. They hurried past the bored-looking attendant at the front desk and the concierge who greeted them like royalty. Ivan acknowledged the bearded man with a smile and slight nod, and he picked up his pace, almost running for the elevator.

As the brass doors slid open, Ivan stepped into the elevator and pulled Jaden into an embrace, falling clumsily against the glass wall. They clawed at one another, practically tearing their clothes off, and it took her a minute to realize the elevator wasn't moving. She looked at Ivan and found he had come to the same conclusion, and he smiled sheepishly while reaching over to press the button marked P.

"We're going to the parking garage?" Jaden teased. "I thought you had more class than that, doctor."

"P isn't for parking, trust me," Ivan grunted and crushed her against the wall again.

She could feel his excitement growing as his eager hands found her breasts. She rested her head against the glass, her heart beating wildly as he plucked and flicked her nipples through the fabric, eliciting a moan of pleasure from deep within her. Jaden reached down and grasped his zipper. Lowering it and gripping him firmly, she was pleased to discover that Mr. Oh So Sexy was also Mr. Oh So Well Equipped.

The elevator halted, and Ivan hastily stepped back and zipped his pants. As he turned, Jaden moved behind him and slipped her hands into his pants pockets.

He groaned. "I am exercising great restraint right now," he informed her. Luckily, they didn't have far to go. Ivan took only two short steps to arrive at the threshold of bliss. He fished in his jacket pocket for the swipe card, and the door to the room swept open.

A touch of the light switch revealed an elegant room with rich leather furnishings in the sitting area and a large plasma TV above the fireplace. A cherry table and chairs sat off to the side, and bold, modern artworks adorned the walls.

Jaden watched curiously as Ivan crossed to examine a gift basket and two very expensive-looking bottles of wine in black velvet bags sitting atop the table. Plucking the card from the gift basket, he tore it open and read its contents.

"What's that?" Jaden asked.

"It's a thank you from tonight's winery," he replied, tossing the card on the table. "Good business clients and much better friends."

Who the hell is this guy? Jaden wondered. *First a VIP table and now the penthouse suite at the fanciest hotel in Sarasota?* But her attention was diverted as Ivan disappeared into the adjoining room. He returned a minute later without his torn jacket and came to where Jaden stood beside the sofa. She felt as nervous as a girl on her way to prom. He took her hand and led her out onto the balcony. The night air had a cold snap now, but she barely realized it. Her body still burned with the passion they'd shared in the limo.

"It's stunning," Jaden breathed, her voice carried away by the wind as she surveyed the spectacular view of the beach and the moonlight reflecting off the ocean. A small, cast iron bistro table and two chairs sat in the corner of the terrace surrounded by lush green plants. Jaden inched closer to the railing and leaned over to glance at the water below. After a moment she relaxed into the sensation of his warmth pressed against her from behind.

"Do you have any idea how beautiful you are?" he whispered. Turning her to face him, he twisted his hands into her hair as his mouth once again found hers—tasting, teasing, tormenting while he moved her back against the glass door. His hands roved her body and trailed down to lift the hem of her dress, pressing her harder against the barrier. Breaking the kiss, Ivan brought his mouth to her breast, and Jaden felt her nipple grow taut in his mouth as he drew her in. "Oh, God, Ivan," she moaned as his skillful tongue ravished her.

They stumbled backward across the patio until she could feel the cold metal table on her exposed thighs. Ivan continued nipping at her breasts through the silk of her dress as his hands slid the hem up, exposing even more of her legs. Taking his hand in hers, Jaden guided the tips of his fingers languidly across her body. Gradually his hands dropped lower and his thumbs traced the satin band around her hips. Jaden was keenly aware that this was the last barrier between them, and he could not move quickly enough.

Pushing aside the silky fabric of her panties, Ivan pressed his fingers against her sex, gently at first, then more urgently as his fingers dipped teasingly into the warmth of her body. He stroked her slowly and evenly, his hand moving in time with the crashing of the waves. Jaden could feel warmth pooling in the bottom of her belly, coiling and weaving through her as it overwhelmed her senses. She'd never felt it before, not like this. Ivan's skillful fingers had her nearly undone, but she needed to feel him inside her — the pulse of his cock throbbing against her, filling her. And she needed it *now*.

Forcing Ivan's hands away, Jaden reached down and in one motion unzipped his pants as she knelt in front of him. She yanked his pants and briefs down his legs until they lay crumpled around his feet, and without licking or teasing, Jaden took him in her mouth, every luscious inch of him.

"Fuuuuuck," Ivan groaned, and Jaden knew she must be tormenting him with her hands and mouth. After a few more delirious moments, he took her firmly by the shoulders and helped her stand before he gently guided her to lay on the tabletop. Positioning his body between her legs, Ivan nudged them apart, running his hands up the length of her thighs before stopping at the hem of her dress.

The intricate pattern cut into the tabletop was biting into Jaden's back, but one look into Ivan's glassy, sex-crazed stare and her body surrendered. Her lust ignited as she watched him reach down between them, roll a condom over his length, and guide himself into her. When she felt the tip of his shaft pressing heavily against her, Jaden let her head fall back, lost in pleasure. Ivan once again grabbed the thin strip of satin that encircled her hips, and this time he ripped it away as he plunged into the warmth of her body.

Jaden stifled a cry as he brought her almost immediately to a precipice. The fact that she'd wanted this from the second she laid eyes on him made it all the more powerful. The promise of release mounted within her with each relentless stroke of his cock, and pure lust engulfed her as each and every luscious movement brought her closer to ecstasy. Gazing at him, she watched his hair swing back and forth in the moonlight as he focused intently on penetrating her completely.

"Fuck me harder," Jaden pleaded, the words escaping her lips before she could stop them. *What?* She'd never been much of a dirty talker, but fuck, this was good. Ivan smiled, looking even more sex crazed than before, and he upped his tempo without missing a beat.

"Please," Jaden cried, not knowing exactly what she was begging for. The glorious sensation of having him fill her so completely was almost too much to bear. Their bodies moved in unison as she reached an orgasm she'd never even known possible, coming so hard her blood pounded in her head. But Ivan remained relentless, raising one of her legs over his shoulder to stimulate her from a different angle.

He'd taken himself to a new level as well, apparently, because his groans grew primal and his speed increased to a frantic pace. Jaden moaned her pleasure, and Ivan's strokes deepened as he prepared to join her in bliss. She felt his cock swell within her and knew he was on the brink of release. Grabbing his tie, she pulled Ivan toward her and lifted her hips to meet his every last thrust, increasing his penetration and sending him over the edge. Gripping the leg draped over his shoulder, he grunted and buried his cock completely, finding his release deep within her. His movements slowed and his head fell back, revealing a look of complete satisfaction and leaving Jaden unable to move in the aftermath of their passion.

As the delirium ebbed to a subtle buzz, Ivan kicked his pants off completely and swept Jaden up into his arms. He carried her inside, passing through the sitting area and into the bedroom. After placing her gently in the middle of the king-size bed, he carefully removed her dress along with his shirt and tie, the only clothing that remained on his muscular frame.

A heap of silk, wool, and satin piled on the floor beside the bed, and soon they lay naked in each other's arms. Suddenly self-conscious, Jaden tried to cloak her body with her arms and hands.

"No, don't," Ivan whispered. "You're magnificent. I want to see you."

"I…"

"You're breathtaking," he replied and silenced her with his mouth.

The luxurious cotton linens tantalized her skin, but they were nothing compared to the feel of Ivan's toned body as he lowered himself over her again. Jaden traced the smooth curves of his muscles as they flexed with each movement of his body. Her hands trailed down the ridges of his stomach, each of her fingers ascending and descending as they skimmed over the well-defined muscles.

Ivan kissed her softly on the mouth, and they settled into the bed, a tangled mass of arms and legs. As passion gave way to drowsiness and comfort, Jaden found it nearly impossible to tell where one body began and the other ended. She fell asleep wrapped in his embrace and blanketed with his scent.

CHAPTER 4

"Where Are You Going"

The early morning sun sent brilliant rays streaming through the open doors of the penthouse-suite balcony, bringing with them a breeze off the ocean. Jaden awoke to the odd sensation of her bare skin being both warmed and cooled at the same time. Strong arms encircled her waist, and a million questions bombarded her mind as she took in the bronzed specimen who lay beside her. *What happened last night? Where am I? He has a tattoo…of a pole-dancing snake? How did I not see that before? And for the love of God—what the hell is his name?*

Jaden fought through the fog of hangover that threatened to blow up in her head. As she closed her eyes and forced herself to focus, memories slowly swam to the surface. She remembered Tasha introducing her to some hottie before the two of them took off for the dance floor. Jaden also remembered watching a gorgeous guy at one of the VIP tables. Was it he who lay next to her now? Turning to look at the man who hugged her possessively, naked and glorious in the light of day, she absorbed every detail: a mane of thick brown hair that hung messily across his shoulders, full lips—the top one slightly smaller than the bottom—stretched in a satisfied smile across his face, and a chiseled body that looked as if it was carved in fine Italian marble… It was him!

The thought of statues and marble sparked another more sultry memory from the night before: a grand fountain in the middle of a garden, the sudden smell of cigars and intoxicating cologne, and Prince Charming singing softly in her ear as they swayed on a grassy dance floor. These memories all led to… *Oh, God,* Jaden screamed silently. *What the hell is his name?* Still staving off the inevitable headache, she closed her eyes more tightly and concentrated. Doctor something or other…Evan maybe? Igor? Jaden gritted her teeth in frustration.

Her eyes opened to look at him again, his face so peaceful and content against the softness of the down pillows. Excitement, pleasure, fear, and nerves crashed over her like a tidal wave. Here she was, lying beside the most gorgeous man she'd ever seen, wanting to wake him and demand a repeat performance, but she couldn't even remember his name.

Taking great care not to wake him, Jaden gently lifted his arm from around her waist. He shifted and stayed sleeping, but her movement caused the dam in her head to break, and it exploded with pain. Rolling over on her side, Jaden searched the floor for her clothes, which were nowhere to be found. She stifled a groan and sat up on the side of the bed, using a corner of the sheet to cover herself. If she tried to gather more of the sheet, Mr. Oh So Sexy might wake up, and that was the last thing she wanted. She needed a few minutes alone to compose her thoughts.

Struggling to get off the bed, Jaden stood and snuck over to the balcony doors, untying the sash of the curtains as she hurried past—but a wine bottle caught her attention. Peeking through the remaining sliver of space between the drapes, Jaden saw the cast iron table in the corner and began to recall what they'd shared under the stars…the sights, the sounds, the feelings. *Oh, God, the feelings.* A shiver ran up her spine at the memory of him — and everything he'd done to her. *Damn it! Why can't I remember his name?*

Taking another quick scan of the room, Jaden still couldn't locate her clothes. Making a beeline for the bathroom, she snatched her purse from the dresser as she scurried past, and with great care, she noiselessly shut the door behind her. Hanging on the hook was the worse-for-wear jacket she'd all but ripped from Ivan's body in the back of the limo. *Ivan! That's it!* She silently rejoiced. Taking the jacket from the hook—*Mmmm, Ralph Lauren*—she wrapped it around her naked form. His wonderful scent—what *was* that cologne?—still lingered on the fabric, and she inhaled deeply and immediately smiled.

Jaden turned to the ornate, gilded mirror on the wall above the sink, and the reflection staring back at her was not one she recognized. A mass of tangled black hair pointed out in every direction, and lines of mascara and lipstick smeared her face. Retrieving a washcloth from the rack, she turned on the faucet and ran the hot water until steam rose in the air. With a whole lot of soap, Jaden scrubbed at her face until not a trace of makeup remained. Once satisfied that she no longer looked like a raccoon, she opened the drawer and rifled for a brush. Instead she found a toothbrush, a razor, and a fine-toothed comb. Picking up the comb, she diligently worked it through her long hair until it looked somewhat presentable.

Scarcely noticing the details of the luxurious bathroom, she perched on the side of the tub and dug through her purse for her cell phone. If she couldn't find her clothes, she'd have to call Tasha, and that was one thing she wanted to avoid at all costs. As she touched the screen of her phone, a notification popped up to inform her that she'd missed four text messages. Swiftly, Jaden opened the first message and began reading.

> OMG! Do you have any idea who you're with right now?
> I knew he had to be important to be at the VIP table,
> but this is beyond ridiculous.
> Mr. Oh So Sexy is all that and then some!

Beneath the text message was a bright blue link. Why the heck would Tasha use a link when a simple description would suffice? Jaden tapped the screen, and the link opened up in the browser window. The heading of the article said it all: *Dr. Ivan Rusilko crowned Mr. USA.*

Jaden skimmed the article until she reached another juicy tidbit: *Dr. Rusilko will now begin his preparations to represent the USA at the world's largest international male modeling competition, which will be hosted in Incheon, Korea.*

After reading a bit more, she scrolled to the bottom of the page where there was a link to a photo gallery. Flipping through the pictures, Jaden realized her memories of the night before weren't one bit skewed. Every gorgeous inch of him was real—real and rock solid. A grin crept over her face as she returned to the text messages.

Tasha hadn't even bothered to type anything with the next message. It was only another link: *Dr. Ivan Rusilko joins world class medical spa in Miami.*

"What? No way he lives in Miami," Jaden whispered. Feeling a little giddy, she fought to suppress a laugh. "And a *medical* doctor. Whoa." *Expertise includes weight loss, wellness, physical enhancement, and sexual improvement...*

Sexual improvement? She could vouch for his expertise in that area. Jaden wondered briefly what a medical spa might be, but there were still more unread texts. The third message simply said *Lucky you,* and included yet another bright blue link. Jaden could barely contain her excitement as she waited for the page to load: *Ivan Rusilko and Irena Stang call it quits!*

Irena Stang...the name sounded familiar, but Jaden couldn't place it. She continued reading.

After a much-publicized relationship, Ivan Rusilko, renowned doctor and international male model, and Irena Stang, Italian beauty queen and actress, have broken up. Publicists report that it is an amicable breakup, and the couple will remain friends. This is just one in a string of several public breakups for the good doctor, who seems to have made a career out of dating models, actresses, and beauty queens.

Jaden cursed under her breath. That's why the name sounded so familiar. Irena Stang was rapidly becoming one of the most sought-after actresses in Hollywood. The euphoria the first two messages had created now began dissolving into blackness. Beauty queens, models, actresses... How could a chef ever compete with that?

Standing up, Jaden returned to the mirror. For the first time in a long time she despised the person she saw. Sure, she worked hard to keep in shape, but just like nearly every other woman, from time to time Jaden struggled with self-image. Her hair was too dark, her bust too small. She had nothing to offer a man used to such perfection. Disheartened, she opened the fourth and final message.

Going to breakfast with Micky.
Want me to wait around,
or are you going to hitch a ride back to Miami with Mr. Oh So Sexy?
Either way, be ready to dish out ALL the juicy details, girl!

Still wearing nothing but Ivan's suit jacket, Jaden tiptoed back into the main room. She now saw that speckled marble and plush carpeting blanketed the floor. A flat screen TV hung above a fully stocked mahogany bar, and a baby grand piano in the corner of the room completed the décor. The splendor of the room had gone mostly unnoticed last night when Jaden had passed through in a drunken, lust-infused stupor. But still no clothes to be found. Jaden took a deep, calming breath and mustered every last bit of courage before returning to the bedroom. She silently circled around to where Ivan slept peacefully. Peeking out from underneath this side of the bed was a thin, black strap that resembled her bra. Getting down on her hands and knees, Jaden rummaged under the bed until she'd retrieved her dress and favorite bra, but no panties. Oh well, something was better than nothing. After making her way back to the bathroom, crumpled clothes in hand, Jaden traded Ivan's suit jacket for her dress before making a beeline to the exit.

Pausing beside the partially open bedroom door, Jaden watched Ivan sleep. Tears welled up in her eyes. She longed to stay, but she'd surely be setting herself up for heartbreak. How could she ever compete with all the beautiful, wealthy women he'd dated? Yet her heart still told her leaving could be one of the biggest mistakes of her life. Nevertheless, without so much as a farewell note or goodbye kiss, Jaden walked out of the suite leaving Ivan alone in bed.

As she reached the lobby, Jaden still fought back tears. She nodded silently to the doorman, who immediately hailed one of the taxis sitting at the fringe of the parking lot. Jaden slipped quietly into the back, watching with regret as the hotel and her mysterious man disappeared.

Chapter 5

"Cannonball"

Jaden opened the door and entered the hotel room she and Tasha had planned to share, noting its contrast to the penthouse suite where she'd spent the night. She flopped down on the closest bed and buried her face in a pillow. Unable to hold them at bay any longer, her tears came out in a rush, and Jaden wondered if she'd made the right choice by leaving. A part of her now regretted that she hadn't so much as left a note for him, but there was nothing to be done about it now. Ivan certainly wouldn't want anything to do with her after she'd left him. Besides, she was probably just another notch on his belt, another conquest on his ever-growing list of women he'd bedded. Well, he'd have her panties as a trophy, a memento of their one and only night together. *Ah, the balcony,* Jaden finally realized. That's where she'd left them. He'd ripped them off in the heat of the moment.

Rolling over, Jaden noticed their suitcases beside the door, packed and ready to go. The clock on the night table flashed 11:29. Tasha was out with Michael — or Micky, as she seemed to be calling him — and there was still an hour and a half before checkout. Summoning the energy to get up, Jaden stood and pulled her suitcase up onto the bed, unzipping and rummaging through it for a change of clothes. She ignored the pounding in her head and shuffled clumsily toward the bathroom. Maybe a nice, hot shower would ease the massive hangover wreaking havoc on her body and clear the jumbled thoughts from her mind.

Jaden turned on the faucet before slipping out of her dress and tossing it aside. Pulling back the shower curtain, she stepped in and let the heat seep into her pores. Hot water flowed over her, washing away some of her tension and taking with it the faint, spicy scent of Ivan that clung to every inch of her body—a scent forever embedded in her memory.

The sound of the hotel room door opening brought Jaden back to her senses. Turning off the water, she wrapped a towel tightly around herself. A chorus of laughter echoed into the bathroom, and for a brief second, Jaden was jealous of her best friend. After slipping on her jeans and T-shirt, she towel-dried her hair and pulled it into a ponytail, then opened the bathroom door.

Tasha and Michael lay in a heap in the center of the other bed, kissing and groping each other, though they were thankfully still fully dressed. Jaden cleared her throat to alert them to her presence but still had to avert her eyes when Michael rolled over, revealing plainly visible evidence of his arousal.

"Oh, wow!" Tasha blurted and moved to untangle herself. "This is awkward."

"Sorry," Jaden replied, and turned toward the door. "I'll give you two some privacy."

"Hey, wait a minute!" Tasha jumped up and stopped Jaden before she could leave the room. "Is everything okay?" she asked quietly. "You look kind of…upset."

"I'm fine," Jaden lied. "I just need some coffee."

"Let me get my purse, and we'll come with you."

Jaden glanced over to where Michael lay on the bed, covering himself with a pillow and grinning from ear to ear. "There's only an hour left until checkout, and I think your new friend wants to say goodbye. Why don't I go down and get a coffee, and you can meet me in the lobby when you're ready to go?"

"Are you sure?" Tasha asked, her eyes already drifting back to the bed. "I mean, I'll come with you if you want."

"Please, you can't leave the poor man hanging like that," Jaden said with forced enthusiasm.

Tasha grabbed Jaden and hugged her. "Thank you," she whispered. "I owe you one."

"Yeah, you do."

Jaden could hear the giggling commence as the door shut behind her. The elevator ride to the lobby was punctuated by gaudy music from the overhead speakers, which intensified her already throbbing headache. Making her way through the people lined up to check out, Jaden entered the restaurant and found a small booth by the front with a clear view of the elevators. Thankfully the hour passed quickly, because her mind once again began churning through the images of a night she needed to forget. Yet somehow she knew they'd already burned themselves into her memory. Jaden was working on her second cup of coffee when Tasha and Michael emerged from the elevator, Tasha beaming and Michael laden with their luggage. Flagging down the waitress, she ordered three coffees to go before joining them at the front desk to check out.

"Feeling better?" Tasha asked as she approached.

"A bit." Jaden juggled the Styrofoam cups as she carefully handed one to each of them.

Checkout was swift, and Jaden was glad to see her SUV at the end of the parking lot. The sooner they left Sarasota, the better. Digging the keys out of her purse, she unlocked the door and slipped into the driver's seat, giving Tasha and Michael a few more minutes of privacy to say their goodbyes. She watched through the rearview mirror, envious that they looked like a committed couple after having shared only one night together.

"So now do you want to tell me what the hell's going on?" Tasha demanded the minute she slipped into the passenger seat. "You cannot be sad after spending the night with a fine gentleman like Mr. Oh So Sexy."

"Can we please talk about something else?" Jaden grumbled as she put the car in reverse and backed out of the parking spot. "What gives with you and *Micky?* The two of you looked awful cozy together. I'm sensing this is more than a one-night deal."

Tasha flushed and looked away. "I don't know. I hope it's more than a one-night thing."

"Start talking," Jaden said. "I want all the juicy details."

Tasha returned her smile and launched into a full account of her night. She prattled on for a few minutes, but then grew quiet before announcing, "And OMG he's hung like a bull. I swear the guy has it going on. And his tongue…good Lord, the man knows how to use it. He must've been down there an hour — or at least it felt like it."

At this point Jaden expected Tasha to turn red, but her grin just widened as she carried on with her far-too-detailed description.

"At first he tried to stop me from returning the favor, but no way was I letting him get away without a taste, so then I —"

Jaden burst out laughing. The happiness that lit up Tasha's face was enough to sweep Ivan out of Jaden's thoughts. "When are you going to see him again?"

"He lives in Fort Lauderdale, and he has to work next weekend, but probably the weekend after that. He mentioned something about having tickets to a basketball game, or maybe it was baseball." She shrugged and sighed. "I hope you don't mind, I said he could crash at our place," Tasha added after a moment. "I mean, if you don't want him there, we can always get a room or something."

"Are you kidding me? Why would I care if he comes over for the weekend? Last time I checked, both our names were on the lease."

Tasha fell silent, and she shifted in the seat to face Jaden. "So are you ready to talk yet?"

"What's there to talk about?" Jaden asked. "We spent the night together, it was great, and now it's over."

"That's it? You're never going to see him again?"

"That's it." Jaden shrugged.

"You're joking, right? You're going to let a guy like that walk away?" Tasha bellowed, her voice echoing loudly in the car. "Are you out of your freaking mind?"

"What else is there to do?" Jaden replied sharply, her tone harsher than she'd intended. She realized that not once during their entire evening together had Ivan asked her name. Feeling used and dejected, she forced back a fresh wave of tears. "The guy only dates celebrities and models, and I certainly do not fall into either of those categories."

"What did Ivan say when you told him this? I doubt he'd just let you leave without talking this over."

"I told you already, there's nothing to talk about. I'm sure he was relieved to wake up to an empty bed. Based on all those articles you sent me, I'd say 'no strings attached' is his favorite mantra."

"You didn't even talk to him before you left?" Tasha asked, dumbfounded. "After all he went through last night to get your attention? The least you could've done was let him know you were leaving."

"What do you mean, after all he went through? What are you talking about?" Jaden glanced over at Tasha, almost veering into the oncoming lane. After swerving to the right, she pulled the SUV over and turned to face Tasha. "What exactly did he do to get my attention? He didn't even know my name!"

"That's not true. Last night while Michael and I were dancing, Ivan found me and asked if he could cut in, which, might I add, Michael was none too happy about. As we danced he asked me all these questions about you. I told him your name, that you were single, and that you'd just accepted the head chef position at Bianca in Miami. By the time we finished talking, you'd disappeared somewhere, and he took off after you like a bat out of hell. That's why I sent that text message. I kind of figured I wouldn't be seeing you again until this morning."

"Oh." Jaden sighed and stared blankly out the window. How could such a brief interlude with a man she didn't even know evoke such strong feelings of regret? Unable to hold back the tears any longer, she buried her face in her hands. "Oh, God, what have I done? I blew it!"

"You sure did! That guy was seriously into you." Then Tasha spoke again, her voice soothing. "You know, you could always Google him and probably find his number, or at the very least his email address."

"I can't do that. He probably hates me by now." Rummaging in the cubby between the seats, Jaden found a napkin and wiped her face. "Look at me! I don't even know the guy, and I'm crying over him. How pathetic is that?"

"It's only pathetic if you sit on your ass and don't do anything," Tasha said. "It's obvious he has a thing for you. Find his number and give him a call. If you don't, you'll only have yourself to blame for letting him get away."

Jaden said nothing but took a deep breath, signaled, and pulled back onto the highway. Turning up the volume on the stereo, she soon lost herself in thoughts of work. She was determined to erase all traces of Ivan from her mind, even if it meant she'd be absolutely miserable.

CHAPTER 6

"Run"

Ivan's eyes began to burn as he stared at the computer monitor, his finger poised directly above the enter key, as it had been for the past five minutes.

Jaden had made her choice when she left him high and dry, alone in the suite that they'd shared for one monumental night, he told himself. And even though her friend had given him the name of the restaurant where Jaden was head chef, after her abrupt departure he'd been determined to push it from his mind. Yet here he sat, behind his glass desk with a stack of patient folders waiting for his attention—each representing someone who hoped he'd help them defeat Mother Nature—and all Ivan could think about was Jaden. Despite the picturesque view of the water from his office window, Ivan could only focus on one thing: seeing her again. Hastily, he typed "Bianca" into the search bar, and his finger trembled above the enter key. Finally, summoning his nerve and following his heart, Ivan tapped the button.

The first link on the page of search results led to the restaurant's website. Taking another deep breath, he clicked. Jaden's picture flashed across the home page, along with a brief bio of their new chef. She looked just as stunning as he remembered: long obsidian locks cascaded down her shoulders, and her emerald green eyes sparkled at him from the screen, her mouth curved into a smile.

The sight of her ignited the same feelings it had several nights ago — when for one brief moment in time she'd been his. He needed to see her, to put this demon to rest. But how could he just walk into the restaurant? He needed a reason to be there, to confront the woman who'd stolen his breath on a warm September evening.

Forming an idea, Ivan logged into his email account and began composing a strategic message, addressed to several of the people who'd attended the Winemaker's Dinner with him. His fingers moved swiftly across the keyboard as he typed.

> Hey, guys!
>
> Wanted to say it was fantastic to see each of you at the dinner last weekend. Sorry I left in a hurry, but I'm sure everyone had a good time. It's been brought to my attention that a fantastic new chef has recently taken over at Bianca, and I was wondering if you'd like to check it out, for business reasons, of course. Ha ha! It would be a pleasure if you'd join me for lunch this Friday at 12:30 — it's on me! Let me know if you can make it.
>
> Cheers,
>
> Ivan

His invitation was accepted. The RSVPs rolled in, and the week seemed to fly by. Before he was certain he was ready, Ivan found himself approaching the door to Bianca. A mounting ball of tension, anticipation, lingering anger, and even a touch of fear weighed heavily on his shoulders. A part of him was still pissed that Jaden had left without so much as a note, but he also wanted to understand how she must have felt. He needed to let her know he wanted more than just a one-night stand, and with any luck, this would be his chance to do that. He smiled as the chattering voices behind him reminded him he wouldn't have to face this alone. Opening the door, he stepped aside and allowed his associates to enter.

The wait staff moved efficiently throughout the dining room as guests chortled and made small talk over their meals. Classical music filtered through the dimly lit room, creating an ambiance of elegance. The smell of truffles and tarragon tantalized as the group followed the hostess to their table, passing a large framed portrait of the restaurant's new executive chef. Ivan paused briefly to admire the picture, and the sight of Jaden, looking so beautiful and demure, caught him off guard. A wave of queasiness washed over him, and he waited for it to pass before following the group.

By the time Ivan reached the table, everyone had taken their seats, leaving only one: the head of the table. As he sat, a slender, redheaded waitress approached and handed each of them a menu.

"Good afternoon, and welcome to Bianca. My name is Susan, and I'll be your server today. You've picked a good day to join us. The chef has just added many new selections to the menu, including a grilled ahi tuna prepared with fresh lime and mint."

Stunned, Ivan snatched the menu off the table and scanned the page. Sure enough, the menu offered the tuna served at the Wine-maker's Dinner, although it appeared from the ingredients that Jaden had put her own twist on the dish. He grinned. *Nice work, Jaden.*

After taking their drink orders, the waitress turned to leave, but Ivan tapped her lightly on the arm. "Excuse me, but is Chef Thorne preparing lunch?" he asked quietly.

"Yes, she is today," the waitress replied.

"Good, would you please ensure that she's the one who prepares our meals personally? My associates work in the industry and have been looking forward to trying her dishes."

The waitress glanced around the table and nodded. "Yes, sir, of course."

Ivan watched as she hurried toward the kitchen and disappeared behind the double doors. This was it. The stage was set, and he would soon have answers to the questions that had plagued him for the past week. He had to know if there was even the slightest possibility for him and Jaden to have a future.

As they settled in at the table, Dirk, a tall Latino playboy dressed to the nines, glanced casually around the restaurant. "So, is this place gonna make it?"

"Sure. Great location, interesting name…" chirped Jay, a maga-zine executive with a brown, scruffy beard, "and as long as they keep hiring waitresses like that." He tilted his head toward a busty blonde as she disappeared behind the kitchen door.

"We shall see," Stephen, a food critic, interjected. "The food better be damn good. You can't eat the waitresses."

"I bet you wouldn't mind taking a bite out of that," the equally busty blonde sitting beside Ivan jibed. He grinned, shaking his head at their one-track minds, but a moment later their waitress returned, and Ivan felt another rush of nervousness. Why was *she* making him so nervous? It's not like this girl had any idea who he was, and there was no way Jaden could know he was sitting less than twenty yards away from her in the dining room. But still, his stomach fluttered.

"May I take your orders?" she inquired politely.

One by one each of Ivan's guests placed their orders, and Ivan knew exactly what he wanted. "I'll have the tuna, my dear," he said with a smile and added a wink for good measure.

The waitress nodded and once again disappeared behind the doors to the kitchen. The friendly banter between his lunch companions grew livelier as they discussed the merits of having a sommelier on staff.

"Every great establishment should have one available," said Stacey on his right. "Don't you think, Ivan?"

"Hmm?" Ivan hummed. His thoughts remained focused on his impending liaison with Jaden.

"I was saying, do you not agree that every great restaurant should have a sommelier on staff?" she repeated with a smartass giggle.

Ivan sat upright, forcing himself to pay attention to the conversation. He was, after all, the one who'd invited them to lunch. "I do agree. Sommeliers are a crutch that the rich—and by that I mean the drunk with too much money—use to hide their lack of knowledge about wine. Why not have someone on staff to capitalize on such ignorance?" he said, grinning. "Isn't that why you like them so much?" His lunch companions roared.

"You ass," Stacey snapped back as she laughed with the others.

Dirk now turned to stare at the picture of Jaden in the entrance to the restaurant. "So about this chef…What did they do? Dress up some model and put a spatula in her hand? I mean, come on, chefs don't look like that. I've seen Emeril sweat out five pounds during a show—ten if he has to do any retakes."

Ivan sat back and listened, laughing silently to himself. He wasn't the only one who found Jaden more than stunning.

"She must be able to turn off a stove if she landed herself the head chef position," Stephen added from across the table. "I've heard good things, but I must say, if the food is substandard she'll sink like the *Titanic*."

Ivan felt a knot tighten in his stomach. Maybe he shouldn't have brought everyone. What if she wasn't such a great chef? He really had no idea. *Oh, Jesus.* How embarrassing would that be? These people were professionals, and if they discovered he'd brought them here on a romantic whim, they'd crucify him. Maybe he shouldn't have told them he'd tried the food and she was the best new chef in town. Grabbing his glass from the table, Ivan took a long sip of his wine. Where was his faith? *She'll do great,* he reassured himself.

Susan hurried through the double doors and into the crowded kitchen teeming with *sous* chefs in their bright kitchen whites. Snaking past the sinks, she found Jaden at the back of the kitchen. "Excuse me, Chef Thorne."

Jaden looked up from the pot of cream sauce she'd been stirring. "Yes?"

"There's a group of people in the dining room that have specifically requested you cook their meal." Retrieving the order slip from her apron, Susan handed it over.

"Like I don't already have enough to do," Jaden sighed. Taking the slip of paper from the waitress, she read their orders: two ahi tuna, two beef tenderloin medallions, and a grilled shrimp skewer. She stuffed the piece of paper into her jacket pocket and nodded. "At least they didn't order the soufflé."

"There's something else, Chef," Susan added hesitantly. "I recognize one of the men at the table from the restaurant I worked at before. He's a food critic for the *Herald*."

"What?" Jaden gasped. "What's he doing here? Critics never review a new chef during the first month. God, which order was his?"

"One of the tunas."

"Thanks, Sue," Jaden replied.

Susan watched as she took a deep, steadying breath and went to work.

Half an hour later, Ivan saw the waitress returning to their table, this time bearing a huge tray with their meals. They smiled appreciatively as she placed the delectable dishes in front of them. Their friendly banter, laced with business, continued throughout lunch and grew more animated with each bottle of wine consumed. Looking around the table, Ivan noticed everyone had cleaned their plates. He smiled as he polished off the last of his wine and motioned for the waitress.

"Pardon me," Ivan said, feeling more confident thanks to the generous liquid portion of his lunch. "Would it be possible to speak with the chef? We'd like to offer our personal kudos on such a spectacular meal."

A rumble of agreement passed among the others. "Yes, please do ask her to join us," Stacey added.

Ivan smiled broadly, pleased that they'd enjoyed the meal as much as he had. Jaden's take on the Winemaker's Dinner dish had just gained her the attention of some very important people.

"Of course, I'll go get her," Susan replied.

Moments later, Ivan felt his breath catch as Jaden emerged from the kitchen's double doors. He wasn't surprised at the glances she received from curious customers as she made her way to their table.

"Good Lord, I am eating here more often," Jay murmured as she approached.

Ivan chuckled. *You should see her naked,* he added silently. Even at work in a hot kitchen she was stunning. Her red dress was now replaced by a crisp white chef's coat and slim black pants, her Manolos exchanged for the typical chef's clogs. Her flowing hair was tucked neatly under the traditional white hat, all of which made her even sexier in Ivan's eyes. Her pace slowed as she drew near the table, appearing to take in each face seated there but not yet meeting Ivan's eyes.

Stephen wasted no time and jumped up to compliment her. "Ah, my dear!" he bellowed. "Cheers to a job well done. That was the finest grilled tuna I've had…well, to be frank, ever!"

"Thank you." Jaden took his outstretched hand. "I'm glad you enjoyed your meal."

"Absolutely great meal from a beautiful woman," Jay added, nearly running to shake her hand.

"Ah, you are too kind," Jaden replied gracefully.

Preserving his usual aura of cool, Dirk spoke from his seat. "It was fantastic, dear. I'm looking forward to seeing where this goes."

"Darling, it was delish," Stacey said as she stood. Ivan could tell his blond companion had her wheels turning about this new chef.

"Thank you all so very much." Jaden beamed and blushed. "It was my pleasure to cook for you today, and I'm honored by your compliments. I hope you'll join…" Her voice faded as her eyes finally found Ivan's and locked. An odd mix of lust and hurt rushed through him in that moment, and he suspected the fire in his eyes whispered, *I want to fuck you*, while his demeanor demanded, *Why did you fuck me?* Whatever message he sent, it looked to be a bit overwhelming for Jaden. After a moment she reached for the back of a chair, seeming to need the support.

"Ah, please join us again soon," she stuttered, finally seeming to come to her senses. "Now if you'll excuse, me, I'm needed in the kitchen."

Jaden turned on her heel and dashed off, but Ivan locked eyes with her again as she peered back over her shoulder. He tossed his linen napkin on the table and stood. "Would you pardon me for a moment?"

Ivan didn't wait for a response as he turned to chase Jaden through the crowded restaurant, bumping into waiters and knocking over dessert trays like an NFL linebacker. "Jaden," he called after her, earning him a few disapproving stares. He pressed on, crashing through the double doors to the kitchen. "Jaden, please wait!"

Ivan screeched to a halt, almost colliding with her as Jaden came to an abrupt stop directly in front of him. He gently touched her shoulder and turned her to face him. His heart lurched at the sight of her tear-stained face, and she looked decidedly hostile, her arms crossed. Wordlessly, he wiped away her tears. Being this close to her, his pulse quickened. Her scent of jasmine and coconut overpowered even the kitchen's succulent aromas of grilling meat and oregano.

"What are you doing here?" she asked, fighting back tears.

"I have to know."

"Know what?" Jaden demanded.

"Well, for starters, I have to know why you left without even saying goodbye." Without thinking, he caressed the soft curve of her cheek with his thumb, stroking it affectionately as he stared into her green eyes. "But more importantly, I need to know why a woman I barely know has left such a gaping hole in my chest, why when I open my eyes in the morning I'm disappointed that you aren't there, and why every song on the radio sounds like Frank Sinatra. Why is it that one night with you felt more like a thousand?"

"Ivan, please don't do this to me," she begged. "I'm not the one for you, and I think we both know that. It was a night of fun. Let's leave it at that, okay?"

"What's that supposed to mean?" he asked. "Do you honestly think I'm a one-night-stand sort of guy?"

"Well, I've seen the articles written about you," she shot back, but when he said nothing, she seemed to soften. "Look at me." Jaden motioned toward her sauce-smeared uniform. "I've seen pictures of the women you've dated, and I'm pretty sure they didn't come home smelling like grease."

Ivan frowned, realizing his past had caught up with him yet again. "Is that what this is about?" he asked sharply. "Is that why you left without so much as a goodbye?"

"No," she responded, looking at the floor. "Do you really want to know why I left?" Raising her hand, Jaden used the tips of her fingers to count off her points. "You're a doctor, a model, a world traveler, and you date actresses and beauty queens like they're going out of style. I'm nothing more than a chef from Colorado. I make my living *cooking* for people like you." She paused for a moment, appearing to fight back tears again. "Let's face facts. I'm me, you're you, and forget about social circles — there's a million miles between us on that front. I'm surprised you even remembered my name."

Ivan stood, unmoving and completely befuddled. How could a woman with such amazing beauty view herself as so inferior? "Is that what you honestly think? That I'm some James Bond international playboy who makes a career out of serial-dating famous women?"

Tucking aside a loose strand of her hair, he cupped her face in his hands. "If that's the type of guy I am, then why am I here right now, making a complete ass out of myself in front of a bunch of people I've never met?" He motioned to the crowd of waiters and kitchen staff that stood captivated by the spectacle unfolding before them. "You're so unbelievably gorgeous, and you don't even know it. You act like working as a chef is simple or somehow degrading, but I think it's amazing. You have a gift! Sure, I've traveled the world and done things some people only dream of doing. So what? That's what I've done, not who I am. Right now I'm just a guy…desperate for you to give him a chance. Nothing more."

His monologue finished, Ivan looked sheepishly around the kitchen and held his breath, waiting for Jaden's response. Had he gotten through to her?

After staring ferociously at him for a few moments, she finally blushed again and studied the floor. When she looked up, her eyes glowed warm. "Ivan, I'm sorry for leaving the way I did. You deserve so much better—"

Ivan pressed a finger gently to her lips, silencing her. "That's the past. What is, is, and what was, was. All I ask is that you let me take you on a proper date: flowers, chocolates, dinner. No sex, no expectations, just a real first date. Let me prove to you that assumptions never lead to anything good."

Jaden tried to hold back a laugh, but she failed miserably. "Well… I do love chocolate."

The sound of her laughter was contagious, and Ivan smiled broadly. "So is that a yes?"

"Yes."

Bringing his lips to hers, Ivan kissed her. He could taste the lingering saltiness of her tears but never had a kiss been so sweet. Wrapping his arms around her waist, he pulled her tightly against his chest. But the emotion soon gave way to passion, and Jaden returned his kiss urgently. Ivan's heart thrilled at her touch, heat spreading through his body.

Riotous cat calls and applause from the kitchen staff soon reminded them of their onlookers, and Jaden pulled back, trying to compose herself. But Ivan wasn't ready to let her go. Grasping her waist, he lifted Jaden off the ground, holding her even more tightly and kissing her again, despite her half-hearted attempts to struggle free. In the midst of their passion, her movement knocked them off balance, and Ivan set her down, only to stumble backward into the counter and knock over a pot of cream sauce. Despite his best dodge, the sauce spilled down the leg of his pants and pooled on the floor.

"We've got to stop doing this." The smile that lit up Ivan's face betrayed his harsh tone, and he burst out laughing. "You do realize this is the second thousand-dollar suit we've ruined in a week, don't you?"

A blush colored her cheeks as another round of applause filled the kitchen. "Okay, guys, back to work," Jaden ordered. "There's nothing to see here."

Ivan captured her in his arms and brought his lips to her neck, drawing a line of tender kisses as he whispered gently against her skin. "You can ruin every suit I own, as long as you promise to say yes every time."

CHAPTER 7

"Gimme Shelter"

"Wear the black one," Tasha yelled from the adjoining bedroom. Then she burst back into Jaden's room and tossed her a green scarf. "Try this with it."

"Tasha," Jaden moaned, "it's still summer. You want me to wear a scarf? I'll sweat my makeup off in two seconds flat before it cools off."

"That's the price you pay for beauty, my dear. This will be fantastic with your eyes." She rummaged through the dresses in Jaden's closet before emerging and passing one to Jaden. "Now this is a dress that will make any man weep, and it shows off those legs of yours."

"Hey, Tash, have you seen the remote?" Michael asked as he rounded the corner. He stopped dead in his tracks at the sight of Jaden standing in nothing but her bra and panties. "Oh, God, I'm so sorry."

"If you're so sorry, why are you still standing there staring?" Tasha teased. She picked up the towel lying on the bed beside her and threw it at him. "You're such a dork."

"It's okay, Michael," Jaden assured him. "I'm sure it's nothing you haven't seen before."

His face turned a bright purplish red as he scuttled off down the hall.

"You and Michael seem to be getting pretty cozy," Jaden observed. "It's been less than two weeks, and he's already taking his vacation days to come see you."

"He is great, isn't he?"

The dreamy look on Tasha's face spoke volumes, and Jaden knew she was a goner. Only girls in love wore that silly grin — the one so many single women envied. Jaden slid the little black dress over her head, loving the way the silky fabric caressed her skin and hugged her body, coming to rest halfway up her thigh. Tasha was right. It accentuated all her best features and made her glad to be five-foot-ten. Retrieving the makeup case from the top of her dresser, she sat down on the bed. "Can you do the thing with my eyes that you did last weekend?"

"I wonder where he's taking you," Tasha mused as she set to work creating the smoky eyes she'd long ago perfected. "I bet it's some fancy restaurant, or maybe an art gallery."

"I don't think it'll be anything like that. He mentioned something about a private party."

"Hmmm…" Tasha said. "Hold still. There. There you go."

Jaden picked up the scarf and draped it around her neck. "Okay, how's that?"

Tasha smiled, evidently pleased with her creation. "Just one more thing." She disappeared from the room and returned a minute later to take Jaden's hand in hers. As she did she placed a gold-and-diamond bangle around her wrist. "Perfect!"

"Tasha, I can't wear this. It was your mom's. What if I break it, or worse, lose it?"

"You won't," she said confidently.

Jaden hugged her. "Thank you."

"Stop it now." Tasha pushed her away. "You're going to ruin your makeup, and I don't have time to do it again."

Just as Jaden looked down at her watch, the phone rang, and she rushed to pick it up. "Hello?"

"Good evening, Ms. Thorne. There's a Dr. Rusilko here to see you."

"Would you please send him up?" Jaden asked, her palms slick with sweat just knowing Ivan was in the lobby.

"Yes, ma'am."

Jaden hung up and paced the living room, her black high heels clacking on the hardwood with every anxious step. Moving to the full-length mirror in the hall, she gave herself the once over.

"You look great," Michael assured her from the sofa. "If he doesn't think you're smokin', the guy has a serious problem."

Jaden tried to think of a witty remark, but her mind refused to cooperate and she just smiled. Somehow, a knock at the door startled all three occupants of the condo.

"One second," Jaden yelled and muttered a muffled, "Shit," as she ran to the mirror for a final appraising glance. She looked over her shoulder to Tasha. "How do I look?"

"Just like Micky said, smokin'." Tasha giggled as she sat down on the sofa beside him.

Jaden shook her head. They made quite the eager audience. "It's show time," she said as she approached the door. She twisted the knob, and the door slowly opened, revealing a man who looked like Ivan, but not quite. Instead of his usual tousle, Ivan's hair had been pulled into a sleek ponytail at the back of his neck, and his expressive eyes seemed brighter and softer all at once. A fitted white button-down shirt tucked smoothly into a pair of black pants, and all traces of his boyish charm seemed to have vanished — replaced by pure masculine sexuality. Jaden leaned in to give him a hug, prepared to inhale his fantastic scent, and was surprised when Ivan took a hesitant step backward.

"Umm…now this is one of my favorite shirts. You aren't going to rip it or spill sauce on it, are you?" he joked. Without giving her a chance to respond, he grabbed her by the hand and kissed her softly on the mouth.

The affectionate gesture left Jaden feeling weak in the knees. She clung to him for support, stunned that something so simple and innocent could make her feel this way.

"And this, my lady, is for you," he whispered, extricating himself enough to reach into his pocket and place something in her hand.

Jaden looked at the small, familiar box of Amedei chocolates. "But this is — " she stammered. "How did you know these are my favorite?"

"I thought they were everyone's favorite," Ivan said and winked before sneaking another quick kiss. "And no first date is complete without flowers."

Ivan hummed as he revealed a simple stem of pale pink orchids from behind his back.

"Thank you," she said with a sigh. "They're beautiful." Wrapping her arms around his neck, Jaden stood on her toes and kissed him hard on the mouth, pressing her body against his as she tried to close the distance between them. He smelled just as delicious as ever.

"Jaden," Ivan gasped as he broke the frenzied kiss. "This sort of kissing on a first date? Why, Ms. Thorne, I had no idea!"

"Are you always this big a smartass?" she asked with a smirk.

"Remember, I promised to be the perfect gentleman tonight, and if we don't stop now…" He shook his head.

A sly smile lit up her face as she moved closer to whisper in his ear. "What will happen if we don't stop now?"

"If we don't stop now, I can't be held responsible for my actions," Ivan whispered back, adjusting his pants.

A cocky grin spread across Jaden's face. Supermodels and actresses be damned—she'd succeeded in driving him wild in less than five minutes!

"That's all we get, a kiss? Come on, you guys can do better than that," Michael heckled from the couch.

Jaden turned to see Tasha elbow him in the ribs.

"Be back by ten," Tasha added in a motherly tone. "And no funny business."

Ivan smiled as he took Jaden's hand and led her out the door. "Don't worry, I'll have her back by eleven," he called, giving Jaden a wink.

"I hope that's a.m.!" Tasha shouted as the door closed. "Have fun tonight!"

They descended in the elevator, crossed the lobby, and exited the building hand in hand. An unusually cool late summer breeze greeted them as they stepped outside, and Jaden felt invigorated and ready to face the night ahead.

She watched as Ivan handed his ticket to the valet, remembering each curve of his muscular form and the way he'd felt when pressed against her in the heat of the moment. But the vehicle creeping out of the parking garage diverted her attention. Rather than a Mercedes or some sort of exotic sports car, an old-school Jeep Wrangler with its top down rolled to a stop in front of them. Jaden slowly turned toward Ivan and watched as an ear-to-ear grin spread across his face. She began to laugh.

"Your chariot, my dear," Ivan chirped in a phony Australian accent as he helped her into the black beast, its oversized tires raising it an extra two inches off the ground. Shutting the door, he laughed. "Assumptions, baby girl, are never right!"

Ivan hopped in the driver's side, clicked on the stereo, and blasted a live version of Jimmy Buffet's "Margaritaville." He hit the gas and tore out of the parking lot, screeching the tires and leaving the valet standing on the curb with a stunned, pissed off look on his face.

Who is this guy? He's full of surprises, Jaden thought. She smiled because she'd loved everyone one of them so far and couldn't wait to see what happened next.

CHAPTER 8

"Wild Nights"

Jimmy's coconut-rum-flavored voice echoed from the stereo, nearly drowning out the wind as they screamed down the road.

"So, where are we off to?" Jaden asked as the whipping breeze threatened to mess up the hair she'd spent the past two hours perfecting.

Turning down the tropical tunes, Ivan responded, "Patience is a virtue, girl." He seemed quite proud of his joke until he glanced over at the annoyed look Jaden couldn't keep off her face. "We're off to a friend's birthday party," he said immediately, motioning to the high rises in the distance. "It's in the penthouse of one of those bad boys."

Suddenly fearful, Jaden could feel the bile rising in the back of her throat. It was her job to cook for the rich and famous, not mingle with them. She was fresh meat about to be tossed in the lion's den. "Who will be there?" she asked, trying not to sound too nervous.

"It'll be mostly professionals — lawyers, doctors, socialites, CEOs."

She must have been broadcasting her unease, because Ivan placed a reassuring hand on her knee. "Jaden, these people are no better than you. They eat, they sleep, and they have sex the exact same way you do… Oh, well, not sure on that last one. Actually, I'm pretty sure they *don't* have sex like you do, because that's like fu — er, sorry. You know what I mean." He gave her a goofy smile and rubbed her thigh playfully. "The only difference is the size of their bank accounts. Just follow my lead, and you'll do fine. After all, you're going to be the most beautiful thing that walks through the door tonight."

"Great," she mumbled. "You're used to this sort of thing. I'm not."

"Well, practice makes perfect. I'm horrible with names but I've perfected a technique to get people to say their name without me having to ask. Pay attention and you'll see. Plus, you'd better get used to mingling. One of these days it's going to be you people are flocking to see. Jaden Thorne, chef extraordinaire—I can see cooking show written all over it."

Jaden rolled her eyes, but she couldn't help being flattered by his confidence in her—even if he was just trying to be his charming self and make her feel more at ease. She swallowed hard as they pulled up in front of the lavish condo, forcing back her queasiness. Looking up, Jaden noticed they were now at the Point—the southernmost tip of South Beach and a place she jogged every morning because of its beauty. Many mornings she'd run by and wondered what it would be like to live here, and now she was about to find out.

It looked much different in the evening. Red and green lights flickered and danced along the columns of the boardwalk, and the water glistened in the dull orange light cast by the port on the other side of the inlet, miles away. There was a certain peace about it now, when it was devoid of the dog walkers, joggers, and sightseers that crowded it during the day.

"Hello, sir. Are you here for the party?" asked a valet in a crisp red and white uniform.

"You betcha," Ivan responded as he opened the door, slid out of the driver's seat, and rushed around to Jaden's door. Offering her his arm, he helped her out of the Jeep. "Mmmmm," he murmured appreciatively as she slid down his body to exit.

Jaden couldn't help but smile in spite of her nerves. *Maybe this guy is for real…*

Large glass doors and windows lined the front of the building, and they were immediately greeted by a rush of cold-air refreshment that poured over their bodies as they entered. Jaden shivered and her nipples stood at attention as the chill assaulted her body. She was immediately thankful that her little black dress did a good job of hiding her body's reaction to frigid temperatures—among other things.

Walking across the lobby, they passed assorted Miami Beachers dressed to the hilt and scurrying about as they prepared for Saturday night.

Beyond the people, the lobby itself was a sight to behold. Picasso-style paintings adorned the walls, but the *pièce de résistance* was the waterfall sculpture in the middle of the floor, which emanated the sounds of trickling water and soft glow of iridescent light. Bright red carpeting lay scattered in no particular pattern across the white-tile floor, and coordinating ruby red sofas and glass coffee tables completed the elegant décor.

As they passed one of the sitting areas, Jaden couldn't help but notice a fancy epicurean magazine she'd never even heard of before, and briefly imagined herself gracing the cover. *One day…*she thought, embracing Ivan's confidence.

They approached the concierge, and he looked up immediately. "May I help you?"

"Yes, we're for the Shaunnessey party," Ivan replied.

"Your name, sir?"

"Dr. Rusilko, plus one," he replied nonchalantly, probably having said the phrase a thousand times before.

The concierge leafed through the papers on his desk and scrolled through the names. Finding the one he was looking for, he checked it off, and then motioned toward the other side of the lobby where a bank of golden elevators lined the wall. "Please use the second set of elevators on your left."

"Are you okay?" Ivan asked as they approached the elevators.

Jaden willed herself to smile. "So far, so good," her voice cracked. "But I swear, if you leave me alone for one second…"

"Leave you alone, are you kidding me? I'm gonna have to stand guard to make sure you don't get swept off your feet by some millionaire banker. So help me God, if that happens…" Ivan joked, successfully eliciting a smile.

"We're going to the parking garage again?" she asked facetiously when he pressed the P button, just as he had before.

"Damn right! Only the best for you, girl." He winked and chuckled under his breath.

The elevator glided smoothly toward the top floor, and Jaden leaned against the glass, the memory of their previous night in an elevator replaying in her mind like a movie. Trying to conceal a grin, she lost the battle and laughed. She looked up at Ivan, and his smirk told her he was thinking about the same thing. They smiled together as the elevator halted.

"You ready to rock and roll?" Ivan wrapped his arm tightly around her waist.

For a moment, Jaden felt as if she were the only woman on earth, and it was his sworn duty to protect her. Confidence swelled within her, and she smiled. "Always."

"That's my girl."

The doors of the elevator slid open, and riotous music and laughter bombarded them as they stepped into the most lavish apartment Jaden had ever seen. Her eyes widened as she realized it filled the entire floor.

Two women in black-and-white designer gowns and one-hundred-watt smiles greeted them, brandishing trays of rose-colored wine. Ivan reached for a glass and handed it to Jaden before retrieving one for himself. "Gracias," he thanked them.

Moving further into the lion's den, Jaden noticed the elaborate kitchen. Four cooks busied themselves with tonight's dinner preparations, and it took every ounce of her willpower not to jump in and start making corrections to their obvious mistakes. "Rookies," she whispered under her breath.

"Fair is fair," Ivan whispered back. "If I'm not allowed to think about sex, you're not allowed to think about work."

Jaden shivered, his sultry voice melting her like butter. "You know, Dr. Rusilko, some rules are meant to be broken," she replied, which left Ivan speechless and grinning that quirky little grin she was beginning to adore.

Then Jaden froze as a sea of people engulfed her. Socialites, businessmen, and chesty women in high heels who could have stepped off the pages of a magazine swirled around her. The furniture in the home's main room had been removed, and in its place they'd constructed a dance floor with a DJ booth, which now pumped out the latest chart toppers.

"So, whatcha think?" Ivan asked.

"Wow!" Jaden shook her head. "Are all these people friends of the birthday boy?"

Ivan bellowed more than laughed. "When you're this wealthy, everyone's your friend."

"What does he do?" Jaden asked, curiously.

"His primary business is financial stuff that I don't even pretend to understand, but he's also a partner in a TV station, among other things," Ivan shouted above the music. "He does a bunch of random stuff really, but he's a great guy."

Jaden nodded, but she must have looked as overwhelmed as she was feeling.

"Let's check out the balcony," Ivan suggested with a warm smile.

As they made their way through a sea of silicon, Botox, and spray tans, Ivan introduced her to everyone who stopped to greet them. Jaden smiled politely, making small talk and appreciating Ivan's efforts. From fabulously dressed bigwigs to local business professionals, the party was a networking paradise—if Jaden had enjoyed networking.

Only once on their trek through the crowd did Ivan insist that she meet someone in particular. He pulled her eagerly toward an impeccably dressed, overly tan gentleman surrounded by a swarm of beautiful women. Walking right past the fashionistas, Ivan didn't so much as cast a second look in their direction as he interrupted the man's conversation with a hearty greeting. They shared a warm hug and a few laughs before Ivan guided Jaden front and center. "Jaden I want you to meet—"

"Ah, this must be the Ms. Thorne I've heard so much about from my colleagues," the man said, interrupting Ivan's introduction. "How are you doing, my dear? Are you enjoying the party?"

"Yes, it's great. Thank you so much for having me."

"Well, eat and drink to your heart's content. Patty's footing the bill." He paused to chuckle at his own joke. "It's a delight to have met you. I apologize that I must leave so abruptly, but my driver awaits."

Kissing Jaden's hand, the tan man turned to Ivan and winked before jetting off toward the elevator with the harem of gorgeous women in his wake.

Utterly confused, Jaden turned to look at Ivan. "Who was—"

"Don't worry about it, babe," he replied indifferently.

Jaden opened her mouth to inquire further, but they were on to the next greetings. As they moved gradually toward the balcony, Jaden took note of Ivan's name trick, and couldn't help but laugh to herself. He said he was terrible with names, but he'd gone to great lengths to discover hers, she reminded herself. Finally, just feet from their balcony destination, they stumbled upon the birthday boy — engaged in a political discussion with several of his guests.

"Dr. Shaunnessey, trying to save the world again," Ivan said with a smile, apparently diffusing a heated debate.

"Always trying, doc," he said. Motioning to Jaden, he asked, "And who might this be?"

"She was the escort service's top girl for the night. Not too shabby, eh?" Jaden's eyes widened, but Ivan maintained a complete poker face as everyone around them fell silent. He allowed Dr. Shaunnessey to turn a bright shade of red before bursting out laughing and properly introducing Jaden. "This beautiful woman is my date, Jaden Thorne. She's the new head chef at Bianca."

"Is that right?" Dr. Shaunnessey asked, raising his eyebrow. "I'm Patrico Shaunnessey, but please call me Patty. I've heard marvelous things about that place and your culinary expertise. I had to decline Ivan's lunch invitation because of a previous commitment, so it's an honor to finally meet you, my dear."

"I might say the same thing, if I knew for sure which side of that argument you were defending a moment ago," Jaden replied. She could practically feel Ivan's heart jump into his throat, along with the birthday boy's, but just as Ivan had done, Jaden let the joke linger to the point of awkwardness before giving in to giggles and poking Ivan in the ribs. "Sorry, I had to get him back for that escort barb," she explained to Patty with a smile.

The group erupted in laughter as Ivan took Jaden's hand and raised it to his lips. "Apparently, she's a comedian as well!"

"My dear, you've made my night," Patty responded, and he gave Jaden a gentlemanly peck on the cheek before returning his attention to Ivan. "You got lucky, my friend."

Ivan's gaze fell intently on Jaden, and she felt warm under his stare. "You have no idea how lucky," he said.

Finally stepping out onto the balcony that overlooked the port inlet, Jaden sighed as she looked out across the open water, transfixed by the breathtaking view. The cool summer breeze cut the humidity and washed over her skin, raising goose bumps on her arms. The

Miami skyline shimmered in the distance, its reflection dancing on the water below.

Ivan leaned in and placed his hands around her waist, smoothing the silky fabric of her dress. "A bit different from up here, eh?"

"It's exquisite." Jaden sighed, shaking her head. "Thank you for bringing me."

"No, thank you," he whispered.

"For what?" She turned from the view to find something equally dazzling before her. Ivan drank her in with his eyes, as if he were trying to memorize every detail. She felt a swell of emotion and lifted her head as he brought his mouth to meet hers.

"Mmmm…pineapple," he softly murmured, and Jaden smiled into his kiss. "Thank you for making this moment perfect." Sensing that they'd become a peepshow on the balcony, she stepped back, and they parted as smoothly as they'd come together.

"Let's get a drink," Ivan suggested, taking her hand. Jaden's heart thumped as they fell into step like they'd been dating for years.

As they wove back through the crowd and across the room, Jaden examined the trays of appetizers being passed and noted the effort that had gone into their presentation. She had no doubt that a great deal had been invested in the evening's menu. Jaden looked toward the kitchen, where the cooks were preparing the next round of appetizers, and noticed her—the blond-haired bimbo who'd been weighing on her mind. She'd been draped on Ivan at the Winemaker's Dinner, and then she'd been part of the group that came to the restaurant. *Who is this woman?* Jaden wondered, and she cringed as jealousy crept over her. She hoped they'd be able to sidestep her, but the moment the woman saw them, she made a beeline for Ivan. *Damn.*

"Ivan, darling, how are you?" the blonde called as she hurried across the room.

Jaden tempered her glare, hoping desperately that a pleasant look settled on her face. Close up, the woman, probably in her early thirties, showcased a warm Latina complexion, light hair, and a trim, athletic body. *God didn't make those,* Jaden noted to herself as she observed the telltale all-too-perfect breasts and matching ass. Despite this, she could see why men, including Ivan, would find her attractive.

"Jaden Thorne," the woman enthused a little too loudly after making eyes at Ivan for a moment. "How are you? Are you enjoying yourself?" Lifting her chin and giving her best impression of enthusiasm, Jaden replied, "I'm doing fine, thank you. Who wouldn't enjoy herself at a party like this?"

"You weren't kidding, were you, Ivan? She *is* a stunning little thing." The blonde tossed Jaden an appraising glance. "You're a lucky man."

"So I've been told." Ivan smiled and squeezed Jaden's hand.

"How do you like Miami?" the woman asked Jaden, barely pausing for her response before she followed up with a succession of personal questions ranging from where Jaden was from to her five-year plan, and even touching on her family.

Jaden answered with as much grace and humor as she could muster, impressing even herself with how naturally she was able to do it. Maybe Ivan was right. They were just people.

"Well, sweetheart, I do have to run and find my friends," she finally said, touching Jaden lightly on the arm. "But I've heard so much about you that I had to have a moment to talk with you. I'll be in touch." She turned to Ivan and winked. "And you, let's do lunch soon. We have so much to chat about."

"Sounds good, doll. Be safe." Ivan waved as she slinked away into the crowd.

What was that all about? Jaden's curiosity was piqued, and *shit!*—she still didn't know the woman's name. During all those rapid-fire questions, the blonde hadn't said a thing about herself. Jaden accepted a glass of wine from Ivan, but remained preoccupied with the odd conversation. "Who was she?" Jaden wondered aloud.

"Her? Oh, she's a friend I've known for a while now. She's a peach," Ivan said with a laugh. "Are you having fun, girl?"

"I started having fun the second I saw that black beast of yours turn the corner," Jaden responded cheerfully, though a part of her still wondered about the blonde.

Forcing the issue from her mind, Jaden returned to mingling and working the crowd like a pro. Laughs were laughed, drinks were drunk, and relationships were forged, all while Ivan stood by her side, beaming.

Finally Jaden glanced down at her watch, expecting it to have gotten late, but still shocked to see it was four in the morning. She gasped. "Time sure does fly…"

"Are you ready to go home?" Ivan asked, looking pretty convinced that's what he wanted.

"Almost," Jaden smiled, still amazed she'd finally managed to feel at ease in this crowd. "I just need to find a ladies' room."

"I'll show you where it is." He put his hand at the small of her back and guided her down a long, narrow corridor to the guest bathroom. Finding the door locked, he leaned against the wall and pulled her to his chest. He ran his fingers through her hair. "Did you have fun tonight?"

Looking up, Jaden smiled. "I did—although I think I'm exhausted."

Ivan smiled, took her in his arms, and kissed her softly, unrushed and uninhibited. Jaden felt warmth rush over her as the kiss deepened, and she felt pulled toward him as if by an unseen magnetic force.

She fell into him, her inhibitions slipping away. The need to feel his touch, his skin against hers, was almost more than she could bear. The feeling of him growing hard against her thigh was enough to pull her apart at the seams, so she just held him tighter.

Breaking away from the kiss, Ivan seemed to struggle for words—and for breath. "Uh, well, I'm glad you had fun."

"It's a lot to digest, but I think I'll manage," Jaden said, smiling at his momentary loss of composure.

The bathroom door opened and a disheveled woman stumbled out into the hall. Ivan released his grip on Jaden and straightened up. "How about we make our exit?"

"I couldn't agree more," Jaden whispered as she snuck past him. "Just give me a minute to freshen up." As she passed, she gave his package the most casual of grabs.

"Oh, you're in for it now, girl," Ivan managed. Jaden batted her eyes as she slipped into the marble bathroom, leaving him at full attention.

A few minutes later Jaden emerged from the bathroom, pleased to see she still had Ivan's attention. He shook his head and adjusted slightly before taking her hand with a smile.

Returning to the overcrowded main room of the penthouse felt like walking into a raging inferno. Even though it was after four, the party remained in full force, and Jaden swore there were more people here now than when they'd first arrived. She suspected that more than just alcohol kept some of the partiers going at such a pace.

Taking one last look around, Jaden soaked up the sights and let the memory cement into her mind. This was a real Miami party, not something you'd see on cheesy reality TV. She chuckled silently, wondering how she'd gone from a simple Colorado life to this absolute craziness in just a short few months.

"Let's hit it before we get sucked into another conversation," Ivan suggested, flashing her favorite cocky grin with a side of lust. They slinked through the crowd, avoiding all eye contact, and made it to the elevator unscathed.

Not able to hold back a second longer, Jaden barely waited until the doors had shut behind them before wrapping her arms around Ivan's neck and kissing him with a passion that rivaled the heat of the sun. She pushed herself against him for a moment, just enough to awaken his desire for a second time. Then, sensing she'd provoked him adequately for the time being, Jaden pulled away, letting the knowledge of her intentions sink in.

"I…Jaden…" he breathed.

Interlocking their fingers, she turned and pulled his arms around her, taking notice of their reflection in the mirrored side of the elevator. They looked good together. They were a natural fit, and she couldn't help but smile.

Ivan leaned heavily against the glass, and Jaden cuddled into his warmth. "Is this how all Miami parties end?" she asked seductively, unbuttoning the top button of his shirt and stroking the newly exposed patch of skin.

"Well, that all depends," he whispered, his voice low and gravelly.

"On what?"

"It all depends on where you want to wake up in the morning," Ivan replied, his voice thick with naughty intentions. "But wait—this is our first date," he quickly caught himself.

Jaden looked down demurely for a moment. "Since I've lived in Miami, I've only been to the beach during the day. I think it's time that changed," she said, adding her own cocky grin and silly wink. She pulled him from the elevator, telling him silently that their night was nowhere near over.

"Ah, sounds perfect," Ivan murmured, his eyes now aflame.

Wordlessly, they walked through the empty lobby, past the lone desk clerk, and out the front doors, their pace quickening with each step.

"Do you have your ticket, sir?" the valet inquired.

"Umm…we're not quite ready to leave yet. My date wants to look for sea turtles," Ivan tossed out on the fly, never breaking his stride. Jaden nearly collapsed in laughter as the valet stood dumbfounded. Gripping each other as if they were glued together, they headed straight for the beach.

CHAPTER 9

Arm in arm they strolled the boardwalk, and Jaden felt safe and secure. They walked the one hundred yards to the beach, their time together wonderful even without words.

Reaching the sand, Ivan took off his shoes, then lowered himself to one knee to remove Jaden's heels one at a time. He led her off the boardwalk and on to the soft, sandy beach—a far cry from the chaos they'd just left. Salt in the air replaced the overwhelming mix of perfumes and colognes. The rhythmic waves crashing against the beach were a much better background than the DJ's boisterous beats, and the stars more elegant than any interior. Only the cool summer breeze they'd felt on the balcony remained the same.

"Well, here we are, Miami Beach in all its glory. Beautiful, isn't it?" Ivan said as he stared up at the inky sky.

"Yes," Jaden replied. "Yes, it is."

Grasping her wrist, Ivan led Jaden to the water's edge, where the sand was damp and washed smooth. Turning north, they began their moonlight stroll.

"I'd like to think it was an okay date," he mused, looking at her from the corner of his eye.

"Meh…I'd give it a B plus," she teased and squeezed his hand.

"B plus, are you joking?" he protested. "That hurts! It's a good thing you're a chef and not a teacher. I'd hate for you to flunk me."

"Well, there is one thing that can get you some extra—ouch!" Jaden stumbled forward, her foot suddenly throbbing.

Ivan grabbed her before she could fall over, and she steadied herself with his shoulders. "What's wrong?" he asked.

"I don't know," she said. "I stepped on something." She scoured the beach, trying to find the source of her pain. Nearby she spied several drops of blood, which appeared black in the semi-darkness and stood out against the grayish sand. Not far from there was a shard of broken seashell, the culprit for this hitch in their near-perfect night. "I think it was a shell."

"Here, let me help you." Ivan held out his hand. He lowered her gently onto the sand and sat cross-legged beside her on the beach.

Jaden flinched as he placed her leg across his lap. He lifted her foot and, using the light of the moon, examined it as thoroughly as possible. "I think I may need to amputate. I'm a doctor, you know."

"Ha, ha." Jaden twisted her foot to get a better look at the damage. Congealed blood and sand coated the inch-long wound.

"It needs to be cleaned," Ivan said, turning it back toward him and gently prodding with the tips of his fingers.

She watched in wonder as he continued to examine her. A mixture of concentration and concern played across his face, sparking something within her soul. It had been a long time since a man had cared for her wellbeing. The thought both intrigued and frightened her.

"Hold on just a second," he said as he picked up one of his shoes and headed for the water's edge. He dipped it into the ocean, then hurried back to her. "This is going to sting a little."

"That's okay," Jaden said with a smile. "I'm a big girl. I can take it."

Her eyes followed Ivan's every move as he tended to her wound, cleaning it until no traces of sand or blood remained. Only once did she flinch when salt water flooded the laceration. Her eyes widened in surprise when Ivan then unbuttoned his shirt and removed it. He gripped it in both hands and pulled, easily tearing it in two. Choosing the smaller piece, he wrapped the cloth tightly around her foot and secured it with a knot.

"That should stop any bleeding," he said seriously, and then an impish smile crept across his face as he looked up at her. "We have *got* to stop ruining my clothes like this. Pretty soon I'll have nothing to wear."

"Hmm…I could get used to that." Jaden raised her eyebrow.

"Girl, you are really something," Ivan responded with a laugh, but without warning, his pants became tight and restrictive. *Mmmmm, baby girl…* He couldn't pinpoint what it was — nor did he care to analyze it at this very moment — but something about Jaden sparked a flame deep within him. She was beautiful, but also generous, caring, and kind hearted, and at that moment he realized he might never tire of her. He could happily spend of the rest of his life ruining clothes and laughing, as long as she was by his side.

He lifted Jaden's foot to his mouth, tenderly kissing her toes. Evidently pleased, Jaden sighed and lay back in the sand. Her legs parted slightly, and his passionate onslaught began. When his kisses reached the hem of her dress, a smile danced across his face, and Ivan knew they would break his vow of no sex. He didn't have the willpower or the desire to resist the goddess before him. Setting her leg back on the ground, and taking care not to jostle her injured foot, Ivan placed his hands under her thighs, supporting her weight. A million thoughts muddled his mind, all of them arriving at a single conclusion: *I need to taste her.*

Ivan slowly and torturously worked his way up her thigh to where a layer of satin was all that separated him from her sweetness. Tonguing the fabric ever so gently, he could feel Jaden writhe, and she grabbed fistfuls of his hair in her hands. The subtle moans and gasping breath that escaped her were like shots of adrenaline to his growing passion. Hastily moving her panties aside with his finger, Ivan took her in one long, luscious lick.

"IIIIIIvan…" she moaned, evidently unable to finish her thought as pure pleasure enveloped her. Ivan continued his work, lapping at her with unrelenting strokes, and Jaden soon thrashed wildly beneath him. Her voice echoed in the night air as she screamed out his name.

Without warning, she gripped his shoulders and pushed him onto his back. With unsteady movements, she sat up and straddled his legs. She fumbled with his zipper, and he sighed in relief as his pants came undone and then struggled for a moment to reach into his pocket. He thrust the foil packet at her, and Jaden slowed her movements to tease the condom into place. She seemed to search for something deep within his eyes as she positioned herself above him and began to lower her body, her warmth encompassing his throbbing cock with each downward stroke of her hips.

Ivan guided her rhythmic movements with his hands on her waist and stroked deeper into her luscious body, bringing them both one step closer to release. Tilting her head back, Jaden ran her hands through her hair as she screamed out her pleasure. Then she collapsed on top of him and parted his lips, driving her tongue deep into his mouth. The sound of her ecstasy echoed in his ear, increasing his passion to an impossible level. He thrust deeper into her, the sounds of flesh on flesh filling the night air. Push by push, Ivan brought his hips away from the sandy beach and deeper into her. Jaden welcomed every inch of him, sending them into an orbit of sexual bliss. Minutes felt like hours as their bodies crashed into each other, the tension mounting with every upward stroke of Ivan's hips and downward thrust of Jaden's body as they fought for release. Ivan twitched as Jaden's warmth tightened and pulsed around his cock. As their bodies swayed in unison, quivers of satisfaction engulfed him, and they screamed out their release in tandem.

Out of breath but full of life, Ivan collapsed in the sand with Jaden draped over him. There were no words to describe what they'd just shared. They breathed in gasps for a time, but as they lay under the stars, Ivan felt himself relax, fully and completely, and soon he and Jaden had matched their breathing into a slow, even rhythm.

"Well, I guess we broke that rule, babe," Ivan said, finally breaking their silence.

"I'm glad we did," Jaden said contentedly, not lifting her head from his chest. For a moment she patted his arm in time with his heartbeat.

With the sun beginning to crest above the horizon, they gathered their belongings and walked back to the building where the Jeep remained parked. Despite his offer to carry her, Jaden insisted she could walk, and she even managed to get her shoe onto her bandaged foot. The air smelled cleaner and the breeze felt fresher as they slowly walked the length of the boardwalk, dodging the dog walkers and early-bird joggers.

Ivan could tell the valet didn't quite know what to make of them — he shirtless and Jaden a little worse for the wear, both of them covered in sand — as they approached. "Man, those sea turtles are rough," he joked as the handed the valet his ticket. Jaden laughed, but the valet managed only a nervous titter before he ran to retrieve the Jeep.

Minutes later he rounded the corner and pulled to a stop in front of them. Ivan opened the passenger door and helped Jaden in. He tipped the still-speechless valet generously and hopped into the driver's seat, thanking him again before pulling out onto the nearly deserted Miami streets.

Ivan took the scenic route along Ocean Drive in the hopes of stealing just a few more minutes with her. He clung tightly to her hand, occasionally lifting it to his mouth for a kiss, and they watched as the sun begin to rise as they drove. By the time Ivan pulled up in front of her building, light had crept across the sky. Releasing Jaden's hand, he jumped out and quickly rounded the Jeep to help her down, admiring her tight form and once again stirring his arousal in the process.

"That was…magical," he said, drawing her close for another lingering kiss. He whispered softly against her lips, "When can I see you again?"

Jaden beamed but couldn't seem to find any words.

"There is going to be a second date, isn't there?" he asked.

"Only if you think you can top this one," Jaden breathed and kissed him on the mouth.

"Hmm…I think I can do that," Ivan said as he drew her closer, the taste of her pineapple gloss flooding his mouth as he nibbled her bottom lip. "Why don't I call you later tonight, babe? I think we could both use a shower and a nap."

Reluctantly, he allowed Jaden to slip out of his embrace. She insisted she didn't need help upstairs, and promised to wash her cut foot again thoroughly, so he had nothing to do but watch her go. She was still an amazing sight in her short black dress, and the look of pure satisfaction on her face caused Ivan to smirk.

Jumping back into the Jeep, he shook his head, laughed to himself, and cranked the stereo up full blast as he headed for home.

Chapter 10

"More Than A Feeling"

As quietly as possible, Jaden slipped the key into the lock and turned the handle. What she really needed was a hot shower and good sleep. What she didn't need was a million questions from Tasha. Jaden took her heels off in the hall before entering the apartment, but as the door opened, the sound of someone rustling around in the living room let her know at least one of them was awake. Rounding the corner, she saw Michael sitting on the couch, tying his sneakers.

"You're up early," Jaden said groggily as she rubbed her eyes.

"I'm just going for a jog," Michael replied as he sat up and saw her. Eyes wide, he looked her up and down. "Rough night?"

"Yeah, something like that." Jaden set her purse on the table and turned to leave, but Michael's voice held her in place.

"You look like you've been mugged. Have you even been to bed?"

"No, I haven't been to bed, and it all depends on your definition of mugged." Jaden shot him a half-assed smile. "I thought you were hitting the pavement?"

"No way. Not now — I don't want to miss the main event. The minute you walked out the door last night, I knew you wouldn't be coming home, but Tasha stayed up until four waiting for you."

"She did what?" Jaden asked in disbelief. "She didn't have to wait up for me."

"Let's face it, Jade. It's not like you really know the guy yet."

Jaden hated when Michael called her Jade, but he had a good point. She now knew Ivan would never do anything to hurt her, but her friends had no way of understanding that. "Okay, I'll go talk to her."

Briefly setting aside her need for a shower and sleep, Jaden knocked softly on Tasha's door. "Tasha, are you are you awake?" she whispered. After not getting a response, she opened the door and let herself in. She sat on the side of the bed and gently shook her friend's shoulder. "Wake up."

"Hmm…" Tasha mumbled and rolled over, pulling the blanket over her head. "What time is it?"

"I think it's about six a.m."

Jaden could hear Michael approaching and sensed him in the doorway behind her. Did he think there was going to be a catfight or something? Ignoring the hilarious image that shot through her mind, Jaden returned to shaking Tasha's shoulder. "Sweetie, I'm home."

"Good," Tasha grumbled. "I'm glad Ivan's not a psycho or anything, but can I please go back to sleep now?"

Jaden chuckled under her breath and stood up, knowing this was nowhere near the end of their conversation. She closed the door behind her and turned her attention back to Michael. "Not what you were expecting, huh?"

"It could've done with some whipped cream or mud."

"Maybe next time," Jaden shot back.

"Promises, promises," he sighed. "I'm off to jog."

Moving slowly and favoring her foot, Jaden limped to the bathroom. Grabbing a towel from the rack, she stripped out of her clothes. She turned on the tap and stepped into the flow of hot water, revelling in the feel of it cascading down her body and washing away the sand that that still clung to her.

The water dancing across her skin reminded her of Ivan's fingers trailing over her body. Never before had Jaden felt so completely satisfied or content with a man—and the thought terrified her. She was the type of girl who could drink beer with the boys and laugh at all their dirty jokes — their friend, not a serious love interest. But maybe this was her chance at happiness, her chance to be the object of a man's true affection, not just his lust.

Smiling, she squirted a generous amount of lavender body wash onto the sponge and cleansed away the apprehension her feelings about Ivan had built up. It wasn't exactly love she was feeling — not yet — but it was certainly something she'd never expected to find at the Winemaker's Dinner, and never so quickly. After a thorough rinse — particularly her foot, which seemed to be a minor injury despite the initial pain — she turned off the water and wrapped herself snugly in the towel.

The trek to her room was no more than twenty feet, but as exhaustion weighed her down, it felt like a mile. Not even bothering with pajamas, Jaden collapsed in the middle of the bed and immediately drifted off to sleep.

"Wake up!" Tasha screeched what seemed to be moments later. She bounced on the side of the bed. "I want to hear everything."

"Can't it wait until later?" Jaden glanced bleary eyed at the clock on her night table.

"Come on, get up. We'll go out for lunch — your treat."

Jaden smiled as she struggled to sit up, momentarily forgetting that all she wore was a towel. Still half asleep, she grumbled, "Pass me my robe, please."

Tasha sprung from the bed and retrieved the terrycloth robe from the back of the door. "Are you going to get up or not?" she asked stubbornly. "I waited up till four this morning. The least you can do is buy me lunch somewhere on Lincoln Road."

"Lincoln?" Jaden guffawed. "All you want to do is people watch."

"Guilty!" Tasha confessed. "But it's Sunday, and anything is better than football."

"Fine," Jaden conceded. "But give me a bit to get ready."

Jaden rummaged through her closet and settled on a pair of plain white capris and a yellow cami. She pulled her hair up into a tight knot and applied a barely there layer of makeup. After a quick onceover in the mirror, she joined Tasha in the living room.

"Ready?"

"Yep." Tasha jumped up from the sofa.

Just a few minutes later, the afternoon sun beat down on them as they walked along the boulevard, stopping every now and then to window shop or sneak in for a better look at the latest pair of Jimmy Choos. The patios were filled with people, and locals and tourists alike decorated the street with their bright, flower-patterned beachwear.

"What about this place?" Tasha asked, pointing to the sign that read Books & Books.

A good-sized crowd already dined under the comfort of the restaurant's enormous blue umbrellas. "Sure, why not," Jaden agreed. "I've heard they have good food."

The question now was inside or out, and in this heat, it was a no brainer. They opted for the refreshing sensation of artificially cooled air. As they took their seats at the back of the restaurant, Jaden prepared for the barrage of questions she knew was coming.

"Can I start you off with a drink?" the fair-skinned waiter asked as he handed each of them a menu.

"I'll have a cappuccino, please," Jaden said.

"Oh, that sounds good. I'll have the same."

As the waiter retreated, Tasha's demeanor shifted from cool to curious. "Soooo," she began and immediately launched into attack mode. She bombarded Jaden with question after question without giving her a chance to answer.

"Slow down. You're gonna give me whiplash if you talk any faster," Jaden teased. "One question at a time."

"Where did he take you?" Tasha gushed after taking a millisecond to catch her breath.

"We went to his friend's birthday party at the Continuum — that gorgeous building on the Point." Jaden sat back and closed her mouth, purposely tormenting Tasha with her silence. It seemed to be working.

"Micky told me how rough you looked this morning when you got home," Tasha tried again. "There's no way you'd look like *that* from going to a birthday party."

Jaden couldn't help her grin.

"Come on, Jaden. I tell you everything about Micky and me. Spill the beans."

"Yes, you do," Jaden responded. "Too much sometimes."

The waiter returned with their drinks and placed them on the table, then pulled out his pad for their lunch orders: pan Asian chicken for Jaden, South Beach Cobb salad for Tasha.

After the waiter left and she'd taken a long sip of her frothy coffee, Jaden recounted the details of the party.

"What happened then?" Tasha asked, sitting on the edge of her seat. "Did he make it out of the elevator in one piece?"

"Please…it's not like I jumped him in the elevator. I have more restraint than that."

"Like hell you do. Remember the time in college when Jim Noon took you to the State Championships? Need I say more?"

Jaden laughed, almost spitting her drink as she remembered that weekend, which seemed a lifetime ago. "Yes, but I never actually gave it up to Jim."

"You mean you two never—" Tasha poked her forefinger into a circle made by her thumb and forefinger on the other hand. "I always thought you did…"

"Jim wanted everyone to think that but nothing major ever happened."

"But it did last night, right? I mean, you and Ivan were pretty hot and heavy when you left."

"After the party, Ivan wanted to show me how to hunt for sea turtles," Jaden said nonchalantly, then shrugged.

"Sea turtles? Why the hell would you go looking for sea turtles in the middle of the night?" Tasha demanded. But after a moment, a light turned on. "Ohhhh! That would explain the sand in the bottom of the tub this morning. Beach sex!"

Jaden blushed and turned away. "Yeah, something like that."

"Oh my God, you're falling for him," Tasha crowed.

"What?" Jaden retorted. "I am not."

"Yes you are. I'd know that look anywhere."

When lunch was finished and the cappuccinos drunk dry, the waiter returned with the check. As he looked at her credit card, Jaden noticed an odd look cross his face. He turned to leave but hesitated.

"Is something wrong?" Jaden asked.

"No, ma'am, but you're… Are you Chef Jaden Thorne?"

"Well, yes," she sputtered. "Why do you ask?"

The waiter looked at Jaden with reverence. Finally gaining the testicular fortitude to speak up, he continued, "I just wanted to say that I love what Dirk D said about you on his blog last week."

"Who? What?"

"Dirk D. He's *the* Miami Beach social blogger — parties, people, places to go, where to eat, 'why I won't date you' type things… He ate at your place recently, and he linked to your bio on the restaurant website. That's how I recognized you, from the picture." The waiter beamed. "I'm a full-time culinary student. I only work here to pay for school, and it's so nice to read success stories like yours. Maybe one day I'll be as famous as you."

Jaden managed to formulate a response without laughing. "Famous? Oh, I wouldn't say famous, but thank you for the compliment. You've made my day."

"Well, it's been great meeting you." He still looked a little star-struck as he reached across to shake her hand.

"The pleasure is all mine. I hope to see you there sometime."

"Okay, thanks." He retreated from the table with a boyish giggle.

Jaden glared at Tasha, who burst into a laugh that may have registered on the Richter scale.

"See, you're famous now. You can afford to pay for lunch."

"Don't start with me," Jaden warned. "But I wonder who that Dirk D guy is. I'll have to Google him when I get home."

Still laughing as they exited the restaurant, Jaden and Tasha linked arms and headed to the boutique down the street.

A short time later Jaden picked up a slinky teddy before returning it to its rightful place on the rack. Satin and silk in rich colors surrounded her. It'd been a while since she'd purchased lingerie, and she felt a little lost.

"What about this?" Tasha asked, peering over a pile of satin bathrobes. She held up a cute bra and panty set.

"Too…pink."

"Jaden," Tasha complained. "We've been here an hour. There has to be something you like."

"There's a lot I like, but it's just not what I'm looking for, and it's been fifteen minutes, smartass."

"Maybe we should try that other store on Fifth."

Jaden shook her head and continued flipping through the items on the rack. But she stopped when a little black ensemble caught her eye. The bra and thong were slick black satin and would flatter her figure, giving her a lift where she needed it most. The garter was intricate lace, which matched the black lace trim of the bra.

"Wait!" Jaden exclaimed. "This is perfect."

Tasha laughed again. "And you say you're not falling for him?"

Jaden flipped over the price tag and just about choked. She hadn't spent this much on her last pair of Fluevogs. "What the hell," she said, more to herself than Tasha, who was already on the way to the cash register. Picking out a pair of stockings from the rack, she placed them on the counter beside her new spoils, smirking as she imagined the look she'd soon see on Ivan's face.

CHAPTER II

"Dream On"

onight, the kitchen seemed a bit different: the smells more powerful, the fluorescent lights less piercing, and the mundane tasks that occupied ninety percent of her time less, well, mundane. She'd noticed a new trend in the days since realizing Dirk D had featured her on his blog—which she still hadn't checked out. Orders for tuna had tripled in the last week, there'd been more requests for dining room appearances, and she'd been told that the nights she worked in the restaurant were busier than usual.

Rather than delegating all the duties to her *sous* chefs, Jaden now involved herself with the hands-on preparation of every single dish that left her kitchen when she was there. And it wasn't just the kitchen and wait staff noticing the changes. The owner, Geoff, had also noticed an upswing in sales. On the nights Jaden personally cooked meals, revenue significantly increased, he told her, and Geoff had made sure to show her his appreciation with a nice bonus check. He'd also designated a table at the front of the dining room as the chef's table, ensuring that VIPs and Jaden's personal guests had the best seats in the house.

Jaden had also decided to take things up a notch in terms of her appearance while working. Her hair had to stay back, but she'd begun highlighting her features with salmon lipstick, a hint of blush, and hazel eye shadow that made her eyes gleam like newly polished emeralds. Who knew when she might be asked to make a dining room appearance? Jaden had quickly come to realize that in Miami, image was *everything*.

This evening her black slacks complemented a perfectly pressed chef's jacket, embroidered with Chef Thorne across the left lapel. She'd made sure the jacket bordered on the small side for a more flattering fit. Having taken charge of all aspects of her work life, Jaden now felt prepared for almost anything.

Now, despite the gauntlet of semi-seared tuna and vegetable side dish ingredients laid out before her, Jaden couldn't help but wonder what Ivan was doing. Where was he? Was his hair slicked back in a ponytail or hanging savagely around his face and shoulders? What was he wearing? *Not now*. She pushed the vivid images aside. *I'll see him soon enough…all of him.* But when?

They still hadn't made plans for their next rendezvous. The restaurant always wanted more of her, and Ivan had been slammed with work, putting in long hours even after he finished seeing patients as he prepared to roll out a new diet plan at the clinic. He also squeezed in a photo shoot on occasion, and always had a plan brewing for some sort of new investment. He was a man who tried to do everything. Jaden laughed to herself. But as long as he was doing her… She cut herself off as her mind transitioned from PG to X in no time.

Maybe she could send him a little hello to make him smile that cocky-cute smile she loved. Grabbing her phone, her fingers went to work:

> Wanted to say I miss the feel of you…
> Inside of me ;)

The second text followed the first after just a few moment's delay. *That should get some blood flowing.* Within seconds a response flashed across her screen:

> Dios mio! Me gusta, chica. Can't wait to taste your lips…

Jaden forced herself back to work, trying not to think too much about which lips he meant. Dirty boy. The thought of him between her legs made her vision a little blurry. Willing her mind to focus on the task at hand, she began to slice a medley of vegetables. Then, finding her rhythm, she transitioned quickly and efficiently to the fish, adding spices and tenderizing it at the same time. Cranking the dial to high and pouring extra virgin olive oil into the pan, she prepared to sear. Not once did she miss a beat, and when she looked up, a group of *sous* chefs had stopped to watch her. "Get back to work," she admonished them with a blush, but flying through her first batch of orders, and perhaps just a teeny bit distracted, Jaden impressed even herself.

"Now all I need is a TV show," Jaden joked under her breath as she put the finishing touches on a Carpaccio salad.

Susan burst through the kitchen's double doors and screeched the moment they closed behind her. "He's back!"

Jaden's heart fluttered. How had he gotten here so quickly? He must've read her mind — or been on the way even before she texted? She began to play out the situation in her head: Ivan tasting the pineapple lip gloss she now wore on a daily basis as his lips, soft and sweet, met hers in a tender kiss. But her fantasy came to an abrupt end as Susan finished what she'd been saying: "That food critic guy Chef Thorne's boyfriend knows."

"He's not my boyfriend, and we aren't in fifth grade," Jaden said, somewhat startled. Not that Susan's use of the word *boyfriend* bothered her… It was a little nerve-wracking, but also comforting, something she could get very used to. Then it hit her: the food critic was sitting in her dining room *again*. This had to be a good sign, right?

"Oh, Jesus," she cursed. All thoughts of Ivan were temporarily sidelined as she switched into high gear. "Make sure he knows I'm on hand, and I'll happily cook anything he'd like."

"Okay, will do," Susan said as she hurried out the door. "And he's with that fake-looking blonde," she added. "The one with the big…you know."

Her again! Who the hell is she? Jaden mentally screamed. *Okay, focus. This is the second time this month he's been here, so he must like your food — or maybe it's just a coincidence.* Jaden scrambled around the kitchen making sure everything was ready.

"Here we go," Susan announced when she reappeared. "They want one grouper, one lamb, one duck, and of-freaking-course, a soufflé!"

A sampling order! This had just been upgraded from casual dinner preparation to a culinary SAT exam. "Okay people, listen up," Jaden yelled. "We have some VIPs in the house tonight, so let's get this right the first time around, shall we?"

Jaden was pleased to see postures straightened, shirts and collars readjusted, and sleeves rolled up as the army of *sous* chefs and wait staff readied themselves for a cooking war. Jaden knew she was in the zone. Whether it was the excitement of her first big shot, the thrill of being under pressure, or the confidence Ivan had left her with, she wasn't sure—but it was working in her favor.

Her first priority was ensuring that the soufflé was started. After that, she flew through frying the grouper and preparing the lamb and duck. When plating them, Jaden took special care to create a presentation that looked like art. Remembering that the menacing blonde liked wine, she added a complimentary bottle of pinot noir for them to try during their taste test. Susan hurriedly swiped up the dishes and headed for the chef's table.

Though there were certainly other orders to attend to, Jaden kept one eye on the kitchen doors until Susan finally returned.

"They're finished," she reported. "Should I bring the soufflé out?"

"Didn't you hear or see anything?" Jaden asked, pacing in front of the stove. "Did they at least look like they were enjoying it?"

Susan finally cracked a smile. "They loved it!" she gushed. "While I was waiting on the table next to them, I caught a bit of what they were saying. They were really focused on the presentation, which they loved, and the blonde kept mentioning how personable and pretty you were."

"What the hell does that have to do with my cooking?"

"The critic said he wouldn't have changed a thing," Susan continued. "He was particularly fond of the duck," she said with a giggle.

"Here, take it." Jaden carefully passed Susan the soufflé. She was physically, mentally, and emotionally exhausted but beyond happy that they'd enjoyed the meal. Between work, Ivan, and food critics, she was beat, but in the best possible way.

Seconds turned to minutes once again as the time ticked by on the 1950s-style clock that hung on the tiled wall of the kitchen. Jaden continued her pacing until Susan finally returned with an elated look on her face.

"They loved it!" she screamed and ran to Jaden, throwing her arms around her. "Congrats, you deserve it!"

Jaden, for a moment, jumped up and down beside Susan like a kindergartener, but she quickly regained her composure and smiled cockily. "I knew they would."

"They want to have a word with you real quick, but they're in a hurry, so get out there before they leave."

"What? How do I look?"

"You look like a freaking supermodel masquerading as a chef. Now get your ass out there!" Taking a towel from the counter, Susan brushed flour off the sleeve of Jaden's coat.

"Thanks!" With a deep breath, Jaden once again walked through the doors toward fate. The blond woman and the critic were already standing up and organizing their belongings as they prepared to leave. Jaden expertly navigated the dining room, rushing to meet with them, but halfway she was met with a barrage of red, white, and yellow roses. Ducking out of the way, she slid past the men who carried them but was halted by the maître d', who stepped in front of her.

"Chef Thorne, you need to sign for these," he said in his snooty French accent.

"These are for me?" *No way.*

"Yes," he replied, clearly annoyed by the onslaught of what looked to be close to eight-dozen long-stemmed roses.

"There has to be some sort of mistake."

"No, Chef Thorne, it says right here on the card: *To Jaden, my fellow turtle watcher*," he replied. "I shan't even ask what that is referring to." He huffed as he passed her the small white envelope that had accompanied the flowers.

Oh my God, he didn't. She took the card from the maître d's outstretched hand. *Oh my God, he did.*

The culinary critiquers now walked toward her, and she panicked. "Wait here. I'll be right back," Jaden said to the maître d' and returned her attention to the VIPs.

"Chef Thorne, it's so nice to see you again," the bald man exclaimed, offering her his hand. "I'm Stephen Watson, food critic for the *Herald*."

"I'm happy to finally officially meet you, Mr. Watson. I hope you enjoyed your meal," Jaden stammered, trying to suppress her excitement.

"Another culinary masterpiece," her arch nemesis cackled in a too-tight pink dress.

"It's so nice to see you again." Jaden smiled.

"Unfortunately, we do have to run," explained Mr. Watson, fidgeting with the top button on his shirt. "But keep your eye on the paper over the next few days. I think you'll be pleased with one of my upcoming articles." He smiled and added a wink that sent Jaden's mind soaring.

"I definitely will, and thank you again for stopping in. It's always a pleasure." Jaden was once more interrupted by the maître d'.

"Chef Thorne, can you please sign for these? These men need to leave."

Jaden smiled politely as she imagined wringing his little fucking French neck for interrupting the most important moment of her culinary life.

"Well, apparently we aren't the only ones impressed with you, are we?" the blonde said with what might have been just a hint of jealousy in her voice.

Jaden, now embarrassed, could only laugh at the situation. She hurried over, snatched the pen out of the maître d's hand, and scribbled her name across the delivery slip. Turning her attention back to the critic and the blonde, Jaden replied, "I hope to see you again, and I look forward your article, Mr. Watson."

"Yes, next time you must *join* us for dinner."

"Certainly," Jaden agreed. "Please let me know when you'll be coming, and I'd be honored to join you for dinner."

The blond woman leaned in for a high society, half-assed hug. "I'll be in touch," she called, and both of them waved as they headed for the exit.

Goddamn it! She still hadn't gotten the woman's name, but no matter. In her mind, she'd just won the Super Bowl, and it was time to celebrate. But first she had to take care of another matter: eight-dozen roses! She smiled at the entire floral shop that now filled the restaurant and decided to have the flowers placed throughout the dining room for the remainder of the evening. As soon as Jaden had this happy inconvenience sorted, she returned the kitchen and poured herself a glass of her favorite Australian shiraz, the one she'd come to love since her night in Sarasota.

Digging her phone out of her pocket, she quickly checked it for messages. This time there was an email from Ivan:

> Some say give a woman a bouquet of roses and she'll smile.
>
> Give her two bouquets of roses and she'll think about you.
>
> Give her three bouquets of roses and she'll forgive you.
>
> Give her four and she'll fall in love with you.
>
> I doubled that, and all I ask is for a second date.
>
> Would you do me honor, Ms. Thorne, of accompanying me on a second date this Friday?
>
> Your fellow turtle watcher,
>
> Ivan

Jaden's smile threatened to overtake her face. At this precise moment, her life was perfect. But an edge of fear lingered nearby because with every peak comes an inevitable valley. Friday…oh, God! There were no special events, so surely she could prep early and duck out for the evening. She closed her eyes for a moment and calmed herself. Tonight's events had been too much to fully absorb. Tomorrow she'd worry about the dangers of too much perfection, but not tonight. Tonight was hers.

She looked down at her phone for a second before responding, then typed:

> Ninety-six roses couldn't have made me smile or think of you any more than I already was, but yes, they won you a second date. Let's find some more turtles!

Filling her glass once more, Jaden saluted herself and downed the contents before returning to work a new woman…a complete woman.

Chapter 12

"Young Lust"

*L*ynyrd Skynyrd's "Free Bird" screeched from the nightstand as the alarm clock on Ivan's phone reached five thirty a.m. The sound woke him from near-comatose sleep. Classic rock was a complete one-eighty from the tranquil sounds of the rainforest he'd fallen asleep to.

"Ay…Ay…Ay…" was all he could muster as he rubbed his eyes. His mind immediately began running in circles over everything he had to do today. Somehow he'd have to fit in his usual exercise sessions before preparing and presenting a fantastic night for his new baby girl. *God*, he thought to himself. *I have to stop calling her that.*

He shivered as frigid air assaulted him. Since moving to Miami two years ago, Ivan had insisted on having the air conditioner cranked up full blast during the night to help him sleep. It reminded him of the freezing northwestern Pennsylvania winters he'd been accustomed to growing up.

As he lifted the blanket, determined to start the day, his cock greeted him, hard and erect against his stomach. He must've been having one fantastic dream because the air was freezing cold, and he still managed to stand at full salute.

"Damn, girl." His thoughts drifted to Jaden, and he wondered what her morning routine was like. Did she sleep naked, or wear a thong? Boy shorts? Some other kind of frilly shit he didn't even know existed but no doubt looked great hugging that amazing ass of hers? Would she say yes if he asked her to spend the night so he could observe firsthand, or was it too soon?

He couldn't resist gliding his hand over his erection as thoughts of her sleek form cleared his morning haze. How would she wake him in the morning? A tender kiss, a gentle shake of his shoulder, or would she surprise him with a kiss of a different sort? The thought of Jaden's sweet, soft lips soon had him gripping his cock in earnest. He began stroking it slowly, then harder and faster as his fantasy grew. He kicked off the blankets and sheets completely as the image of Jaden's warmth against his cold flesh replayed over and over in his mind: the taste of her laid out on the beach, the sight of her in front of him on the balcony, her perfume mixing with their animalistic lust. His hand worked his cock in ever-quickening strokes as he imagined Jaden in the short black dress that hugged her tight ass and perfect tits kneeling before him, her mouth taking him in. In an instant he came hard and fast. He lay spread-eagled and breathing heavy, his body spent.

When he'd recovered and finally rolled out of bed, Ivan was greeted by a cold floor. He hop-shuffled over to the window of his twelfth-floor condo on the bay side of Miami Beach to sneak a peek at the weather for his early-morning jog. The faint orange glow illuminating the clouds above the distant Miami skyline meant the possibility of rain, but that didn't matter. He was up, and this was his routine.

He flipped on the light, illuminating his room and all his familiar, favorite things. An M.C. Escher print hung on the cardinal red wall above his bed. His blue sunburst guitar sat on its pedestal in the corner next to his grandmother's favorite denim chair, one of the only things he'd brought with him from home. He'd positioned his chestnut dresser beneath the ocean-facing window so on even his busiest days he'd have the view to remind him that life was beautiful and precious.

"Shit, it's cold," he muttered as if to reassure himself he wasn't imagining the chill. Pulling on a pair of clean briefs, white shorts, and his favorite Pink Floyd T-shirt, he headed for the bathroom.

Ivan splashed his face with cold water and drenched his hair in an attempt to spark a shot of adrenaline for his seven-mile daily jaunt ahead. He watched the water drip from his face in the mirror and started smiling. Forget the water. The image of Jaden running her hands through her hair on the beach as the moonlight painted her in an ethereal glow gave him just the jumpstart he needed for the run.

Then his mind circled back to his packed day ahead, and the excitement was short lived: exercise, patients at the spa, a lunch meeting about the new weight loss program's debut, then back to work, more exercise, and *then* his second date with his sweet new addiction.

Tonight he planned to offer Jaden a completely different experience—and he was both excited and paralyzed by the possibilities. Returning to his bedroom, he sat on the bed to put on his old sneakers. He'd estimated they had around one thousand miles on them, and they were on the verge of being retired. After lacing them up, he gave a half-assed attempt at a stretch before grabbing his phone and completing the ritual that unfolded each and every morning. Passing through the still-dark living room, Ivan entered the kitchen, snagged a bottle of water from the fridge and chugged it, hoping to get enough fluid in his system to counteract the muggy morning.

Closing the fridge door, he retreated back through his apartment and out the front door. On his way to the elevator, his obligations—both business and pleasure—crept back for another spin around his head, and he cranked up the tunes. But he soon realized his attempt to divert his attention with even the melodies of Pink Floyd was futile. Work receded into the background, but he couldn't stop wondering what Jaden might wear on their date—or *not* wear, if he had his way.

Sundress? No, too casual. Evening dress? Too formal. Sexy police officer outfit? Now we're talking, but unlikely. Whatever it might be, Ivan knew it would look great. Jaden would look sexy in a clown costume.

As he stepped into the elevator, Ivan continued his daydreaming and personal predictions. *Hair up or down? Heels or flats? Floral or fruity perfume? Heavy or minimal makeup? Thong or*—He stopped himself. *God, I am terrible. But thong for sure*, his mind snuck in. He had a particular fetish for the strappy little pieces of dental floss that women called underwear, not to mention skirts that barely concealed them.

When the elevator came to rest on the ground floor, Ivan exited with an extra jump in his step, his blood pumping with fantasies of the knockout he was courting. *Courting?* Is that what he was doing?

Did this relationship with Jaden have the potential to be more than just great sea-turtle watching? The answer came to him as naturally as breathing: *Yes.*

Ivan was still shaking his head, shocked that he hadn't come to this conclusion sooner, when he left the air-conditioned lobby and an extra-muggy heat wave crashed over him like a ton of bricks. Setting out into the wet furnace that was Miami Beach, he jogged the short distance to the beach. He took extra-long strides, hoping to elongate his leg muscles, which felt like they were back in bed. Less than five minutes in the heat and a thin sheen of sweat covered his body. He yanked his shirt over his head and tucked it in the back of his shorts.

A woman jogging by slowed her pace to watch. His biceps flexed as he reached above his head for a final stretch. She nearly tripped and fell headfirst into the sand. "You okay?" Ivan asked as he heard her gasp, but with his thoughts focused on Jaden, he hardly even saw her.

As he began to run, he wondered if the way he was pursuing Jaden was proper. He'd never really pursued a girl before, and being so forward was foreign to him. All of his past relationships had either been a set up by a friend or his agent, so the game he now played was different. But there was something different about Jaden.

He recalled the second he'd laid eyes on her. The presence she carried when she stepped out onto the dance floor was palpable—the way her red dress had outlined her slender form, the searching look on her face. In the first moments of seeing her, Ivan knew this woman was worth taking a chance on.

Yeah, he'd been around the world and been with beauty queens, actresses, singers, and socialites, but this girl in the red dress had blown his mind and altered his world before he'd even learned her name. And *since* he'd learned her name? She'd only cranked up the heat.

Ivan had finished his warm-up and now faced another choice: run on the path constructed at the sand's edge or go off-road on the sand. He reminded himself that he'd moved to Miami to live on the beach and chose the latter. Giving his neck a final crack and his back a rotating twist, Ivan turned his attention to the psychedelic rhythm of his music and set off for six more miles of sand and sweat. He couldn't stop grinning.

CHAPTER 13

"Shakin'"

Jaden circled the kitchen for what seemed like the fiftieth time, reading and rereading the text message she'd received during her lunch break:

> Wishing you a beautiful day, and I hope you're up for a magical night. I'm looking forward to getting to know the real Jaden Thorne tonight, inside and out. Hope you're hungry, and think casual!

Hungry? That was easy. But casual? What was that? A dress, blue jeans, shorts? This Miami Beach lingo was a language she needed to learn, and fast. But even if she came to understand the language, she might not be very fluent, Jaden worried. Her wardrobe was on the modest side, and not many of her clothes actually carried designer labels. Fearing she might be in over her head, Jaden ever-so-casually asked her *sous* chef—and fashionable Miami native—what Ivan meant by casual.

Chuckling, Bert took her to peek through the restaurant's kitchen doors. "Do you see that lady in the blue top and nice jeans? That's casual." He pointed to a woman sitting at the bar. "The lady over there in the red dress and high heels? That's smart casual. As for formal, think celebrity wedding. There you go! Miami Beach Clothing one-oh-one."

"Gotcha!" Jaden said, feeling better as they returned to work.

She could do that, and now that she knew what to aim for, all she needed was for her day to end. But the time crawled by as she prepped for the evening's rush, which gave Jaden a chance to mentally scan her closet and audition outfit possibilities. When she finally felt satisfied she was leaving the evening's kitchen staff in good shape, she sailed out the door. It was amazing to have an actual weekend ahead of her, instead of putting in the endless hours she was becoming accustomed to.

Practically running to her car, and breaking every speed limit on the way home, Jaden didn't even wait for the elevator to arrive and instead ran up the four flights of stairs to her apartment, praying that Tasha was home to help her get ready. In her frantic attempt to unlock the door, she fumbled with the keys and dropped them on the ground. She cursed herself for wasting time. Bursting into the apartment, she was met by luck: Tasha sat in front of the computer, and Michael was nowhere to be seen. Success!

"Slow down, killer," Tasha said as Jaden ran past her in a blur "Where's the fire?"

"No fire," Jaden called from her bedroom. "But I need help getting ready. Ivan's picking me up in two hours, so we need to get moving."

"Take deep, calming breaths and relax." Tasha laughed. "Do you think he's acting this insane getting ready for you?"

Ivan snapped his computer shut and left his office within moments of finishing his last consultation. He tossed a pile of paperwork and a round of goodbyes to the ladies at the reception desk and strolled out through the lobby of the Four Seasons. He mounted his black Ducati and began the trip back across the bridge to his apartment, the bike lane allowing him to speed past the standstill traffic as he tended to do. He'd decided against his helmet, a rarity for him, but the temperature was too perfect, and he loved the feel of the wind sliding through his hair — even if it meant taking a stupid risk.

With his usual button-down shirt now unbuttoned halfway down, Ivan finally gave himself over completely to his anticipation of the evening's events. He felt on top of the world and ready for anything. His aviator sunglasses gleamed in the five o'clock sun and nearly flew from his face as made a particularly high-speed turn into the parking lot. Ivan parked the bike in front of Betty, his Jeep, and trotted toward the door. He felt a bit shaky now and was surprised by his concern, not about what he was going to wear, but about how clean his apartment was (or wasn't) and what to cook.

His plan for the evening involved sharing his love of the culinary arts with Jaden. Ivan hadn't told her—or anyone else, actually—but he would've loved to become a chef. He might have pursued it if he hadn't gotten caught up in the modeling and doctoring gigs.

He'd grown up in a family that relished big meals accompanied by even bigger smiles, and he'd learned to cook not only by watching his mom but also his dad. His mother's Italian family gave him a flair for the perfect pasta sauce and a love of holiday traditions like ham-and-cheese pie and the Seven Fishes of Italy—a dish he looked forward to cooking every Christmas Eve in his Santa suit. His father's side brought the Russian flavor of pigs in a blanket and *halupki*, a stuffed cabbage dish. As he grew older and learned more about nutrition for his medical career, he'd taught himself the basics of roasting a turkey and stir-frying vegetables, and he'd studied up on simple, healthy, cooking-from-scratch techniques.

He wanted to show Jaden he shared her love for cooking and prepare her a meal from start to finish. Normally Ivan would have thought it wasn't such a good idea to cook dinner for a chef, but this was Jaden—*and* he felt confident he had the upper hand. Not only would he cook her a meal fit for a queen, if needed, he could top it off with a bottle of the wine he and his father made every year.

But exactly *what* to make for her still weighed heavily on his mind. If he made something easy, she wouldn't be impressed. If he tried something hard and ruined it, he'd be embarrassed. He needed to find middle ground. Ivan checked his watch. He had two hours to make up his mind, buy the groceries, get himself ready, clean the condo, and, of course, get her some little token of his affection. Brought up to respect women, he tried to do something special on each date. Corny? Yes. But he enjoyed it.

Bursting back out of his apartment, keys once again in hand, Ivan formulated a mental game plan and set to work plotting a night he hoped would capture Jaden's heart once and for all.

The first hour flew by as the girls searched frantically for the perfect "casual" outfit. Despite Jaden's mental calculations at work, her confusion returned the moment she opened her closet door. Tasha to the rescue! After a quick shower, Jaden now sat in front of her mirror wearing a pair of jeans accentuated by an oversized brown belt and a white, low-cut top. Tasha's skilled hands put on the finishing touches, ensuring that Jaden's makeup and hair looked like she'd just stepped out of a salon.

Jaden's phone beeped, startling both of them, and she saw there was a new text. It was still fifteen minutes before Ivan was supposed to be there.

There's no way that's him, she told herself. Miami Standard Time usually ran thirty minutes behind schedule.

"Don't move," Tasha cautioned. "I don't want to ruin this 'casual' look." She giggled, rolling her eyes. "I'll get it for you."

Picking up Jaden's phone, Tasha read the message:

> I'm on my way, young lady. I'll be there in 5.
> Hope your hair isn't done up.

"So much for all my work. I think we did your hair for nothing," Tasha sighed, giving Jaden a phony menacing glare. "I smell another lunch in my future."

Jaden's heart skipped a beat as the unknown drew near. She'd tormented herself all day trying to figure it out, and finally the evening was about to unfold. She quickly typed back:

> Okay, I'll be in the lobby waiting.

Smoothing her hair into a neat ponytail, Jaden grabbed the small leather bag she'd pre-packed with all the essentials: toothbrush, makeup, change of clothes, and the new items she'd picked up on Lincoln. Slipping into stylish sandals, she kissed Tasha on the cheek, smiling knowingly. "I owe you one."

"Yes, you do," Tasha said. She returned the kiss, adding, "Oh, and try not to come back tonight. I want all the juicy details tomorrow morning."

Jaden smiled nervously. She had no idea if Ivan would even ask her, and she wasn't at all sure she was ready to spend the night just yet. But who was she kidding? The bag hanging over her shoulder was proof enough it was something she wanted.

Jaden was a little disappointed not to see Ivan when she stepped out of the elevators, and as she left the lobby, she saw no sign of the black beast that had picked her up last time. What did catch her eye was a hot-looking motorcycle sitting in front of her building. So sexy, and so Miami Beach.

Yep, there he was, some pretty boy straddling the monster. Dark blue denim hugged his legs, and a short-sleeved green polo shirt stretched tightly around the ridged muscles of his arms. The bike roared to life and crept along the curb, coming to rest just inches from Jaden's feet, leaving her both startled and annoyed. *Who does this asshole think he is?*

Wordlessly, the asshole raised the shield hiding his face. Eyeing her inquisitively, Ivan asked, "Are you making assumptions again, young lady?"

Feeling like a complete idiot, Jaden burst out in laughter. "Really? Do you honestly think I look like a biker chick? Now you're the one making assumptions, doctor."

Stepping off the bike, Ivan removed his helmet, releasing hair that flowed over his shoulders. Jaden smiled, remembering the way Ivan's hair had felt as she wrapped her hands around it, and the intoxicating scent that came off him in waves as he heated up. A shiver swept across her skin as she approached the bike.

"*This* is why I was hoping you hadn't spent too much time on your hair," Ivan said as he revealed another helmet.

"Oh, of course not," Jaden said sarcastically. "I just threw everything together."

"Well done. You look delicious." Ivan pulled her close and kissed her cheek. "There's only one thing missing," he added, and Jaden saw the small box in his hand.

She gasped as he opened the box to show her, and then slowly turned her around. He brushed aside her hair and draped the silver necklace around her neck, securing the tiny clasp from the back. Hanging from the chain was a golden sea turtle. Jaden reached up and ran her fingers over its smooth surface.

"I've never been so jealous of a turtle!" Ivan smiled and kissed the silky skin at the nape of her neck.

Jaden turned to face him and inhaled deeply. Her passion for this man overpowered her, and she kissed him with fervor. "You're too good to me. What did I do to deserve you?"

"The night has just begun, baby," he whispered against her skin.

"Well, thank you. You have no idea how much this means to me." Jaden had always been happy with the simple things in life, and she found the greatest joy in small, meaningful gestures. Overwhelmed by feelings, she leaned in and kissed him again. "If you're lucky, I may just show you *how* grateful I am."

"Mmmmmm…" Ivan cleared his throat and stepped back, appearing to catch his breath. "Okay! Will you be all right riding this bad boy?"

"There's a first time for everything," Jaden replied, also a bit breathless.

She put on the helmet Ivan handed her and slid on to the back of the Ducati. She admired its smooth lines and the way her arms naturally fit with the curves of his body and her ass with the curves of the bike. It almost seemed built for sex. She grasped him firmly around the waist, and after retrieving his sunglasses from his pocket, Ivan started the bike. Instantly vibrations danced up Jaden's thighs, surprising her, but if she was going to be a biker chick, she needed to be one with the bike, right?

As Ivan picked up speed, the purr of the engine massaged her pussy, and she squirmed with pleasure, gripping Ivan more tightly. Was she going to cum before they made their destination? And where was their destination? Jaden had just begun to wonder how she could ask Ivan about that when he revved the engine, sending a fresh cascade of tingles all through her, and then snaked a hand between them. He rubbed her sweet spot gently and intently, which soon sent her over the edge—at sixty miles per hour. That was a first. And Ivan, of course, had chosen to travel Ocean Drive, the busiest street on the beach right now. Sunbathers and happy hour patrons gawked as the smiling couple sped by.

She'd gathered herself together, and Jaden's mind began to turn as they pulled up at Mirador, a boutique high-rise building on the beach. It obviously wasn't a restaurant… As the bike came to a stop at the front entrance, Ivan cut the engine and helped her down. He smiled wickedly, but said nothing.

"Where are we?" Jaden could no longer contain her curiosity.

"Like I said, I hope you're hungry!" Ivan grinned as he took her hand and led her into the lobby. He waved as they passed the front deskman, who gave him a nod in return.

As they waited for the elevators, Jaden whispered, "I have a sneaking suspicion you live here."

"What?" Ivan said, eyes wide. "Can't you just let a guy surprise you?"

As they entered the elevator, confident she was right, Jaden began to imagine the night ahead. An evening at home! Possibilities both sweet and extreme flashed through her mind, and she concluded she still had no damn clue what to expect.

As the elevators opened, Ivan took Jaden's hand again, this time entwining his fingers with hers. He gave her a look, as if to test her reaction. Jaden's heart warmed at the romantic gesture, and his cautious attention to her feelings. She squeezed his hand and smiled as they walked down the corridor.

Chapter 14

"Today"

Ivan fumbled with his keys, and Jaden almost smacked them right out of his hand as she slugged his shoulder. "I was right! This is your place."

"That's gonna leave a bruise you know!"

"Please," she scoffed. "I barely touched you."

"Yeah, yeah, you win." Ivan laughed as he unlocked the door and pushed it open. "After you, madam."

As she entered, Jaden first noticed the refreshing splash of cold air. Then she was captivated by the view. Through the windows, downtown Miami had begun to light up in the distance. Only then did she turn her attention to the place itself. It was filled with all sorts of things, yet somehow managed to seem organized. *Sort of like Ivan himself,* she thought with a laugh.

"Okay, I admit it! I have a cleaning lady come in from time to time," Ivan confessed.

"Good to know." Jaden snickered again as she continued her look around. As she moved farther into the space, she detected the faint scent of vanilla spice. There must be a candle somewhere. Or was he baking? You never knew with this one…

Intrigued by all that surrounded her, she walked over to examine a collection of frames in varying shapes and sizes. There were pictures of Ivan hugging sea lions, holding koalas, climbing rocks, and engaging in a variety of activities with people she assumed to be his family.

"You have quite a background, Dr. Ivan. I could make a whole list of things to ask you about now."

He smiled again but with intensity this time. In an instant he'd moved in to wrap his arms around her waist, and his warm breath tickled her skin as he spoke. "Thanks, but tonight isn't about me — it's about *us*."

Jaden was just about to comment on a striking picture of a budding sunflower when Ivan slid his hands down the length of her torso to rest at her hips and positioned himself directly behind her. Shutting her eyes and tucking her head into the crook of his neck, Jaden indulged her senses. Not a sliver of space remained between them as she leaned back and felt his growing erection.

"What brought this on?" she asked breathlessly. "Not that I'm complaining."

"I guess I liked the way you called me Dr. Ivan," he said with a low laugh that was nearly a growl. He slid his hands beneath her top and traced her abdomen, his fingers ascending and descending as he made his way along her ribs to the button of her jeans. He fingered the small, metal button for a moment, and Jaden felt time slow nearly to a stop as he seemed to deliberate about what to do. Her mind raced. What could he be thinking? Was he unsure what she wanted?

Her questions vanished as Ivan began to trace the curve of her ear with his tongue, licking ever so softly, and her body swayed at the sensation. Slowly, he popped the button and slid his hand down the front of her jeans, past the zipper, and to the moist spot between her legs. As his fingers explored the wetness still remaining from her encounter with the Ducati, Jaden shamelessly spread her legs, urging him to continue.

Ivan slid her jeans to her ankles, and she widened her stance. She eyed the couch, wondering if she'd be able to remain standing through the good doctor's treatment but decided she'd best not change a thing as he slid one finger in and began to stroke her clit with his thumb. Jaden quivered, and with his fingers rocking back and forth at a steady pace, she began to moan in ecstasy. Faster and faster his fingers fucked her, drawing her toward yet another orgasm. Just as her body trembled and contracted, Ivan drew his hand upward, pressing his palm hard against her clit. Jaden could barely keep her footing as waves of pleasure engulfed her, and she clung to him for support. "Holy fuck," she whispered after a moment.

Ivan gave her a warm squeeze and kissed her neck. "Are you ready for dinner, my dear?"

Drawing her eyes back into focus and finding the kitchen, Jaden smiled. She now realized what the evening had in store for her. "Yes, doctor, I think I am."

A brown-speckled counter topped the kitchen island where two wine glasses awaited, along with two bar stools. Off to one side, wine decanted in a glass bottle that looked oddly like a chemistry project. Ivan picked up a small black remote, and from somewhere in the distance the sultry voice a familiar artist filled the air: "The Way You Look Tonight" once again. The memory that accompanied the tune brought a smile to both their faces.

"Welcome to *casa de* Ivan, where this evening I will have the honor of cooking for you." He pulled out one of the bar stools and motioned for her to take a seat.

Jaden suddenly didn't care if hot dogs and hamburgers were the only thing on the menu tonight. Ivan was so thoughtful to do something so special and personal for her, and so early in their relationship…"You're too sweet. Thank you," she said, looking meaningfully at him.

She realized this was the first time she'd ever had a boyfriend do something like this for her. *Boyfriend?* Jaden cursed herself. So far everything was going great, but *boyfriend* made it sound so official. This was only their second date, and things weren't that serious yet. Were they? *Get a grip, oh Queen of the Planet of Unrealistic Expectations.* She returned her attention to Ivan, who now busied himself with dinner preparations.

He brought over the decanter full of wine. "I'm cooking," he said. "But don't think you're getting off easy. You have two jobs tonight. First, you're the official DJ, and second, you have to help me polish off a few bottles of fantastic wine."

"Hmm…I have to be the DJ and the bartender, eh? Who's going to be the designated driver after we down all this booze?" she asked playfully.

"We can cross that bridge when we come to it." Ivan winked seductively before setting two glasses next to the decanter.

Jaden looked from the decanter to the empty wine bottle on the counter. *Carnival of Love. How perfect.* She shook her head and smiled. "I think we have ourselves a deal, doc."

She watched in wonder as Ivan moved through the kitchen with the grace and ease of a professional chef, almost as naturally as she did in her own kitchen. "So, what might the good doctor be preparing for us this evening? Hot dogs? Hamburgers?"

"Really? You don't think too much of these culinary skills, do you?" He looked down at his hands in mock disbelief. "I considered going to culinary school, you know, and cooking just so happens to be in my blood, Ms. Thorne."

Ivan laughed, then — doing the worst Sean Connery impersonation she'd ever heard — he began to present the menu. "Tonight we shall dine on a shrimp stir fry including cashews, broccoli, baby corn, and Brussels sprouts with traces of fresh garlic. Accompanying this shall be a side of spaghetti squash laced with hints of cinnamon and butter, but first we shall start with an arugula salad, complete with cherry tomatoes — that's to-*mah*-toes, not to-*may*-toes — and feta cheese topped with a balsamic reduction. Our wine selections for this evening are Australia's finest — some of my favorites of all time."

Ivan motioned to a cluster of bottles on the counter, including one in a velvet bag. Jaden remembered the velvet-shrouded bottles he'd received at the Winemaker's Dinner.

"As for dessert…well, we shall see how dinner goes before we talk of such a thing."

When he'd finished, Jaden didn't know whether to laugh or swoon. Was he serious?

"Not quite hot dogs and hamburgers, is it?" Ivan added, in his regular voice.

Jaden nearly died laughing. "I was genuinely fine with some hot dogs, but since it seems you can talk the talk, now we'll see if you can walk the walk."

She left her stool and slid across the tile floor to where Ivan stood at the counter. She drew him to her, kissing him ever so teasingly, licking and tickling his bottom lip with the tip of her tongue. "I'll be in charge of dessert," she whispered.

"Well, now I'm officially distracted," Ivan announced. "I must have a glass of wine, and Ms. DJ, what's it gonna be? You have more than eight thousand songs to choose from. Don't disappoint!"

"What's wrong with what we have on?" Jaden asked. "I love Sinatra, and I'd say so do you."

"Sold!" Ivan replied cheerfully as Jaden poured the wine.

Handing Ivan his glass, Jaden raised hers in a toast. "To officially finding out who we are tonight."

"And to what our future may hold," Ivan added as their glasses clinked together. His eyes found hers and held them for a moment, unblinking. Then, retreating to the refrigerator, Ivan returned with salad fixings, stir fry vegetables, and a gigantic squash.

"What can I do?" Jaden asked.

"Nothing," Ivan assured her. "I've got it all under control. Just sit back, relax, and talk." He smiled at her. "Where are you from? And I'm not looking for just a city and state. I want details, girl."

"Hmm…let's see." Jaden took another sip of her wine, relieved that the first question was easy. "I grew up in a small town in Colorado called Estes Park. It's basically a giant wildlife preserve. You can't walk out the front door without bumping into some sort of animal." Jaden smiled, remembering her childhood. "If I wasn't in school, I was either at the lake swimming and catching frogs, helping out at my grandparent's farm, or fishing with my Poppy. In the winter we'd find the biggest hill and spend the entire day tobogganing."

"We? You have brothers and sisters?" Ivan moved methodically as he chopped vegetables. "What do your parents do?"

"Hey, that's three questions you've asked. Not fair," Jaden teased. She took another long sip of her wine.

"I have one sister and one brother, and we're all pretty different from each other. My sister is in her last year of high school. Everyone thinks she's a drama queen because she's the youngest, but underneath all the makeup, gossip, and sassy talk, she's really sweet. My brother, on the other hand, is a little rougher around the edges. He's a tattoo-covered metal head who spends far too much time playing video games, drinking beer, and goofing off with his friends. Dad is a park ranger, which is probably where I inherited my love of animals and nature, and my mom has her hands full trying to keep us all in line."

Determined not to talk this much the entire evening, Jaden threw out a question before Ivan got a chance to reload. "Okay, now your turn, Mr. USA. What about your family?"

"Ha ha—I see you're fluent in Google, huh?" Ivan moved on to mixing the salad. "Well, much like you, I came from a very small town. Mine's in northwest Pennsylvania where the only places open past ten p.m. are Walmart and Perkins. My dad is a chiropractor, and he's the reason I became a doctor. I had a few other options available after college, but that was the right choice, especially with my Pap there to guide me. My mom has her masters in psychology, but chose a much harder profession: raising us. She's a woman of faith, always praying for us, and I think it's *her* faith and love for our family that's kept me on the straight and narrow. My brother is a well-established reconstructive urologist. I call him Captain Cock since his main focus is correcting dick issues."

Ivan's eyes twinkled, and Jaden could see the respect and love he had for his brother.

"He's also my role model," Ivan added. "And my little sis is a physician's assistant at an oncology clinic. She might actually outdo my crazy father on the wild scale. And did I mention she's great at helping me pick up girls?"

Jaden tilted her head and looked at him expectantly.

"Used to be," he countered quickly. "Won't need her assistance any more."

Jaden now felt a little homesick for her own family. "So what did you do growing up? I'm sure you have a few stories to tell."

"My dad thought it would build character if I worked on a farm, so my childhood days consisted of milking cows, bailing hay, and shoveling shit!" Ivan laughed, but his eyes never left hers, and he paused, seemingly just to look at her for a moment. He opened the cupboard and retrieved two plates before continuing. "I hated farm work, but I'm so glad I did it. It gave me an appreciation of the simple things in life—and the value of a hard-earned dollar. But I didn't only work on the farm. I also played hockey all the way through school. I was the tough guy, and I played the part well. Once I even had a chance to go pro," he said, shaking his head. "But I was doing well with school and had just gotten accepted into an advanced medical program, so instead I skipped my last year of college and went directly into medical school. I had a choice between a sure thing and a boyhood dream. After a lot of consideration, and some very careful guidance from my dad, I chose the sure thing. But mind you, not a day goes by that I don't wonder what might've happened if I'd followed that dream."

The salads now finished, Ivan poured the dressing and passed Jaden her plate. "Here's round one. I hope you like. And by the way, you're slacking! We're both bone dry." Ivan looked pointedly at their empty wine glasses.

Still surprised they had such similar backgrounds, Jaden snagged the wine and poured them each a hefty glass. "There you go. And to be fair, I guess you get the next question."

"What are your turn-ons and turn-offs?" Ivan shot back without hesitation. "Besides sea turtles, of course."

Jaden laughed. "Absolutely. Sea turtles, of course, are one of my biggest turn-ons. And bar none, the things I hate the most are smoking, cockiness, and laziness. If any of those three are present, then it's *adios amigo*."

"That's a fantastic answer—about sums it up for me too. Smoking is my biggest turn off," Ivan said, punching holes in the oversized squash.

As he placed it in the microwave, Jaden raised the stakes. "Ex-girlfriends: what went wrong?"

Ivan froze with his arms in midair. "You want to go there, eh?"

Jaden could detect a slight deer-in-the-headlights look in his eyes when he turned around, but then he smiled. "Okay, but you know the gloves are off, right?" Ivan picked up his glass and downed it in one gulp. "What do you want to know about them? Ask and you shall receive. I'm an open book."

"What happened? How did you meet them?" Jaden asked.

"As you'll eventually come to find out, I'm actually a rather shy person. Despite the charade you may read about on the internet, I am not some womanizer, playboy, or pimp. Minus high school sweethearts, I was introduced to each of my ex-girlfriends by a friend, an agent, or a manager in a very business-like fashion. Without that,

I'd have been single for the last five years. But every relationship I've had, though it ended, was wonderful in its own right. I've always combated heartache with a quote I found in the most unusual of places: 'Don't cry because it's over, smile because it happened.'"

Jaden rested her chin in her hand. "That's a good one."

"I can't believe you know that quote," he said, smiling broadly. "I've relied on it in every hard situation I've faced," he admitted. "I've been lucky to share some amazing things with some extraordinary women, and I'll always cherish that, but time and distance can break even the strongest of bonds. I attempted to prove this wrong many times, but it's one thing I've promised myself I'll never do again. It's too hard to let something slip away just because you aren't there."

Wow, Jaden thought. *My assumptions were way off once again.* It seemed Ivan had truly loved and lost. Adrift in her thoughts for a moment, Jaden snapped back to the present when Ivan gently took her hand.

"So what about you," he asked warmly. "How many guys do I have to thank for passing up their chance to be with you?"

"Not many. I had a few high school boyfriends. My senior year, I dated a guy — he was really geeky and quirky, not my usual type, but we hit it off really well. I fell hard for him over the two years that we dated. Then one summer I went to visit family on the coast, and when I got home, I found he'd been cheating on me with one of my best friends. It broke my heart. After that I kept to casual dating until I finished college. I've had a few semi-serious relationships since then, but nothing that's sent me running down the aisle. If I wasn't such a coward when it comes to guys, I probably would've had more luck in the romance department."

"Hahaha…I've got you beat there, girl." Ivan laughed. "I can assure you, I'm the biggest chickenshit you'll ever meet when it comes to talking to the ladies."

"Oh, come on. You bashful?" Jaden interrupted. "You were the furthest thing from bashful at the Winemaker's Dinner! And I've watched a few of your quite chatty interviews online, if you must know…" Jaden blushed and studied her wine.

"Giving interviews on things like fashion or bodybuilding is nothing," Ivan protested, pointing at her with a huge raw shrimp. "Discussing things I'm passionate about like diet and exercise, or children's health? Piece of cake. But surrendering my ego and opening my heart to someone I barely know scares me to death," he proclaimed.

"Then why am I here right now?" Jaden asked in the sexiest way possible, dipping her finger into her wine and twirling it around the rim before licking a drop from the tip of her finger.

"There's a first time for everything," Ivan said, shrugging as he dried his hands with a paper towel. "And watching you walk into that dinner, I knew you were going be that first for me. I can't even explain what went through my mind when you stepped into my field of vision that night."

Biting her lower lip, Jaden tried to suppress an enormous smile. "I'm so happy you did," she responded demurely.

Standing up on the legs of her stool, she leaned across the table as Ivan met her halfway to exchange a smoldering kiss. "Okay, I've got one more," she said, slinking back into her seat as the music transitioned into something more upbeat, lightening the mood. "What about your tattoos? Not very doctorly to have tattoos, now is it?"

Ivan looked skyward as if he'd had this conversation before. "Well, setting yourself apart is the key—especially in this environment," he said with a hearty laugh. "I'm not exactly a white coat and stethoscope guy, you know? Each of my tattoos is for a family member," he explained. "The padre for Mother, who has Italian heritage, and the cross is Russian Orthodox, for my father who's of Russian descent. The one here on my wrist is the Staff of Asclepius, the symbol for physician, and the wings behind it are for my brother. The red on the snake and the blue on the nail are in remembrance of my Mr. USA run, which was a bigger part of my life than I ever would have imagined. And I still need to get a matching one on my other wrist for my sister. It's a work in progress, I guess you could say. I have to wait for inspiration, and then it's hard to find the time to sit and get them done!" He laughed again. "Now, back to you. I don't see any tattoos—and I've checked thoroughly," he added with a wicked grin. "So I'll have to think of something else…" He tapped his chin as if deep in thought for a moment. "What would you say is your main ambition, your main drive? Why did you move from Colorado to Miami?" Ivan asked as he turned on the stove and began to heat some olive oil.

"Well, I'd been looking for a job out here for a while. I told everyone it was because I wanted to live near the ocean, and that Miami was perfect because Tasha already lived here but…"

"The real reason was?" Ivan asked. "Come on, I made an ass out of myself back there a bit ago, join the party."

Jaden struggled to find the right words as he dumped shrimp into the searing oil, creating a cacophony of sounds and smells. Following Ivan's lead, she picked up her wine and downed it in a single gulp. "I've never told anyone this, and I don't know why I'm telling you. You'll think it's stupid."

Ivan looked at her crossly. "I'll *never* think anything you say or do is stupid."

He did seem genuinely interested, so Jaden swallowed her pride. "Ever since I was little, I've always been infatuated with the celebrity lifestyle. My bedroom walls were plastered with posters of cute guys I dreamed of and beautiful women I admired. I wondered how it would feel to walk by and see myself on a magazine cover, or read about an affair I was supposedly having with some actor—and heaven forbid I ever got the chance to see myself on TV. After I went to culinary school, I knew I was done with New York, and LA was also too big. Chicago was too cold, so I settled on Miami, hoping to somehow make my way onto the scene—and it did help that Tasha was here. I was working at a great restaurant in Estes Park where the chef was amazing and such an inspiration to me, and then I got incredibly lucky with Bianca. My mentor actually put in a good word for me—even though it meant I'd be leaving—and Geoff was willing to take a chance." She paused for just a moment, and Ivan didn't respond. "See, now you think I'm an idiot," she mumbled, nervously toying with her empty wine glass.

Ivan finished adding vegetables to the now crispy frying shrimp, then came to wrap his arms around her, surrounding her with his warmth. "I don't think you're stupid at all. Why do you think I'm here? Why do you think half the people in the city are here? We're all chasing fame and fortune in one way or another. I think it's amazing that you stepped outside your comfort zone and moved here. Ninety percent of the population spends time imagining their future and forgetting that *now* is where we live and breathe. The ten percent who live in the present are the ones who have the stories to tell, the ones who live life the way it's meant to be lived. Stupid? No, I think you're doing a great job of living."

Jaden found herself surprisingly comforted by his words. Perhaps her decision to move here made sense after all. She deserved to take a chance. "Thank you."

"Anytime, baby," he said. He smiled down at her, and then cast an eye toward the stir fry. "Time to eat!" he announced.

Lost in their conversation and wine, Jaden had barely noticed the meal coming together. "It smells delicious," she now noted, taking a deep inhale of the layered aromas. "Do you need any help?"

"Yes, more wine for both of us, and more music."

"I'm on it." Jaden poured them each another glass before scrolling through Ivan's playlists. As she fumbled through the endless artists, she wondered briefly if he was for real. He seemed to have a cheat sheet somewhere with all the right things to say. He'd made her feel at peace about his past relationships, and even assured her that pursuing her dream in Miami wasn't crazy. The enigma that was Dr. Ivan Oh So Sexy Rusilko, international male model, was mostly just a front. Deep down, Ivan was a sincere, sweet guy who appreciated the simple things in life—just like her.

Finally settling on an old-school favorite, Jaden clicked on the Dave Matthews Band. "Does this work?" she called.

"More than you know," Ivan responded, waggling his eyebrows as he put the final touches on the spaghetti squash. Apparently satisfied with his presentation, he scooped up both dishes and presented them to Jaden, as if for judging.

She could only smile and shake her head as she admired the colorful concoction that adorned their plates. "You do actually cook!" she said in amazement. "What don't you do?"

"I think you'd better try it first—make sure it's satisfactory," he said. Raising his glass, Ivan motioned for another toast. "Here's to meeting the real Jaden Thorne. Your beauty took my breath away, but your mind has stopped my heart."

Saluting his glass, Jaden just stared at the man before her. Finally she smiled. For once in her life she needed no convincing that she'd made the right choice.

"Now, let's eat!" Ivan said.

CHAPTER 15

"Sexual Healing"

The beautiful dinners now in front of them on the nearby table, Jaden wanted to be sure they didn't lose the intensity of their conversation. Intrigued, she wanted to get a little more personal with her inquisition of Mr. Oh So Sexy.

"So what about you—why are you here in Miami? Are you a doctor, a model, what?" she asked after swallowing a mouthful of the spaghetti squash. "This is delicious, by the way."

Ivan smiled, clearly pleased she was enjoying his food. "If I gave you an answer now, I'd just be guessing. It changes daily," he said with a laugh. "When I'm at the spa, I'm a doctor. When I'm on a shoot, I'm a model. If I had it my way—and I feel stupid even saying it—"

"Please," Jaden interrupted. "If I'm not allowed to feel stupid, then neither are you. Open books, remember?"

"Yeah, right, open books," Ivan conceded. "Well, I would love to end up in politics. I always joke with myself that I'll retire at forty-three after two terms in office as the president…" He trailed off with a laugh, but Jaden wasn't sure if he was kidding.

"You certainly have the background for it," she said. "And in my opinion you're well on your way. I'd vote for you in a heartbeat."

"There's that comedian coming out again." He smiled as she took a bite of shrimp.

"I love how the vegetables are done, and the garlic is fantastic. Well done, you," Jaden said, truly impressed with his cooking. "You really are a jack of all trades."

"A jack of all trades, but master of none," he responded with a comedic sigh.

Noticing that the decanter now sat empty along with their wine glasses, Jaden remembered her designated job and stood to open the next bottle on the kitchen counter, making sure to slide her finger along Ivan's shoulders as she passed.

"Where you off to? Is the food that bad?"

"Nope, I'm just doing my job. We're running on empty." Jaden motioned to the decanter.

"You're not just a pretty face, are you?" Ivan replied. "Grab the one in the velvet bag."

Jaden nodded. Grasping the bottle and corkscrew, she turned and asked, "So, what do you do at your spa?"

He didn't respond right away, but just watched her efficiently opening the wine. "Ivan? Where have you gone?" Jaden asked in a sultry voice. She twirled the corkscrew through her fingers.

Ivan jumped and blushed slightly. Jaden knew she'd caught him in some sort of fantasy. *A corkscrew? Really? Men.*

"Yes, at work I do medical fitness, anti-aging techniques, and sexual health and weight loss counseling," he explained, suddenly all business. "I'm preparing to introduce a new weight loss program, as I think I've told you. It's bound to make some waves, so I've been dealing with all of that. And then I also do stuff like Botox and set up high-end cosmetic parties for the crème de la crème. That's Miami medicine for you. I make the rich more beautiful and they make me, well, not rich, unfortunately." He laughed.

"And what would you recommend for me?" Jaden asked. Still gripping the bottle of wine in one hand and the corkscrew in the other, she turned a complete circle in the middle of the kitchen floor.

She then poured two glasses and decided to use Ivan's lap as her seat, rather than the chair. Straddling his legs, she handed him his glass of wine.

Eyes wide, he immediately took a hefty gulp before reaching around her to place his glass on the table. As he shifted forward,

Jaden felt his stiffness press into the warmth between her legs. She smiled seductively. "Well?" she asked.

Looking deep into Jaden's eyes, Ivan finally responded. "If I could wake up next to you every day for the rest of my life, with you looking half as good as you do, I'd be a very happy man. Every part of you is perfect—I wouldn't change a thing. But mind you, I may have to get a better look before I can confirm my diagnosis."

Without giving him a chance to say another word, Jaden brought her mouth to his and rubbed her hips against him, their bodies caught in a seductive dance on the seat of the chair. Then she pulled back as quickly as she'd progressed. Leaving Ivan both speechless and breathless, she whispered, "I think it's time for dessert, and I think you do too."

Reaching down, she caressed his cock through his jeans. His response was immediate, his hands gripping the arms of the chair and his hips moving in sync with each stroke of her hand. Slipping from his lap, Jaden slid down his legs and onto her knees as she placed her wine beside his on the table. She shivered with anticipation as she ran her hands up and down his thighs and across the prominent bulge in his pants. Batting her eyelashes, she unbuttoned his jeans and slowly dragged down his zipper. "Why, doctor! Going commando, are we? I'm shocked…and pleased."

A slow smirk played on his lips. "I aim to please."

Jaden reached into his jeans and held him firmly in her hands. "Impressive."

Ivan swallowed hard and reached down to brush the stray hair from her brow. "You're killing me here, Jaden."

Her eyes flickered down to his fully erect cock in her hands and then back to his before she took every luscious inch of him into her mouth. Ivan trembled and began to rock with each downward stroke of her mouth. Jaden took her time, working his cock up and down, her hands grasping the base of his shaft as she took him even deeper down her throat. The salty taste of pre-cum spread across the back of her tongue, and she knew he was close. Wordlessly, she released her grip on him and stood up.

Jaden retrieved her bag and headed for the bathroom, leaving Ivan in the chair, high, dry, and begging for more.

"Heeeyyy!" he protested.

"I'll be right back," she called over her shoulder as she slinked away. "And refill our wine while I'm gone."

Once she'd closed the bathroom door, Jaden quickly changed into her secret weapon, purchased on Lincoln. After a few moments Ivan seemed to have recovered enough to move. She heard him shuffling through assorted music selections and gave a smile when an Al Green number floated through the air. Definitely time for dessert.

Jaden adjusted her minimal ensemble and smoothed her hair, but as she turned to make her grand entrance, she suddenly paused with her hand on the doorknob. This wasn't the first time she and Ivan had been intimate, so why did she feel so nervous? Carefully, she sat on the edge of the tub. Maybe there was a lot more riding on it now. They'd just spent the past two hours pouring their hearts out to each other. But that was a *good* thing.

As her mind raced, she distracted herself with a quick snoop through Ivan's bathroom. Towels under the sink--nice ones too. No prescriptions in the medicine cabinet, just some ginseng and, *whoa*, a lot of vitamins. Willing herself to stop, Jaden still couldn't resist the cobalt blue bottle next to the sink. She removed the silver top and *ooooohh*, there it was — the elusive ingredient in Ivan's unmistakable, signature scent: Polo Blue. She sprayed a little onto her skin and indulged in the smell. Immediately she imagined his warm arms and scent surrounding her. Taking a deep, calming breath, Jaden stood, took one last look in the mirror, opened the door, and stepped out into the hall.

With the lights dimmed and the sultry sound of Marvin Gaye now drifting through the air, Jaden looked across the room to find Ivan lazing on the sofa and looking at her admiringly, as if he'd just won the lottery. Passion, need, and most importantly, affection, were reflected in the depths of his soulful brown eyes. Her momentary jitters gone, Jaden sauntered toward him, drinking in the sight of him as she closed the distance. She knew he liked what he saw, and she felt unbelievably sexy and uninhibited. Stopping just out of reach, she turned around to give him a full rear view of her new lingerie.

"So," Jaden whispered over her shoulder, "what do you think, Dr. Ivan? Do I need any work done?" She bent over slightly, revealing the outline of her black satin thong beneath the lacy garter. Before she could turn around to face him, Ivan was at her back, pressing against her, his stiff cock digging into the small of her back.

"I told you, Ms. Thorne, I need a better look before I can make my diagnosis," he whispered in her ear as he reached between them and unclasped her bra. His fingers grazed her skin as he slid the straps off her shoulders and let it fall to the ground at their feet.

Brushing a tendril of inky hair aside, he laid a kiss on the back of her shoulder. She trembled at his touch. "Hmm…reflexes are just fine," he murmured, trailing his lips tenderly across her back as his hands found her breasts. Jaden felt herself grow taut as he plucked and teased her nipples. Turning her around, Ivan pinned Jaden to the wall and placed his hands on either side of her. His mouth swiftly found hers, his tongue strong and sure as it dove into her mouth and stole the very breath from her chest.

Jaden's legs gave out from the power of his kiss, and she collapsed into his arms, their bodies melding into one as she surrendered to him. Their tongues danced, darting in and out as Ivan drove her half mad with need. He left her fighting for breath when he finally pulled away.

Lowering his head, Ivan's mouth now found her breast and drew in her nipple, suckling and laving until Jaden writhed. Just when she could take no more, Ivan swept her into his arms and carried her the length of the hall to his bedroom, placing her gently at the foot of the bed.

Jaden silently slid to her knees, then looked up with a cocky smile as her hands found the button on his jeans. "Well, doc, what's your diagnosis so far?" she whispered as she lowered the zipper and pulled his jeans to his ankles. Not waiting for his answer, she took the length of him in her hands and slowly brought him to her mouth once again. Now she would finish what she'd started. But before she could, Ivan gripped her arms and raised her from the ground. She could see a primal need in his eyes, a need that called to something within her, soaking the thin strip of satin between her legs.

"There's time for that later," he growled. "Right now I just need you." Ivan turned her to face the bed, and his voice was hoarse as he ordered her to lie down. Obediently, Jaden lay flat on her stomach, her hands propped under her chin as Ivan sat on the edge of the bed and kicked off his jeans. With achingly slow movements, he unclasped one of the stockings from the garter belt and ran his palm across her ass to undo the other. He traced the outline of the black satin thong, and Jaden lifted her hips, allowing Ivan to slip off her panties. He left her stockings and garter belt in place.

Quivering as his fingers brushed her thighs, Jaden glanced over her shoulder at him, inviting him with her eyes to do as he pleased. She got to her knees on the center of the bed and lifted her hips in anticipation. The breath hitched in her throat, and desire shot through her. Her need was just as strong as his own. Clenching the comforter tightly in her hands, Jaden braced herself for what was to come while listening to Ivan cursing as he hurried to roll on a condom.

With one swift thrust, he impaled her. Wet and ready to take him, Jaden gasped as Ivan began stroking into her, his pace quickening as her thrusts met his own. The sounds of flesh on flesh filled the air with the rhythm of their love.

"Ivan…" Jaden struggled for words and breath that would not come. Her body shook as he brought her closer and closer to release. He gripped her shoulders tightly as he drove into her, filling her completely. Jaden cocked her head back, silently pleading for him to be savage, to take what he wanted, as she wanted it too. Ivan obliged her unspoken desire as he grabbed a fist full of her hair, using it as leverage to drive himself deeper within her. His free hand reached around and came to rest at the thatch between her legs, his fingers finding her swollen, wet bud.

One touch sent her over the edge, and Jaden reached back to grip him tightly, milking him as she screamed out her climax, riding the wave of bliss and releasing herself in waves of orgasm, drenching herself and Ivan as he continued to thrust into her. Within moments, his strokes shortened and he filled her with his release.

Jaden's breathing was ragged and her thoughts disorganized as they collapsed in a tangled heap on the bed. Ivan rolled on his side and wrapped her tightly in his arms as he laid a trail of soft kisses across her cheek and shoulders. He began to grow stiff again almost immediately as Jaden grinded her hips into him, begging for more. His lips found her ear and he nibbled gently. "Stay the night," he implored.

Jaden could feel his stiffness pressing into her back, and she smiled. "You're incorrigible, Dr. Rusilko."

Laughing, Ivan held her tighter. They were slippery and sweaty, but Jaden didn't care. In this haze of pleasure, she felt totally at ease, at peace. She settled in and began to trace a pattern up and down his arm with her fingertips.

He sighed into her hair and after a few moments asked, "So why cooking?"

She smiled to herself, happy that Ivan was still interested in knowing her better—not just rocking her body. "My grandmother and I used to cook when I was little," Jaden began. "She loved to share her secret family recipes with me. But for me, cooking was always more of an experiment and a way to express my creativity. I love the connections that come through food as well. It's a great way to spend time with friends and family."

"Absolutely," Ivan murmured. "And I can see the creativity and passion that drive your work at Bianca. You're an artist, babe."

"Well, I don't know about that," Jaden said with a laugh. "But thank you." She knew she was blushing a little and was thankful for the dark. "Okay, my turn," she said. "What got you interested in being Mr. USA—besides all the 'Miss' contestants you got to meet," she asked, wiggling her naked ass into his still semi-erect hard-on.

He gave her hip a playful smack. "Well, it was an accident really. I somehow transitioned from hockey to bodybuilding to modeling. Trust me, I didn't pursue it. It pursued me. I always thought male models were a breed I wanted nothing to do with. Go figure that years later I'd become the US representative of the breed. But I just decided to go with it and enjoy the opportunities it brought my way. After that it was fun. I got to see some amazing places, do things I would never have had the opportunity to do, and meet all sorts of people. It took me from milking cows in Pennsylvania to racing a Mercedes on the Formula One track in Melbourne. Not too bad for a farm boy, eh?"

"And Irena?" Jaden nervously asked, remembering his most famous ex. Silence filled the room, and she could feel his breathing accelerate. Jaden rolled on her side to face him and interlocked her limbs with his, like pieces of a puzzle that fit perfectly together.

"Irena was…amazing. We shared some laughs and experiences that I'll never forget, and I'm thankful for that," he said as his gaze drifted away. "She still holds a place in my heart, but she also left a stain on it. The way it ended wasn't as glamorous as everyone seems to believe, but it's over all the same. That chapter in my life is closed. You can't keep looking over your shoulder, because your future is always in front of you…as it is now."

Ivan's eyes met hers once again, and Jaden felt as if his soul had reached out and touched hers. Suddenly it all made sense and her fears about his past faded away. She just knew. Smiling, she rolled over and pressed her body against his. His arms surrounded her, and they drifted off to sleep in a lovers' embrace.

Chapter 16

"Linger"

Jaden wandered around the unfamiliar kitchen wearing nothing but Ivan's old Mario Lemieux jersey and his too-big slippers, searching the drawers for cutlery. Breakfast in bed was hard to pull off when she didn't have the slightest clue where anything was. After all the trouble Ivan went to cooking dinner for her last night, she was eager to return the favor. Opening the cupboard, she found bottles of spices labeled in terrible penmanship. Selecting a few possibilities, Jaden turned to the fridge to find the rest of the ingredients. She scrounged through the crisper. Eggs, asparagus, Swiss cheese, and prosciutto…a perfect omelet!

A savory aroma filled the kitchen as she hurried to put the finishing touches on breakfast. Rye toast, orange juice, and a halved grapefruit already rested on the tray, and the omelet would be finished in three…two…one… Grabbing the frying pan off the stove, she plated the omelet and added it to tray along with two forks. Jaden balanced carefully as she shuffled down the hall.

She entered the bedroom, placed the tray on the night table, and sat on the edge of the bed. She pulled the blanket low enough to expose Ivan's bare chest, and resting her hand on his shoulder, she gently shook him. "Ivan, wake up. Breakfast is ready," she called, her tone soft and soothing. No response. She tried a second time, this time shaking him more firmly. "Ivan, come on. Wake up. Your breakfast is getting cold."

He mumbled and rolled over, pushing the blanket farther aside as he did. Jaden couldn't help but admire his naked form: the curve of his muscles, his soft, pouty lips that partially opened while he slept, and the tousled brown hair that looked almost savage in the morning light. Jaden chuckled as she noticed Ivan suffering from a severe case of morning wood.

Feeling brassy and still coming down off her high from the night before, she decided to attempt something she'd never done. Slipping out of his slippers, she climbed into bed and took extra care not to wake him as she positioned herself. Straddling his legs, she lowered her mouth until she was just inches away. Her lips parted wide as she took him in. Inch by glorious inch, she swallowed him whole.

In an instant, Ivan was awake—everywhere. His back arched, and only Jaden's quick reflexes kept her in position. Tossing his head back into the pillows, he let out a low, guttural moan. "Good God, Jaden," he gasped, unwittingly thrusting himself deeper into her mouth.

His hands reached for her shoulders, trying to pull her up, but she shrugged him off, determined to finish what she'd started.

"Jaden," Ivan pleaded, his voice rough. "Ay, ay, ay…"

She looked up with knowing eyes. Ivan was close. She could feel it as his body tensed beneath her. Bracing his hips with her hands, she took more of him into her mouth, her tongue caressing him with slow, even strokes. His body jerked just once as he thrust forward forcefully and released himself into her throat.

"Ouch," Jaden moaned as she snuggled up to him moments later. Brilliant rays of mid-afternoon sun streamed in through the windows, warming the skin that wasn't covered by Ivan or the blanket.

"Are you okay?" Ivan asked as he brushed hair from her forehead. "That was amazing."

"I guess I'm a little more out of practice than I thought—at *drinking* that is." Jaden rested her head on his chest with a smirk.

"I have aspirin if you need it."

"Thanks, doc, but I'm good. I think I'll live." A satisfied smile settled on Jaden's face as she snuggled into Ivan's strong arms.

Goose bumps rose along her skin as he traced the outline of her form on the linen sheet. Then he slid his hand beneath the sheet and repeated the outline, trailing his touch lower on her body and settling between her legs. With the lightest of touches, he began to stroke the sensitive bundle of nerves, which Jaden could feel becoming more responsive with every pass of his finger. She tried to wriggle free of his embrace, longing to grant him open access, but Ivan held her firmly in place, teasing and tormenting her clit in a slow, circular motion. Jaden writhed under his touch, her body begging for more. Amazed that he could sense her need, Jaden gasped as Ivan slid two fingers into her wet, swollen pussy. Each thrust of his hand brought her closer to climax, and Jaden arched into him, her body quivering as Ivan placed the pad of thumb to her clit and pressed, driving her body to contract in release.

"It only seemed fair, babe," he told her as the aftershocks of orgasm began to ebb. Then he pulled up the covers and placed a tender kiss on Jaden's forehead as they returned to sleep.

Whether it was three hours or three days later, Jaden couldn't tell, but the brilliant sun had been replaced by a darkening Miami skyline. She felt a little wobbly as she stood up, and holding on to the headboard, wondered where Ivan had wandered off to. As she went to find him, she encountered the luscious aroma of roasted chicken, followed shortly by the sound of pots clashing and Ivan cursing from the vicinity of the kitchen.

Making a quick stop in the bathroom, Jaden rinsed her face. She dug through her overnight bag and pulled her hair into a loose ponytail at the base of her neck. But she still felt sweaty. She could hear Ivan busy in the kitchen, so she opted for a quick shower.

Jaden felt immediate relief as the steam soothed her sore body. Never in her life had she experienced a marathon of sex like the one she'd just completed. Every muscle ached, but it was a good sort of pain — the type that made you blush and brag to your girlfriends. She located some rather masculine smelling shampoo among the bottles in the shower and worked it through her hair. After a final rinse, she felt reenergized and stepped out of the shower. She towel dried her hair before pulling it back into a ponytail. After making herself presentable, Jaden pulled on the robe she found hanging on the back of the door and joined Ivan in the kitchen.

Ivan turned as she approached him from behind. He gathered her in his arms and nuzzled her neck, inhaling deeply. "It's not lavender, but I can live with it."

"How'd you know I use lavender shampoo?"

"I can smell it on you from a mile away." He shrugged. "And combined with your natural scent, it makes for a wonderful fragrance, one I could get *very* used to."

Raising her chin with the tips of his fingers, Ivan brought her lips to his, kissing her hard on the mouth. Jaden again reached for the button on his pants, but he broke the kiss. "There's time for that later. Right now you need to refuel—we both do."

"Well, I did make breakfast…at some point," she said with a laugh. "What ever happened to that?"

"Ahh, sorry," Ivan said. "I'm afraid we got distracted and forgot to eat it. Now we're on to the next meal."

Looking over his shoulder, Jaden saw two large bowls on the counter. "Is that chicken Caesar salad?"

"And not just any Caesar salad," Ivan said with a nod. "That's my famous homemade dressing and multigrain croutons."

"Good, I'm famished."

"It's a beautiful night. I thought we'd eat on the balcony."

Jaden looked past the living room to the open patio doors. He'd set the table and lit large pillar candles, which now reflected brightly off the glass patio doors. "I'd like that."

"I'll grab the wine, and you get the salads," Ivan instructed, releasing her.

A cool breeze danced across Jaden's skin as she stepped on to the patio. She put the salads on the table and looked over the railing. A marbled pool glistened twelve floors below, and Biscayne Bay spread out beyond that, speckled with islands bearing multimillion-dollar homes. The Miami skyline completed the picture. She could hear Ivan fumbling with something behind her, but was too mesmerized to pay him much attention.

"Spectacular view, isn't it? Too bad it's obscured by a robe," he joked as he handed her a glass of wine.

"Ha ha. I thought we were refueling?" Jaden remarked. She lifted the glass to her mouth, and the flavor exploded as it hit her tongue, sending her thoughts straight back to the Winemaker's Dinner. Turning, Jaden noticed the bottle on the table. She smiled. "Hmm…this all seems a little familiar."

"That's my intention."

"You want to have sex on the balcony again?" Jaden looked down at the busy scene below. "I didn't know putting on a show was your type of thing."

Ivan laughed and led her to the table where he pulled out the chair for her. "I was thinking more of new beginnings."

"New beginnings?"

Ivan sat across from her and seemed to take a moment to gather his thoughts. "That night at the Winemaker's Dinner, the night on the balcony — it was something way out of character for me. I'm not a one-night-stand guy, and I hope by now you've realized that."

Jaden tried to speak, but Ivan silenced her with a simple gesture. "I don't make a habit of bringing random girls back to my hotel room. I never have. But that night, there was something about you… The first time I saw you, it was like I already knew you. I knew your taste, your smell, the sound of your laugh — just not your name. I had to catch your attention. There was no way I was letting you slip through my fingers. Things happened, things I wouldn't normally do, but I'm so glad. Jaden, the night I met you, I started feeling life in a whole new way. You showed me something I never knew I was missing."

"Ivan, I —"

"Please, let me finish before I lose my nerve."

He looked at her with such affection that she couldn't help but smile.

"We are so much more than a one-night stand, and more than just sex, so I thought it might be nice if we started fresh…maybe try our luck at a real relationship."

Jaden was shocked by his words — and also not shocked at the very same time. A brief tremor of fear coursed through her, but she knew what she wanted. And what she wanted was Ivan. She smiled impishly and reached across the table for his hand. "You mean boyfriend and girlfriend?" Jaden asked in a girlish tone before turning serious. "Yes, of course. I'd love that."

"So it's official then," Ivan replied, his boyish charm shining through.

"It's official."

The cool breeze caressed her skin as they sat silently on the balcony, drinking wine, eating, and enjoying each other's company. There was no need for words. Just being together was enough.

"Spend the night again, baby girl. I'll drive you home in the morning," Ivan said, finishing a mouthful of salad.

Baby girl? she thought to herself. *That's a new one. I could get used to being Ivan's baby girl...* "I'd love to," Jaden replied with a smile. "But since a certain someone has been occupying my time, I've neglected my emails. I have to catch up before I work again tomorrow."

"Oh, right. You can't forget about your fans now that you're a star," he teased, taking another bite of salad.

"Ha-ha-ha! My boyfriend's a comedian!" The words passed Jaden's lips before she could stop them, but they sounded right.

When dinner was finished, Jaden retreated to the bathroom to change while Ivan cleared the table and did the dishes. She packed her things reluctantly. If she hadn't had so much to catch up on, she would've gladly stayed the night. Heck, she'd stay until she wore out her welcome, but she'd been neglecting laundry, grocery shopping, and emails. No need to let her life fall apart!

Wordlessly, they rode the elevator to the lobby, neither wanting this amazing weekend to end. The cool breeze greeted them again as they exited the lobby and headed for the Jeep. The sounds of Dave Matthews filled the air around them as Ivan took her hand and began to sing along.

Jaden sank back in the seat and let the sound of Ivan's voice lull her into a tranquil state. She longed to disappear with him, just like the song said, and before she knew it, Ivan was shaking her shoulder.

"Hey, baby girl, we're here."

"Already?" Jaden asked as she rubbed sleepily at her eyes. "That was fast."

"No, not really," Ivan replied. "I took the long way back because I didn't have the heart to wake you."

"What time is it?" She looked at the clock on the dash through blurry eyes. "Ten o'clock already?"

"Time flies when you're having fun." Ivan leaned across and un-buckled her seatbelt, slyly sliding in a kiss.

"Why don't you come up for a while?" Jaden said offering a kiss of her own.

"We both know that if I come upstairs, neither one of us will get much sleep tonight—or any work done."

"That's a bit of a double standard, Dr. Rusilko," Jaden said. "Weren't you the one who just invited me to spend the night at your place?"

"Touché," Ivan conceded. "But you're exhausted, and you need your sleep."

Reluctantly, Jaden leaned closer for a parting kiss. The tenderness as their lips met, unrushed and sensual, was the perfect ending to a perfect weekend. Ivan jumped out to open the door for her. With great hesitation, she slid out of the Jeep, pausing to see if Ivan might change his mind.

"Go," he encouraged her and winked. "You need to regain your strength for next weekend."

"Why, what's going on next weekend?" Jaden's brow lifted.

His response was simple and lighthearted. "You'll see."

"I hope you haven't made plans for Sunday."

"Why?" Ivan asked, seeming alarmed. "You never work on Sundays."

"Not usually, but Geoff's booked a private party, and he needs all hands on deck." Jaden watched an unfamiliar expression dance across Ivan's face. "You're not mad, are you?"

"I could never be mad at you, baby girl," Ivan replied. After a moment he managed a smile. "But I am disappointed. I had big plans for next Sunday."

"Well, I guess I'll just have to make it up to you."

After one more lingering kiss, Jaden stood on the curb and watched as Ivan drove out of sight, the taillights of the Jeep growing dim as the distance between them grew. The walk to the apartment seemed longer than usual tonight, and Jaden took the time to collect her thoughts, knowing Tasha would bombard her with questions the minute she walked through the door. Retrieving her keys from her purse, she unlocked the door and entered the apartment, surprised to find that all the lights were out. Tossing her keys on the table, she entered the living room and looked around.

"Tasha, are you here?" she called. Realizing she was alone, Jaden walked over to the desk and switched on the computer. With any luck she'd be able to read through her emails and get to bed before Tasha got home—and the questioning would have to be postponed until the morning.

Jaden sat in the chair as the monitor flickered to life. She brought up her email and soon faced page after page of unread messages. Jaden scrolled though the list, sending spam to the trash folder. She was about to select a message when the name of the sender caught her attention: OD Magazine. *That sounds familiar.* Opening the message, she began to read:

> Dear Chef Thorne,
>
> I write to inform you that you've been selected as a feature chef for an upcoming issue of OD Magazine. After reading a recent blog post, one of our columnists dined at your establishment and speaks very highly of your culinary talent. We'd love to do a story about you and the work you're doing at Bianca.
>
> Please contact me as soon as possible so that we may arrange to have a crew meet with you at the restaurant. One of our staff writers will conduct a brief interview, and a photographer will take some photos. The sooner we can have them meet with you, the better. Given our deadlines, it would be wonderful if we could arrange something before this coming Thursday.
>
> With kindest regards,
>
> Jay Gallo
>
> Editor-in-Chief

Jaden jumped from the chair, screeching as she ran for her purse. Grabbing her phone from the side pocket, she quickly typed out a message to Ivan:

> Oh my God, you're never going to guess what just happened!!

Without waiting for him to respond, Jaden returned to the computer and drafted her reply. Her finger lingered over the send button. Part of her was disappointed Ivan wasn't here to share this. *Of all the nights not to be together...* Taking a deep, calming breath, she grinned from ear to ear as she hit send.

Chapter 17

"Life Is A Highway"

"How does this look? Too much?" Geoff asked, holding up a pair of gold-plated dining utensils before passing them to Jaden for inspection.

"Geoff, I'm sure they aren't going to be concentrating on the type of forks and spoons we use." Jaden eyed her tall, gray-haired boss, a man who'd become more of a friend than a superior over the past few weeks. She fought back a wave of nausea and returned to putting the finishing touches on the plates of hors d'oeuvres to be served during the interview. "The way you're prattling on, you'd think it was you being interrogated today," she said with a smile. "Relax, it's going to work out fine. You'll see."

Fresh off the high of waking up to find a glowing review in the *Miami Herald*, Jaden felt on top of the world. *Beauty and the Feast* decorated the front page of the lifestyle section in today's paper. Stephen had truly kept to his word. His article made Jaden shine like a polished diamond.

"I know, I know, but I'm excited for you…and for the restaurant," he added as an afterthought. "We've never been featured in *OD*, just run ads there. This is so great."

Geoff only added to the pressure with a comment like that. Jaden hadn't thought much about how her interview might impact the restaurant. "It's just a magazine, and I'm sure they aren't going to plaster me on the cover," she said, trying to convince herself it was a long shot but secretly hoping for the best. "And remind me again what *OD* is all about?"

"*OD* is *the* magazine for the what's what and the crème de la crème of Miami Beach. They're known for making or breaking businesses and people," Geoff responded.

Jaden felt her nausea shoot up another notch or two, and it wasn't helped when she saw a small man in plaid wielding an oversized camera enter the restaurant followed by a taller man in gray pants and a white button-down shirt. They approached the hostess, who directed them to the back where she and Geoff waited. Wiping her sweaty palms on the dishcloth tucked into the pocket of her pants, Jaden said, "Well, looks like it's show time."

Geoff stopped pacing and seemed to make an extra effort to pull himself together as he watched the men approach.

"Take this, would you?" Jaden said to Susan as she passed by, handing her the dishcloth.

"Good luck, boss. Knock 'em dead." Susan gave her a warm smile before returning to the kitchen.

As the two men drew closer, Jaden realized she'd actually met the taller of the two before. He'd been at the birthday party Ivan had taken her to for their first date. *Crap, I don't remember is his name! Bill, Bob, Ben… What the hell is his name?* But then she remembered the trick she'd learned from Ivan, and Jaden jumped to speak first and ensure she wouldn't have to call him by name.

"How are you? It's been a while," she announced cheerfully as the men arrived.

"Jaden, it's so great to see you! You look marvelous." Taking her hand, the tall man kissed it before motioning to his colleague. "This is Aaron Resnick, a fantastic photographer for our magazine."

"So nice to meet you, and this is my boss, Geoff Knight," Jaden announced. "He's the owner of Bianca."

Now, if the trick worked, the unknown man would have to divulge his name to her boss. *Please work,* she hoped frantically.

"Hi, Geoff. My name is Rob Sena, and I want to say I've heard great things about this restaurant from so many people. It's a pleasure to finally visit and have the opportunity to talk with the one and only Chef Jaden Thorne."

Jaden barely heard the compliment as she mentally celebrated her success. *His name is Rob!*

As Geoff greeted the two men, he motioned for Rob and Jaden to take a seat at the elegantly set table that had already been furnished with water, a bottle of red wine, and a wide array of appetizers.

"Geoff, if you could please show Aaron around, it would be greatly appreciated," Rob said politely. "We'd like to get some pictures of your restaurant for the magazine."

"Of course," Geoff responded, bowing graciously before scurrying off with the photographer and leaving Jaden on her own.

Turning his attention back to Jaden, Rob wasted no time getting down to business. With his tape recorder out, he shot off his first question: "So, Ms. Thorne, professional chef and beauty queen, do explain."

Totally taken aback, Jaden couldn't help but stutter in response. "Ahh, um, I don't know if I'd call myself a beauty queen," she said. "I just love what I do and try to maintain a professional appearance both in and out of the kitchen."

Rob smiled. "What's your favorite thing about Miami?"

Hesitating and forcing herself not to say the first thing that came to her mind—Ivan and their sexual exploits—Jaden focused and settled on a more appropriate reply. "There's so much to love about a city as diverse as Miami—the people, the activities, the opportunities. It's a magical place. I'm so happy to be an official Miami Beacher now."

Rob forged on. The rest of the interview consisted of questions ranging from her culinary training (CIA, New York) to her favorite dish to cook for herself (pasta al forno with her grandmother's tomato sauce).

As they talked, Jaden caught glimpses of Geoff and the photographer scurrying around the restaurant taking pictures of the kitchen, dining room, wait staff, patrons, and anything else that might look nice and shiny on the glossy pages of the magazine.

As the interview came to a close, Rob asked one final question: "Why should Miami come to eat here at Bianca?"

Jaden answered without hesitation. "Life's too short to not live, laugh, and love. At Bianca you'll do all three at once."

"I must say, Ms. Thorne, it's been an absolute pleasure meeting you," Rob said, reaching across to shake her hand. "I can see that you're well on your way to greatness. Now I can boast that I knew you way back when…" He ended with a laugh. "Your personality confirms the rumors swirling around about how fantastic you are."

Jaden opened her mouth to ask what he meant but closed it immediately when she heard him call to the photographer.

"Okay, let's get her makeup done and get some great shots of this beautiful young lady," he announced.

What? Makeup? Photo shoot? Oh, God! Do I look okay? Why didn't someone tell me what they meant by "some photos"? Jaden screamed inside her head.

Digging deep for the same poise she'd drawn on at Dr. Shaunnessey's birthday party, Jaden smiled and joined the photographer for her makeup. As she sat quietly in the chair, a woman she hadn't noticed until now explained that she'd just soften her eyes and plump her already full lips a bit. Jaden closed her eyes and relaxed as she next went to work on her hair. Her daydreams were brought to a sudden halt as she overheard Rob mumble to Aaron to make sure they got a quality shot of her, and to make sure the sex appeal was high.

Sex appeal? What the hell is talking about? I'm a chef! But Jaden wasn't about to complain. Sitting in that chair, she felt like this was her fifteen minutes of fame, and she was going to suck it up, every last drop.

The stylist handed her a mirror, and the photographer smiled. "You look stunning, Ms. Thorne."

"Please, call me Jaden," she corrected him with a smile.

When she looked in the mirror, Jaden had to take a second glance to make sure it was her. It wasn't a girl staring back at her, it was a gorgeous woman — and for a second, Jaden didn't recognize the face. The stylist had brightened her emerald eyes and accentuated her high cheekbones. Her normally plain-Jane hair was now tucked up in a high-fashion bun with a few ebony tendrils falling free, outlining the soft curves of her face.

Still baffled about the events taking place, Jaden asked, "What am I supposed to wear? All I have is my chef's outfit. Was I supposed to bring a change of clothes?"

Aaron and Rob burst into laughter. "Priceless! No wonder everyone loves you," Tim said. "The chef's outfit is perfect! *That* is what makes you a cup of coffee on a table full of tea!"

Jaden forced a laugh not truly understanding what was funny. Why was everyone making such a big deal out of her?

"Are you ready, Ms. Thorne? I mean, Jaden?" the photographer asked.

"Let's do it," she responded with determination and set off for the kitchen.

They'd be working on Jaden's home field, which not only made her more comfortable, but made a spotless backdrop courtesy of Geoff's diligent planning and foresight.

"Have you ever been photographed before?" Rob asked.

"No, not professionally. This is my first time, so please be gentle," Jaden added with a laugh.

"Well, I tell all my models to imagine a clock in front of them. Strike a pose, then look at one number on the clock and then another. Then switch the pose and repeat. It's simple as pie."

Jaden grasped the concept immediately and summoned her biggest and brightest smile. "Let's do it," she said again.

From the moment she struck her first pose, Jaden felt at ease. This was fun! She used the kitchen in a way she never thought possible, turning the utensils, counters, and pans into objects laced with sexuality.

"How did I do?" Jaden asked as they finished.

"Amazing!" Aaron and Rob replied in unison. "I think we've got everything here. Thanks so much, Ms. Thorne, for a splendid day. We'll be in touch soon. My boss will be very happy."

Jaden escorted the men to the front of the restaurant where Geoff nervously paced in front of the window. After casually saying their goodbyes, Jaden immediately dug out her phone to text Ivan:

Now there are two models in this relationship!

Ivan was about to get a run for his money.

CHAPTER 18

"Here Comes My Girl"

Still riding on the high of her fantastic day parading around like a fashion model, Jaden headed back to the kitchen, no cameras snapping now, and back to reality. Swinging open the double doors, she was met with a round of cheers and hollers.

"You guys…" Jaden said, blushing and averting her gaze from the rowdy kitchen crew. "Thanks for all your help today, but if you don't mind, I need a few minutes to myself. I'm still feeling a bit overwhelmed."

Jaden retired to the small staff room at the back of the kitchen and took the buzzing phone from her pocket to see what Ivan had replied, but to her surprise it was Tasha texting her:

> Great! Now I have two models to deal with.
> Come out front and don't keep me waiting.

Befuddled, Jaden tried to understand the text. Quickly checking her history, she confirmed that she wasn't going crazy — she had, in fact, sent the last text to Ivan as intended. That must mean… Without even finishing her thought, she high-tailed it out the doors and into the restaurant. When she saw them, Jaden couldn't believe her eyes. Ivan and Tasha stood in the corridor of the entrance, Tasha in a flowing, pale yellow minidress and Ivan wearing a slim-cut black shirt and gray jeans with a bouquet of flowers in hand. His hair was tied up in a sleek ponytail, and a five o'clock shadow darkened his face.

Jaden rushed over to them. "Okay, what is going on? What are you doing here together?"

"Ivan suggested the three of us go out tonight to celebrate your big day. How could I disagree with an idea like that?"

"A superstar day calls for a superstar night, right?" Ivan leaned in for a kiss and placed the lush bouquet of orchids in her hand. "Congratulations, baby girl. I hear you did amazing."

His face beamed with pride, causing Jaden to blush even more. "You guys…I wish I could, but I have to work tonight. No rest for the wicked or something like that. And how did you hear that—"

Just then she heard a voice behind her. "Jaden, I hope you weren't thinking of slipping out without letting me say goodbye. It was a fantastic day, and it looks like you're in for a fantastic night! Let me treat you and your friends to dinner, if you have time. You did such a great job today for us. I owe you."

Stunned by, well, just about everything going on right now—Geoff's offer, Ivan and Tasha's surprise visit, the article in this morning's paper, and the apparent success with *OD*—Jaden graciously accepted. "Thanks, Geoff. That'd be great."

"Fantastic! I'll seat you at the chef's table. Fitting, right?" He smiled and motioned for the waitress to show them to *her* table. "Have fun, and remember, it's on the house."

The group expressed their thanks as Geoff strolled off.

Turning to Tasha, Jaden kept her voice to a whisper. "Why didn't you at least give me a hint? I don't have anything to wear."

"You don't have much faith in me, do you?" Tasha gave Jaden a smart-ass look as she motioned to Ivan. "Doctor, if you please."

From nowhere, Ivan produced a cream-colored box secured with a large blue ribbon. He planted a quick kiss before handing her the box. "This is for you, baby girl."

Jaden eagerly untied the ribbon and removed the lid. Within the box was a stunning blue dress—perfect for a fabulous evening. "You're too good to me," she breathed and glanced down at the colorful bouquet in her hand. "And the flowers, I love them. Thank you."

Giving her another soft kiss, Ivan whispered, "Only the best for you."

"Right this way, Chef Thorne," the waitress said, beaming with excitement. The young, woman guided them to the chef's table and seated each of them, placing Jaden at the head of the table.

Taking command, since she knew the menu inside out, Jaden ordered the entire meal for the table, complete with a bottle of shiraz, winking at Ivan. That task complete, Jaden excused herself to change into her new dress. She returned fifteen minutes later, thrilled with Ivan's purchase, and was floored to find him and Tasha chatting away. There was a certain comfort in having her boyfriend and her best friend get along so well. Her last boyfriend had been standoffish and jealous of anyone she knew.

"So how did you two get a hold of each other?" she asked them, slipping back into her seat.

"The internet is a funny thing," Tasha said. "You can contact anyone and their sister if you need to, but it's all Ivan's doing. He's the one who planned it."

Tasha looked at Jaden and grabbed her in a hug. "I'm just so damn proud of you, girl. Would you have believed any of this was going to happen when you decided to move to Miami?"

Jaden looked from one to the other, happy that Ivan had included Tasha in this special night. "No, but it seems I have a lot to be thankful for."

For the next hour they dined and discussed everything in their lives. Tasha prattled on to Ivan about Micky being the one, and Jaden bragged about her and Ivan's relationship, causing Ivan's cheeks to redden on more than one occasion.

"You don't need to sell me on his good points," Tasha teased. "I already know this one's a keeper."

Twenty-one jokes, sixty-three laughs, and four bottles of wine later, the dinner came to a close, but Jaden had a feeling the night was only beginning.

Ivan, who now seemed slightly more than tipsy, cleared his throat importantly. "Well, ladies, now that we've had our fill of great food and wine, it's time to set off on the next leg of our adventure."

"Really? There's more?" Jaden asked.

"Are you kidding me? This is the time the clubs start to get good," Ivan exclaimed. "I was thinking we'd hit LIVE for a few shenanigans."

LIVE. Jaden had heard tales of it, but never imagined she'd hang out there. It was ranked one of the top nightclubs in the world, so the constant line to get in made it seem impossible.

"Awesome!" Tasha cheered. "Let's go."

Jaden looked at Ivan as if to say, yet another story! Feeling ready to conquer the world, she nodded. "I'm in. Let's get this show on the road."

Ivan tossed a tip on the table, and they set out to hail one of the yellow taxis that scurried around Miami Beach like ants on an anthill. They piled into the cab and Tasha called out, "LIVE—and step on it."

As the cab sped away, Jaden wanted to let Ivan know how much she appreciated everything he'd done for her tonight. Showing up unexpectedly with Tasha, the flowers, the dress—this was turning out to be one of the most memorable nights of her life. Discreetly, Jaden untwined her hand from his and reached between his legs to gently caress the other gift she hoped to be unwrapping later tonight.

Ivan leaned in for a lingering kiss, parting Jaden's lips with his tongue, but pulled back when Tasha cleared her throat. "I'm so proud of you," he said, squeezing her hand.

The taxi pulled up to the curb and they could see the line, as usual, five people deep and trailing down the block, with a gigantic guardian keeping watch. A shot of disappointment ran through Jaden, but Ivan didn't seem fazed.

"I don't know," said Jaden. "Looks like we'll have to wait all night. Should we go somewhere else?"

"I'm sure with you two beauties on my arms, this'll be a cinch," Ivan reassured them.

They waded through a mob scene of tourists and locals dressed to the nines with Ivan in the lead. He didn't stop until he'd reached the head of the line. There they were met by a three-hundred-pound monster dressed head to toe in black. He wore an earpiece and a stone cold look as he worked the small velvet rope. Jaden cringed at the thought of being turned away. She wasn't any different than the other people waiting in line.

But as the giant of a man turned to see Ivan, he slowly cracked a smile, lowering his guard for a split second, and then dropped the rope, acknowledging Ivan with a simple nod of his oversized head. Feeling as if she were doing something illegal, Jaden snuck a look at Tasha and glued herself to Ivan's side. Looking over her shoulder, Jaden watched as the behemoth of a man returned to his defensive lineman's stance and fought back the crowd trying to press in after them.

"What was that all about?" Tasha screeched directly into Ivan's ear.

Ivan smiled but ignored Tasha's question as he led them further into the club. Jaden's eyes widened while they made their way around the outskirts of the overcrowded dance floor. The club resembled something out of an X-rated Dr. Seuss book. Dark blue and red neon lights shone brightly against the flat black walls. She ran the palm of her hand along the sleek surface of a massive column that shot up from the floor. Looking up, she could see that the top of the pillar was capped with beautiful women wearing outfits that would make Hugh Hefner blush. The heady air that surrounded them was filled with smoke emanating from a machine and the sparklers on the champagne bottles being delivered by scantily clad waitresses.

Blasting from the speakers was trance-inducing music that filled their ears with a beat created solely for women to get their groove on. Strobe lights danced around them, highlighting dancers and DJs, and the mob in the center of the room resembled a sea of people, all of whom appeared to be looking for a quick lay. Surrounding the trove of lust and alcohol were tables of brightly colored beverages and high-rolling clubbers spending their cold hard cash.

Jaden clung to Ivan's arm, in awe of the sights before them. Making a beeline for the side staircase, they encountered another monstrous guard, but after another acknowledging nod, they headed past the second velvet rope.

As she slowly climbed the stairs in front of Ivan, Jaden suddenly felt his hand snaking up her inner thigh. His fingers trailed along, coming to rest at the edge of her thong. She turned back to see him smile, no doubt pleased to know what she'd been wearing underneath her kitchen whites. Looping his finger around the thin strip of satin between her legs, he pulled it aside and caressed her velvety soft folds. "Damn," he whispered.

Jaden's breath caught in her throat but she maintained her composure. She looked at Tasha, who was occupied with trying to see what awaited them at the top of the stairs, and then looked over her shoulder again at Ivan. "You know you're pushing it, right?"

"Just say the word and I'll stop."

Jaden stopped abruptly on the stair ahead of him, and Ivan's forward momentum caused his hand to slip farther between her legs. "Don't you dare," she warned.

As they topped the stairs, Ivan released Jaden with a little pat, and she turned her attention to the more relaxed section of the club that greeted them. They now overlooked the ocean of flesh below, admiring it from a distance. At the bar a cute little brunette, clad in a miniskirt that hid nothing from view, stood behind the gleaming black counter amidst an array of multicolored bottles and glasses. Ivan ordered a round of shots: lemon drops for the ladies and a whiskey for himself.

Women more silicone than flesh, and men wearing enough gold to significantly reduce the deficit, lounged on plush red sofas and armchairs as Jaden looked around. Rather than the outlandish lighting and smoke effects of the lower level, this area featured track lighting that spanned the length of the room. It wasn't meant for dancing but relaxing, and Jaden liked it very much. This was more her style.

The shots arrived, and Ivan handed them out, raising his in toast. "Here's to good times with great friends. *Arriba abajo al centro pa'dentro!*" he said as he moved the shot glass up, down, in, and down!

The girls followed suit, slamming their shots in a single gulp.

After drinking down the last drop of his whiskey, Ivan turned to order another round of drinks, but Jaden protested. "This round's on me, doc."

Ordering her drink and Tasha's was easy, but Ivan was a complex man with complex tastes, and this wasn't the type of place to order a shiraz. Looking him up and down, she smiled. "Give me one dirty martini, a vodka and cran, and a whiskey on the rocks."

Jaden picked up their drinks, cast Ivan a knowing smile over her shoulder, and maneuvered her way through the scattered tables, sofas, and people to where Tasha had found a spot in the corner. Jaden grinned when she noticed a few eyes following her as she passed.

Jaden arranged the drinks on their table, and they sat, enjoying the people-watching and music around them. Jaden wondered what Ivan had said to the bartender before they left, until within minutes a server showed up with their second round, then the third, and then the forth. "You started a tab, you little sneak," she admonished him.

Jaden now teetered between the edge of tipsy and the black abyss of drunkenness. And she suspected her companions were not far behind.

"I love this song," Tasha announced, loud enough to gain the attention of everyone in the lounge. She jumped to her feet and staggered to the middle of the room, pushing aside the empty tables to make an impromptu dance floor.

"Turn it up!" one of the clubbers yelled, and within seconds he'd joined Tasha in the center of the room.

"You had to bring us to a club, didn't you?" Jaden chided. "You've obviously never seen Tasha drunk."

"Nothing wrong with a little harmless fun every—" Ivan started to say, but abruptly fell silent. Jaden suppressed a giggle as her foot traveled up the inside of his leg. Surrendering to the moment, he spread his legs farther apart and granted her access.

Jaden's foot moved in sync to the beat, her toes massaging him into a heated fury. With everyone in the lounge now dancing, she could've easily snuck beneath the table unseen—and without any protest from Ivan—but she enjoyed watching him squirm under her skillful touch. The look of pure pleasure on his face added to her already incredible high.

Sinking back into his seat, Ivan rested his head on the back of the chair, his eyes rolling in bliss as he squeezed them shut.

As the DJ changed the beat, Jaden's foot retreated. She just had to dance. But she swayed in her seat, not wanting to leave Ivan completely alone.

He eyed her as he adjusted his jeans and sat up straighter in the chair. "Go dance if you want to," he said.

"What, and leave you sitting here by yourself? No way. Not unless you come dance with me."

"Umm, baby girl, that's not gonna happen for a while, not after that little stunt you just pulled." He shifted again in his seat. "Why don't you go dance? I'll join you in a few minutes."

"Are you sure you don't mind?" Jaden asked, but was out of her seat before Ivan had a chance to answer.

The server appeared with their next round of drinks, and Ivan gladly reached for his. He sat back and savored it as he watched Jaden make her way to the middle of the crowd. Stunned at seeing his girl dance for the first time, he couldn't help but watch the way Jaden and Tasha danced together, their bodies pressing and pulsing to the beat. It was enough to drive a gay man straight and a married man single. Sweat coated their bodies, and they glistened in the light of the lounge like a glitter-coated fantasy. Dirty thoughts crowded Ivan's mind as he watched the spectacle unfold, and he strained harder against his jeans.

Slamming down the last of his drink, he joined in the festivities. Hard-on or not, there was no way he was passing up the chance to dance with the two most gorgeous girls in the club. Ivan pushed his way through the thrumming dancers to Jaden's side. It didn't matter that his dancing abilities had been hindered by the alcohol he'd consumed, because with Jaden in front of him and Tasha behind, he looked like a pro.

A man would have to be out of his mind to not want two beautiful women using him as a stripper pole, but Ivan only had eyes for one of them. As untamed as his fantasies might be, Jaden was the only one he wanted.

Everyone surrounding them had stopped to stare at the sweaty tangle of limbs they created. Jaden, leaning against Ivvan's front, worked his lingering hard-on with her ass, and Tasha worked her own kind of magic from behind. But as the music changed to something slower, Ivan noticed the gray pallor that now tinted Tasha's face.

Pulling Jaden closer, he raised his voice to be heard over the music and pointed at Tasha, who was now half-walking, half-crawling back to their table. "I think we'd better get her home."

"I think you're right."

"Wait for me at the table," Ivan told her. "I'll be back in a minute."

Nodding, Jaden hurried across the floor, a little unsteady herself, Ivan noticed, to where Tasha now sat hunched over in a chair.

"That was quite a show you put on out there, hun," the bartender said as Ivan approached.

"Thanks," he murmured as he retrieved his credit card and signed the receipt.

Looking down at the slip of paper, the bartender frowned. "What, no phone number?"

"Maybe next time," Ivan said and shot her a wink. But he knew if he got his way, his bachelorhood would be a thing of the past.

As he moved to rejoin his partners in crime, Tasha's gray complexion became more and more apparent. Picking up his pace, he rushed to the table. Jaden helped him scoop up their friend, and they hurried off, past the party still in full swing, down the stairs, past behemoth number one, through the sea of flesh, past behemoth number two, and onto the sidewalk outside.

"Tasha," Jaden said as they struggled through the doors and onto the street.

Tasha waved her off and steadied herself against the streetlamp. "I'll be okay. Just give me a minute."

Ivan watched as Jaden efficiently lifted Tasha's hair and held it to the side. Sure enough, a loud wail echoed in the muggy Miami night as Tasha leaned over and painted the sidewalk.

"I'll find us a taxi," Ivan offered, turning his attention discreetly away from them.

"Are you okay, sweetie?" he heard Jaden ask. "Do you want me to get you a drink of water or something?"

"I'll be fine," Tasha murmured, and let out another heave.

Just then, a yellow taxi pulled to the curb in front of them. Ivan turned to offer a hand to Tasha and help her into the backseat. "I think we'd better let her have the window seat," he told Jaden with a smile.

"I think you're right." Jaden slid into the center spot, followed by Ivan. She gave the driver their address and emphasized that speed was of the utmost importance.

"If she gets sick in my car, you're paying to have it cleaned," the driver announced in a clipped tone.

"Don't worry about it," Ivan snapped back, his voice more forceful than he'd intended.

Somehow, they made all the lights but one and arrived at the condo in record time. As the taxi pulled to a halt at the front door, Ivan leaped out and rushed to the other side to help Tasha maneuver. With Jaden on one side and himself on the other, they seated her on the bench outside the building.

Jaden looked from Ivan to Tasha and then back to Ivan. "Thank you," she said. Standing on her tiptoes, she leaned in to give him a kiss, soft at first, but becoming more aggressive as she reached down and cupped his bulging crotch in the palm of her hand.

"I think you'd better get Tasha inside," Ivan said breathlessly as he broke the kiss.

"Right again, doc."

"Do you need a hand getting her upstairs?"

"You're not staying?" Ivan could hear the disappointment in her voice.

"Not tonight, baby girl. I think we've both had a little too much to drink, and Tasha needs you more than I do right now."

"You're unbelievable," Jaden whispered as she laid another soft kiss on his lips. "How on earth did I ever get so lucky?"

"I'm the lucky one." Ivan kissed Jaden's cheek before releasing her. "Are you sure you don't need any help getting her inside?"

"No, she can make it."

"Well, I guess I'll go then," Ivan said reluctantly as he took a step backward. Every part of his brain screamed at him to follow Jaden upstairs, but his common sense prevailed, and he took two more steps back to the waiting taxi. "My chariot awaits."

"Call me in the morning," Jaden said as she helped Tasha to her feet.

"'Night, baby girl."

"'Night, Dr. Ivan," he heard Jaden call as he slunk back into the backseat of the taxi.

CHAPTER 19

"How Sweet It Is"

Bright, blinding light seared Jaden's eyes as she made the short walk from her car to the entrance of the restaurant. The dim light of the foyer did little to relieve the massive hangover she was battling, with a throbbing headache that made her ears ring and her vision blur. Pushing thought the double doors to the kitchen, Jaden was met by more blinding light from the fluorescents that lined the ceiling and reflected vibrantly off the white-tiled walls. She ignored the stares and jeers from the kitchen staff as she walked to the back of the kitchen and sat on the bench in front of her locker.

"Morning, boss," Susan said from the bench across from her.

"Morning," Jaden grumbled as she slumped over, resting her head on her arms.

"Did you see it?" Susan asked excitedly.

"Sue, it's not going to be out for at least two or three weeks, and that's if the article even makes it into the next issue." Jaden sighed and squeezed her eyes tighter, trying to block out the last bit of light. No amount of painkillers or coffee was going to rid her of this hangover, and Jaden briefly wondered if she should've used one of her sick days.

"I'm not talking about the article. I'm talking about Dirk D's blog. Your pictures are all over his website."

Jaden's head snapped up, and she immediately squinted against the throbbing pain. "What pictures?"

"The pictures of you and Ivan at that club," Susan replied.

"What are you talking about…?" Jaden's voice trailed off as she dumped the contents of her purse on the floor in front of her, frantically searching for her cell phone. Snatching it from the pile of junk, Jaden touched the screen and the phone sprang to life. Once she'd finally read that first blog post Dirk D had written about her, she'd become a regular follower, so navigating to the page was quick. As the images began to load, Jaden couldn't believe what she was seeing. Pictures of her, Ivan, and Tasha plastered the website. In fact, there were so many that a photo gallery had been created for easy viewing. "Thirty-two pictures?" Jaden stammered in disbelief. She began reading the latest post. "And how in the hell does he know about the *OD Magazine* article already?"

"Word spreads quick in Miami, boss. That's what happens when you're a power couple."

Power couple? A smile lit up Jaden's face. She was a small-town girl from Colorado, and Ivan was a farm boy from Pennsylvania. Together they were a force to be reckoned with.

Over the next few weeks Ivan and Jaden grew as inseparable as their schedules would allow—attending VIP dinners, sharing intimate moments, and networking at high-end events, but also trading phone messages and often substituting texting for time to be together. Susan was right. Miami had labeled them the city's newest power couple, and it felt as though they'd lived a ten-year relationship in just a few short weeks.

Their connection still grew, but it became increasingly apparent that scheduling conflicts could have an impact on the most solid of relationships. Once made public, Ivan's weight loss plan kept him even busier, and Jaden's career took off in several directions at once. Appearing in an array of media outlets, she was truly becoming the Queen of Cuisine in Miami, and the restaurant required more and more of her time. Gone was her leisure time, as nearly every week now seemed to include some special event at Bianca or an appearance somewhere else. Career stepped to the forefront and demanded the intensity from both of them that they'd once reserved for each other. Though they did their best to talk every day, plans often fell by the wayside or occasionally were forgotten entirely in the quest to make just the right media and business connections. Newer to the limelight than her power-couple partner and fueled by a quest for fame, Jaden drove herself relentlessly, lest at any moment it all slip away.

She might have been Miami's Queen of Cuisine, but at the moment, Jaden didn't feel particularly regal at all. The screeching alarm she'd silenced only moments ago was now replaced by an incessant ringing from the phone on the bedside table. Snatching it from the stand, Jaden saw that it was her building's front desk calling.

"Hello?" she muttered through a receding haze of sleep.

"Good morning, Ms. Thorne. There's someone here to see you. He claims he's an acquaintance of Dr. Rusilko."

What the hell? Still a bit foggy, she mumbled, "Okay, let him up. Thank you."

Trying to focus, a million questions drifted through Jaden's mind. She'd dreamed of her photo shoot with *OD Magazine*—a dream that had become more and more frequent in the days leading up to the new issue's release. Would the article be near the front, or at the back with all the advertisements no one bothered to look at? How long would it be? What picture would they use?

Jaden was ripped from her line of self-questioning by a loud banging at the door. *Argh!* She'd said this person could come up. Throwing back the covers and not bothering to get dressed, she stumbled across the room and retrieved her robe from the back of the bedroom door as the knocking turned into a rapid succession of thuds. "Jeez, this better be worth the trouble," she complained before yelling in the direction of the front door, "All right already! I'm coming."

Jaden fumbled with the lock and struggled to look through the peephole to see who had the nerve to wake her up at such a God-awful hour. She was met with only black. Either the person was standing way too close to the peephole or was purposely covering it. Jaden let the door creak open, and encountered a sight no one should have to endure so early in the morning. A person wearing a heart-shaped costume, complete with white limbs and oversized sneakers, stood in the hallway. *What the fuck is this?* Jaden wondered as the giant red heart handed her a package. Taking a step back, the stranger moved awkwardly in the costume as he shuffled his feet and attempted to do some sort of ridiculous dance, concluding with a quick bow.

Still stunned, Jaden managed to blurt out a thank you. She pulled the card from the meticulously wrapped red-and-white gift. As she opened it, she immediately recognized the terrible handwriting:

Jaden,

Over the past weeks I have watched you grow from the mysterious woman in a red dress who took my breath away without uttering a word, into a beautiful, successful, and confident woman who has breathed that very breath back into me. I'm so happy with how far we've come. The memories we've shared eclipse anything I could have imagined for us.

I spend every day looking forward to where we're going and remembering where we've already been, and I anticipate sharing many more years of happiness with you. I know right now our schedules make things tough, but no barrier can ultimately stand between us or the way I feel about you.

I'm so proud of you and of being able to say I knew you before you were the Culinary Queen of South Beach. I'm thrilled that all your dreams are coming true, because mine are as well.

Ivan

PS Check out page 23 and let that ridiculous heart know your answer. I'm sure he's growing impatient by now.

Jaden's eyes welled with tears as she read and reread the note, almost forgetting there was a package yet to be unwrapped. Finally examining the parcel, it hit her, and she screeched, "Oh, my God! The magazine!"

Anxiously tearing through the paper, she found a cardboard box with the words *couldn't make it easy on you,* written on top in the same familiar handwriting. Of course he'd duct taped the box tighter than Fort Knox. Ivan was a smartass — one of the qualities she'd grown to love. Finally ripping through the all the gray tape, she tossed the lid aside and looked in the box.

Jaden held the thick, glossy magazine in her hands and stared. *She* was on the cover. It was one of the first pictures they'd taken. She was cutting a large, raw piece of beef that just so happened to look suggestively like something else. She bit her bottom lip with a look of "come get it" in her eyes. Her white coat sparkled, with the help of Photoshop, of course. Jaden couldn't believe how amazing, how sexy they'd made her look.

Still in shock, she shook the disbelief from her mind and managed to make out the words printed across the bottom of the cover. *Chef Jaden Thorne, Culinary Queen of South Beach, takes her rightful place on the throne. See page 23 for details.* She stood for what felt like twenty minutes, holding back her excitement and a fresh wave of tears. Quickly flipping past all the crap at the front to the magazine, Jaden stopped at page twenty-three, where another cream-colored envelope was stuck between the pages. In the photo on this page, she sat on the countertop with her feet up and her chef's jacket slightly askew, revealing a glimpse of her chest. With her head tilted back and tendrils of jet black hair trickling down her neck, it looked as if her eyes were having sultry sex with the camera lens. The picture spread across both pages and another title ran across the bottom: *Dining out has never been so sexy.*

Quickly shuffling through the article, Jaden noticed that it seemed to be mostly about her and only briefly mentioned the restaurant. There were a few shots of the dining room and kitchen, but the majority of the pictures were her looking sexy in her kitchen whites.

The giant heart standing in front of her coughed and cleared his throat, so tucking the magazine under her arm, Jaden ripped open the second envelope and began reading.

> I know probably the last thing you want to do is read another card right now, but I'm sure that ridiculously dressed heart is getting very impatient.
>
> I would be honored if you'd allow me to treat you to a celebratory outing for your amazing accomplishment. We could either cruise through the Caribbean, where I'm sure we'd find tons of sea turtles, or spend a hillbilly Thanksgiving in northwestern Pennsylvania with my family. Everybody gets to celebrate the holiday, so I know we can schedule this! Please let the heart know your answer.
>
> Ivan

Jaden jumped for joy, and the heart stepped out of the way for his own safety. She'd always dreamed of going on a Caribbean cruise, but she wasn't about to pass up the chance to see where her new love came from and to meet the amazing family she'd heard so much about. Looking at the heart, she offered her reply. "Tell the good doctor that as much as I love turtle watching, I'd much rather meet his family."

The oversized, red heart gave her an oversized thumbs-up. Jaden, thinking the conversation was over, began to shut the door, so she was surprised to see the costumed person shuffle his feet and begin another awkward dance. Now slightly annoyed, she said thank you again, but before she could slip away the heart reached for the zipper at the top of his costume and slowly slid it down. A full head of long brown hair emerged, followed by an ecstatically grinning Ivan.

Jaden stood speechless, her mouth hanging open.

"I would've picked the cruise, baby girl," Ivan said after a moment.

Overcome with emotion, Jaden rushed the costumed fool and jumped into his arms. Ivan lost his balance, and they both toppled into a heap in the center of the hall.

Laughing feverishly, Jaden whispered, "This is better than any magazine cover ever could be. Do you think you can unzip that the all the way down and come in for a second?" She raised her eyebrows meaningfully.

Rushing to get out of the costume, Ivan quickly followed her inside and shut the door behind them.

Chapter 20

"Tempted"

Jaden had officially transitioned into the fast lane of local stardom. Someone recognized her everywhere she went, long lines to get into clubs were a thing of the past, and sought after invitations to the hottest parties in the city rolled in like junk mail. And right by her side was Ivan. Drawing on his long history in the limelight, he offered advice on what to say during interviews and what to expect at events. Not only was she lucky to have him as her boyfriend, he was her stand-in manager as well. After all, she didn't really need a full-time manager. She wasn't that big…yet.

With Ivan away playing doctor in Chicago and promoting his weight loss program, Jaden decided to do something productive to jump-start her day, and she opted for a beach jog. The temperature was soothing this time of the year as October quickly faded away. Looking up and down the beach, she thought of how magical Miami was as winter began. November, they said, was when the rains began to dissipate and the vacationers rolled into town. Events were already in full swing and would stay that way until April when things slowed down for the summer.

With the trip to Ivan's home in Meadville fast approaching, Jaden wanted to make an extra good impression and had been secretly exercising more than usual. Her plan was to surprise Ivan with her new and improved sexy curves, and so far it had been working like a charm.

Before stepping onto the grainy sand, Jaden fished her phone out of her pocket to check her messages one last time before cranking up the tunes and settling in for the long run ahead. Within seconds her email came up on the screen. A message from R&H Casting marked "urgent" topped of the list of unread emails. Perplexed, she opened the message and began to read:

> Hello, Chef Thorne.
>
> My name is Jessie Alexander, and I'm a casting agent based in Miami. I represent various businesses across the US, but primarily my clients are TV networks. We are currently casting for contestants on an upcoming celebrity chef cook-off culinary show that will be based in Los Angeles. Local auditions are being held today at 2 p.m. in Miami Beach. I know this is last minute, but we would love you to come in and audition for the part. Please call my cell and let me know if you'll be able to make it.
>
> Jessie
>
> 814-555-8165

This has to be a joke. Since when was she a celebrity chef? The thought made her laugh out loud. Maybe it was one of Ivan's tricks? But what if it wasn't? Deciding not to risk it, Jaden dialed the number and held her breath as she waited for someone to pick up.

"Hello?" A female voice answered on the third ring.

"Hi, this is Jaden Thorne. I just received an email for a casting—"

"Oh! Chef Thorne," the woman jumped in. "Thank you so much for getting back to me quickly. I had your name come across my desk and wanted to contact you immediately. This is the last day of casting, and we'd love it if you could make it for an audition."

"Well, today must be my lucky day," Jaden replied. "It just so happens I have the day off, and I would love to audition."

"Fabulous!" the woman exclaimed. "I'll email you the directions and instructions on what to bring and wear. Oh, and Jaden, I'm looking forward to meeting you in person."

"I look forward to meeting you too." Jaden ended the call and suddenly felt a little overwhelmed. She turned back to her apartment, and all thoughts of jogging vanished from her mind. It was already twelve fifteen and the audition was scheduled for two.

Jaden burst into her apartment, checking again for new emails as she hurried to get ready. As promised, there was an email from Jessie containing instructions and the address. Scrolling down, she found the list of required items: driver's license and casual wear. That seemed easy enough, and as for the address, 1111 Lincoln Road. Perfect! It wasn't far at all.

Since Jaden had begun wearing makeup and doing her hair on a regular basis, getting ready had become second nature to her. Even the thought of dressing properly didn't frighten her so much now. Throwing on a pair of khaki capris, a moss green tank top, and a pair of brown leather sandals, she was ready to go. Parking this time of day was crazy, so taking a taxi to the location seemed like the best option. Hailing the first cab she saw, Jaden hopped in and set sail for her first casting call.

The same butterflies that had accompanied her on the shoot with *OD Magazine* start to flutter as the taxi pulled up in front of 1111 Lincoln Road. Following the signs that had been placed in the lobby, Jaden took the elevator to the seventh floor, down the hall, and to the door labeled Cooking Casting. She walked through the door and time seemed to stand still as everyone stopped to stare. The room was filled to the rafters with chefs of all shapes and sizes, some of whom she knew as local chefs of rival restaurants, and others who were celebrities of sorts, having already appeared on reality TV shows.

The small, effeminate man at the desk directed her to the sign-in sheet at the other side of the room. Jaden felt a little uneasy because it now appeared she'd dressed too casually, but oh well, too late to change now. Besides, with this caliber of chefs vying to be contestants, she didn't have a prayer. Already having committed to the audition, walking out simply wasn't a possibility, so with a great deal of effort, Jaden swallowed hard and decided to make the best of it. She signed her name across the sheet.

Jaden sat in the back and didn't say a word as one by one the others were called, each of them disappearing into a private room. She could have cut the tension with one of her knives. As she waited, the realization struck that she wasn't exactly sure what she was auditioning for. She'd been contacted at the last minute, but by the looks of it, all the other chefs were prepared.

"Jaden Thorne," the effeminate man who'd greeted her called out.

Hopping up, Jaden crossed the room and continued through a set of large steel doors behind him. She entered an overly bright white room, and Jaden felt as though she'd stepped onto a blank canvas--not a speck of color anywhere, just white walls, white ceilings, and white-tiled floor. In front of her sat three people, two men and a woman she'd guessed was Jessie. A large camera sat in the middle of the room, facing a white high stool. A wave of anxiety crashed over her as she approached the chair from the side. What was she doing here? She should be enjoying her day off, not sweating in front of a camera.

"Hello, Chef Thorne," the woman called. "I'm Jessie, and I'm delighted you could make it on such short notice. These are my colleagues from the network, Paul and Lawrence." Her voice echoed in the vast cavern of the empty room.

Jaden walked over to the table and shook each hand as she made her introduction. The men wore stuffy business suits, making it obvious they were not locals. Jessie, however, had the Miami flair. She wore a flowing dress and a huge smile to match.

The first suit spoke up. "Chef Thorne, here's what's going to happen. We're going to put you in front of the camera, ask you a couple questions, and that's it. Just act natural and stay relaxed. They say the camera adds five pounds, but it amplifies your attitude as well."

Seems easy enough, Jaden thought.

The second suit spoke just as the first finished his spiel. "This audition is for a major network, a syndicated television show. Should you be selected as a contestant, the network requires that you travel to LA for filming. Will that be a problem?"

Major show, syndicated television, Los Angeles…this was too crazy. Jaden's mouth opened before her brain had a chance to formulate a proper response. "No, sir. That won't be a problem."

"Fantastic!" the first suit chimed in. "We were told to pay close attention to you, so good luck, Chef Thorne."

What? Jaden didn't have time to contemplate the remark as the suits' inquisition began. She felt het palms getting sweaty. In a voice as pleasant and calm as possible, she replied, "I'll try not to disappoint."

"Go ahead and take a seat," Jessie said, pointing to the uncomfortable-looking stool. "We can begin whenever you're ready."

Hoisting herself up in the chair, Jaden looked fate directly in the lens and dove right in.

CHAPTER 21

Talk of turkey, stuffing, and overcrowded airports filled the radio waves, alerting Jaden and all of Miami Beach that Thanksgiving was right around the corner—as was her trip to Meadville. She could hardly imagine what it would be like for her and Ivan to have three full days together, uninterrupted. No pots or pans or leering stares. Jaden was so determined to leave work behind that she'd decided not to tell Ivan about the audition. It wasn't like she had a chance in hell of getting the part, and telling him about it would just be a distraction. This weekend was about them. Just them. Besides, then she wouldn't have to look foolish when she got the inevitable email telling her they'd selected someone else.

Their plans were all set to make the two-and-a-half-hour flight aboard the only airline that would take them directly to Pittsburgh, where they would then meet Ivan's mother for an additional ninety-minute ride to the backwoods of northwestern Pennsylvania. It would be a quick trip, as Geoff had begged her not to be away the entire holiday weekend, but it was nevertheless a vacation, and Ivan would be here any minute to whisk her away to his family's traditional Thanksgiving festivities. It was a big step for their budding relationship, but Jaden was looking forward to it. Over the past few months, she'd gown fond of his family through Ivan's stories, and although they'd never actually met them, she felt as though she'd known them her entire life.

As Jaden had packed for the visit, she remembered Ivan's warning not to bring anything formal or expensive. He'd listed the trip's highlights as campfires, canoes, homemade wine, and guns, so it was a safe bet she could leave her high heels behind. She was ready for the cold weather with a collection of jeans, warm sweaters, and fleece jackets she'd brought with her from back home. Growing up in Colorado had prepared her for anything that Mother Nature could throw at her.

She was less prepared for what the sleeping arrangements might be when they got there. Ivan's mom was religious, so did that mean they'd have to sleep in separate beds? Sighing, Jaden made sure to tuck in a sexy set of lingerie to spice things up if they had the chance.

Minutes after getting the call from downstairs, Jaden heard a soft knock on the door and opened it to find Ivan in the doorway wearing his million-dollar smile.

"Are you ready, baby girl?"

"I think a more fitting question is, are *you* ready for your family to meet me?" Jaden replied. Standing on her tiptoes, she placed a soft kiss on his lips. "Did you remember to pick up those things I asked you to get?" She slinked across the floor toward her bedroom. As she'd hoped, Ivan began to follow.

"I did, but I still don't see why you're making such a fuss." "We're barely going to be gone three days, and I'm quite sure Tasha is capable of buying a carton of milk and a loaf of bread. Besides, I thought she said something about going to Fort Lauderdale with Michael for Thanksgiving?"

"I know, but I still feel bad leaving her."

"Tasha's not going to be alone," Ivan reminded her again. "She's going to be with her boyfriend and his family. The last thing she'll be thinking about is whether there's enough milk in the fridge to last until you get home."

Jaden smacked Ivan playfully on the shoulder before leaning in for another kiss. Her hands wandered the hard planes of his chest, dipping beneath his shirt, feeling the warmth of his skin and breathing in that scent she'd grown to crave.

"Jaden," he groaned, not removing his lips from her mouth, "We don't have time for this, baby girl."

"Not even a quickie?" Jaden all but begged. "I'm easy to please."

Ivan tilted his head back and laughed. "Someone's feeling a little lascivious today."

"What's lascivious about a quick fuck before we go?" she fired back, surprising herself and apparently Ivan as well.

"Well, well," he said with a laugh, his eyes glinting.

She tried to steal another kiss, but Ivan grasped her by the shoulders, holding her firmly in place. Certain this little tryst had come to an untimely end, Jaden was shocked when he swiftly flung her around and pinned her against the bedroom wall, firmly planting his hands on either side of her head and caging her in like an animal. A primal lust swept over her when they lowered their hands and fumbled with the zippers on each other's pants, Ivan's falling around his ankles as he tore at the condom and Jaden struggling to get hers off in record time.

Without waiting for her to finish, Ivan grabbed her thighs, hoisted her up and pressed her back firmly into the wall, leaving her jeans to dangle from one foot. His fingers dug into her legs as he lifted her higher. In one hurried movement he entered her and proceeded to stroke into her mercilessly.

Jaden screamed and writhed, bucking wildly as he drove into her with a ferocity she hadn't experienced before. She tried to reposition herself but was pinned by his firm body as they rocked hard against the wall. If she could only move her hips another inch, she could… "Oh, *fuck!*" Jaden screamed as he plunged deeper into her core. Ivan had awakened the sexually liberated, dirty girl within her, and she loved it. Evidently so did he.

Ivan threw her onto the bed, still covered in the clothes she'd decided not to bring. Encircling her waist, he flipped her over as if she were weightless. Then the pounding and pumping continued as he penetrated her from behind. Jaden couldn't tell if she was in pain or sexual nirvana, but as she moaned his name she knew she didn't want this moment to end. Thrust after thrust she took his cock into her, pushing back at his every stroke, matching his pace and passion. Their hips rebounded off of each other and the sounds of sweaty skin smacking filled the room as weeks of frustration and separation were hammered away.

Jaden felt Ivan's hand in her hair and then found her head jerked back toward the ceiling. Her sexual gears cranking further into overdrive, she began to tell him what she wanted him to do to her. "Oh fuck! God, Ivan, fuck me, fuck me, fuck me. Yeah, yeah, yessss! Come on, come on. Harder! Ooooh, fuck, yes, yes, yes!"

When Ivan released her hair to grab her hips, she turned to admire the man who was fucking her brains out. The moment their eyes met she watched him fall over the edge. Pulling out, he locked eyes with her as he poured himself onto the small of her back. Jaden realized she and the good doctor had something else in common. This wouldn't be the last time she begged him to ride her rough.

"Shit!" Ivan yelled, breaking the mood a bit. "We gotta go!" He yanked up his pants.

"Umm…a little help, doctor?" Jaden requested from her all-fours position, her back covered in the product of their passion. "After all, this is your mess."

"Oh! Sorry," Ivan replied. He found a towel and cleaned her off, then helped her to her feet.

Dressing themselves as they ran from the apartment, bags in tow, they hurried down the hall, into the elevator, out of the building, and straight into the waiting taxi.

"I wait twenty-five minutes," the taxi driver shouted as they slipped into the backseat. Not having the time to load their luggage into the trunk, Ivan tossed it in beside them.

"No, you're getting paid for an extra twenty-five minutes," he shot back.

The flight left at four fifteen and it was already three p.m. With the airport twenty minutes away, Jaden silently prayed for no traffic—or any other obstacles that would slow their progress.

"If you get us there on time, I'll make it worth your while," Ivan added.

His words must have worked, because the cabby sank back in his seat and hit the gas.

As they roared to the airport, Jaden scooted close and, with a sultry smile, whispered in Ivan's ear, "I think I figured you out."

"And you as well," he replied, playfully tugging her hair.

Busted, she thought, snuggling against him. He smiled, and for a moment Jaden forgot how dangerously late their fuck-fest had made them.

But as the cab screeched to a stop, it all came flooding back. They jumped out, and Ivan threw the driver a hundred dollar bill, grabbed their belongings, and headed for security. Jaden clung tightly to his hand as he navigated the airport.

"Follow me and don't let go," he instructed.

"What if we miss the plane?"

"We won't," he assured her and winked before turning his attention to hustling through the throngs of holiday travelers.

Luckily, Jaden had taken his advice about never checking bags, and she had only a carry-on and a few personal items. He'd assured her there would be more than enough extra clothes at his house if need be, as his sister was around the same size.

Jaden felt ill when she saw the line of people waiting to take off their shoes and submit their computers for inspection, but Ivan didn't seem concerned. He steered them, her hand interlocked with his, into the business class line. They snaked their way to the metal detectors and easily passed through. Ivan then beelined for the departures monitor.

"Dammit!" he cursed after studying it for a moment. "I hate D60! Of course it would have to be that damn gate." Turning to Jaden he asked in a hurried tone, "Ready, baby girl? We got some work to do."

Jaden glanced at her watch: *3:50 — they've started boarding. Shit!*

Jogging briskly, they found the shuttle that ferried passengers along the terminal. Of course their plane waited at the very end. They hopped aboard the trolley, and time slipped away as the shuttle clunked down the line, finally slowing at their stop. They rushed out of the car and bolted down the stairs to their gate.

When they rounded the corner, Jaden could see the tail end of the line still at the gate. She and Ivan looked at each other and slowed their pace, now walking ever so casually as if they'd made it a point to be fashionably late. Feeling overheated and sweaty, from both the adrenaline rush and the hot sex preceding it, Jaden wiped a thin sheen of perspiration from her forehead.

As they finally made their way down the jet bridge, Ivan looked down at her and chuckled. He kissed her sweetly.

"Well, that was intense," Jaden remarked as they passed through the metal door and into the plane.

"I never doubted us for a second," Ivan shot back with an I'm-obviously-lying look all over his face.

Finding their oversized seats, Ivan and Jaden settled in for the flight, making sure to order their first round of drinks.

"Make mine a double," Jaden said, finally feeling some nerves about the visit ahead. Sitting back, she snuggled into Ivan's arms and made herself comfortable as he gently stroked her hair.

"So, give me a rundown of what I should know about your family," she suggested after their drinks arrived.

"Hmm… Dad's a bit of a party animal and backwoods guru. If you like the wine, laugh at his jokes, and can shoot a gun, you're all set. And I apologize now for any terrible jokes that may come your way."

"I've never shot a gun in my life," Jaden said in a panic.

"Relax, girl," Ivan replied, continuing to stroke her hair. "I'll teach you."

"Is that before or after I shoot myself in the foot?" Jaden took a long, calming sip of her drink. "What about the rest of your family?"

"Mom loves making jewelry. She's the sweetest thing on this earth and my best friend," Ivan replied, his tone sincere. "You'll have no problems there. My brother, PJ, loves all the high-class things and is way more high society than I am. Mention that you like expensive watches or skiing and you'll be best friends."

Jaden couldn't see Ivan's face with her head on his chest, but she'd bet a million bucks that talking about his family had him grinning ear to ear. His love for them was one of the things she adored about him.

"And what about your sister, what's she like?" Jaden asked, almost as an afterthought as her eyes grew heavy with sleep and began to close against her will.

"Ah. Elise. My little sis—she's just like my dad. I have a feeling the two of you will get along just fine… Just relax and get ready to have some fun."

Apparently more tired than she'd realized, from the sex or from the gauntlet they'd just run, Jaden drifted off to sleep under Ivan's the soothing caresses.

Chapter 22

"I Feel Home"

Jaden slowly opened her eyes, awaking to the sound of the captain announcing their final descent into Pittsburgh. She was stunned to find Ivan still stroking her hair. *How sweet*, she thought, straightening her back. Out the window everything was white on the ground. It reminded her of home.

"Did you sleep well, baby girl?" Ivan asked as he unwound his arm from around her shoulder.

"Like a log," Jaden replied, rubbing her eyes.

As the plane touched down and rolled to the gate, Jaden was surprised to find her usual fluttering butterflies hadn't made the trip. Maybe she was getting used to stressful situations, or maybe she just felt comfortable meeting his family. Either way, a calm stomach was a nice sensation.

Ivan grabbed their bags, and they quickly exited the plane. They traveled the long terminal to the transfer train that would take them to meet his mother. On the way Ivan texted his mom with an update, and he laughed when he looked at his phone. "She sent seven messages while we were in the air," he said, shaking his head. "Evidently she's also excited to see us!"

The shuttle slowed to a stop, and Ivan turned to look down at her. "Thank you for this. You have no idea how much it means to me." He kissed her cheek softly.

"No, thank you. You've made the past few months magical for me—and that hasn't been easy with everything else going on. Besides, what's Thanksgiving without family around?" She finished with a smile, but immediately her thoughts went to her own family, likely gathered around the table in Colorado, and she missed them intensely. She'd have to make some time for them soon. They'd been so patient since she moved away.

Ivan smiled again and gathered her into a hug, but as the train lurched to a stop, he was off at nearly a run with Jaden struggling to keep up. As they rounded the corner, Ivan somehow picked up his pace and rushed at a little lady standing beside the airport information sign. He scooped her into a bear hug.

"*Hola, chica!*" he yelled as he lifted her from the ground and spun her around in a circle.

Laughing, she slapped him on the arm. "Oh, stop it."

Without missing a beat, Ivan jumped right into the introduction. "Mom, this is Jaden."

Not settling for a casual hello, Ivan's mom went right for the hug. "So," she said, "this is the girl who could be my future daughter–in–law."

Ivan and Jaden stared silently at one another, their mouths slightly open.

"I had to get him back for embarrassing me like that," Mrs. Rusilko added. She took Jaden's hand. "How are you, dear? I'm Marie, and it's a pleasure to finally meet you. You're much more beautiful in person. That magazine does you no justice."

"You've seen the magazine?" Jaden asked, shooting a look at Ivan, who smiled sheepishly.

"What?" he shrugged. "There was a great article in there about South Beach marine life. Turtle migration, you know."

Jaden stifled a laugh and turned her attention back to his mom. "The pleasure is all mine, and thank you for having me. I couldn't pass up the chance to see where this guy came from." She nodded in Ivan's direction.

"Are you guys ready?" Ivan slung the bags over his shoulder and took each of the women by the hand, leading them through the busy airport terminal toward the parking garage. He practically skipped, Jaden noticed. He was truly glad to be home.

"I hope you're hungry," his mom said. "I packed food for the drive home."

"I could go for a bite to eat," Ivan said with a smile.

Jaden decided she should work immediately on getting to know Ivan's mom, since it seemed his family already knew a thing or two about her. "So Ivan tells me you're quite a Scrabble player, Mrs. Rusilko," she ventured.

Ivan started to laugh.

"He beats me most of the time, but I sneak in a few here and there. Do you play?"

"He hasn't tested me yet." Jaden looked at Ivan and giggled. "I think he's scared of me beating him."

Reaching a Jeep, Ivan's mom produced a set of keys and handed them to her son. "And please, dear, call me Marie. There's no need to be so formal."

Jaden and Ivan, somewhat underdressed for Pennsylvania temperatures, shivered as they stood waiting for the Jeep doors to unlock. After chucking their bags in the trunk, Ivan opened the doors for each of them.

Insisting that Jaden take the front seat, Marie climbed in the back while they continued their conversation. They roamed from topic to topic, and Marie shared a few stories from Ivan's childhood. Jaden felt sure a friendly rapport was being firmly established.

As Ivan started the journey home, the conversation transitioned to Jaden's childhood and her experiences in culinary school, and Marie talked of her passion for making jewelry and traveling.

They were about halfway to their destination when Marie finally asked "How did the two of you meet?"

Jaden and Ivan's eyes locked in surprise, and for a moment Jaden froze, not at all sure how to explain. But Ivan jumped right in.

"Do you remember Mollydooker, the winery those friends of mine own?" Ivan asked.

"Yes, you've commandeered my basement with your stash of their bottles."

"Hahaha…yeah, that's the one. Well, they sponsored the Winemaker's Dinner this year in Sarasota."

"I remember you mentioning something about that."

"That's where I happened to see the most beautiful girl in the world walk past, and I knew I had to get her name. After a little work she finally agreed to go on a date with me. Actually, a *lot* of work, now that I think about it," he added, taking a playful jab at Jaden.

Jaden smiled, silently thankful for his edited version of the events. "I have to give you credit, Marie. You raised one romantic son."

"It was all my dad," Ivan quickly added, eliciting a laugh and a thwack on the back from his mom.

"Yeah, right," Jaden added.

Time moved quickly, right along with the frosted countryside outside the foggy car windows. The gloomy sky threatened snowfall but held off as the Jeep barreled down the highway, bringing Ivan closer to his favorite place on earth. Farms, complete with cows, were scattered across the landscape and reminded Jaden of her winters in Colorado.

"Now, Jaden," Marie warned, "this isn't Miami Beach. It's very simple in comparison."

"Trust me, this has Miami beat, hands down," Jaden reassured her as Ivan veered right onto the Meadville exit.

While they drove through the town, Jaden felt even more at home. Meadville was so similar to her hometown. Plus the lack of traffic, scorching heat, and inconsiderate drivers was a welcome change from Miami Beach.

Jaden also noticed a change in Ivan. In Miami, he was an up-and-comer on the social scene, but here he was a different man. Stripped of his fast-paced lifestyle, he'd almost instantly transitioned from a suit-wearing doctor to a ruggedly handsome outdoorsman. The fact that he loved his family more than anything else in the world only made her fall harder for him. Maybe one day when they'd both retired they could move to a place *just like this*. She smiled, a little ahead of herself she knew.

They rounded the corner and pulled into a driveway. Nestled among a cluster of lush evergreens and maple trees was a brick house, blanketed with nearly a foot of fresh snow. Watching over the house like Swiss Guards at the gates of Vatican City were three dogs: two chocolate labs and a golden retriever, all of whom came tearing up the driveway as the Jeep came to a stop. Ivan opened the door and tried to hold off the mob of fur and paws, but before he could say anything, Jaden jumped out of the Jeep and rushed to his side. Watching him embrace the three pooches melted her heart and reminded her how much she missed her own little bundle of fur back home.

"Settle down," Marie called to the dogs as she came around the car.

"Well, these are my three Pennsylvania girlfriends," Ivan said, rumpling their fur. "The puppy is Gia, the golden is Taylor, and the middle one is Sasha." He petted each of them affectionately on the head as he gave their names.

"I love them!" Jaden exclaimed and offered her cheek for a big ol' sloppy puppy kiss.

"Mom, why don't you take Jaden inside and warm her up? I'll get the luggage."

"I'm okay," Jaden replied, trying to hide her shivering.

"Baby girl, your lips are turning purple. Go inside with Mom, and I'll be right behind."

"Thank you, I'm so glad you brought me here," Jaden whispered and kissed Ivan on the cheek. She stood and took Marie's outstretched hand. "Come on, girls," Jaden yelled, beckoning for the dogs to follow her.

"Traitors! Every last one of you, but especially you, Gia. I thought you were my girl," Ivan teased as the dogs raced off.

A warm blast of air, scented with the smell of home, greeted Jaden as she entered the Rusilkos' kitchen. The scent of a well-used fireplace, home cooking, and fresh country air enveloped her. Jaden admired the simple, cozy kitchen, complete with a gallery of family pictures and evidence of dog treats littering the floor. Yep, she was going to fit in perfectly.

Within minutes of their arrival a gorgeous dirty blonde bounced into the kitchen. Jaden recognized her from the family photo at Ivan's condo, and she also wore a smile identical to that of her brother.

"What's up, girl?" the blonde bellowed, squeezing Jaden in a hug. "It's so great to finally meet you."

"It's great to meet you too, Elise!" Jaden said, offering a hug in return. It seemed the word *girl* was a staple in this house.

"You must be thirsty. What do you want to drink?" Elise asked.

"I wouldn't mind a glass of water," Jaden said politely.

"Umm, water?" Elise stopped in her tracks. "You didn't make that trip to end up drinking water, especially in this house. You'll need a stiff drink. Trust me!"

"Okay," Jaden said with a giggle. "Surprise me."

"You're a brave girl." Elise laughed as she pulled out three glasses. "Mom, you want the usual Seven and Seven?"

"Sure, why not." Marie pulled out a chair and sat at the kitchen table.

Elise poured three cocktails, handed them out, and raised her glass in a toast. "Here's to a kick-ass Thanksgiving weekend."

"To a kick-ass Thanksgiving," Jaden echoed. Ivan was right, his sister was a rock star. Just then he burst through the door with the luggage, and Elise pounced immediately.

"All this time and you didn't even pour me a drink? Jeez!" he exclaimed, dropping the bags to twirl her in a hug.

"Big brother!" Elise screeched. "It's been too damn long!"

Setting Elise back down, Ivan pulled out a chair for Jaden at the table. "Have a seat. Make yourself at home."

Jaden obliged and joined the friendly banter, smiling at Ivan from time to time as she could feel him watching her. They discussed the Miami Beach lifestyle, Elise's work in Pittsburgh, and the major happenings in Meadville, which included a new menu at Perkins. A little while later another vehicle rumbled in the driveway, and Ivan took Jaden's hand and squeezed.

"Brace yourself," he told her. "Papa bear is home."

Then, with a Fu Man Chu mustache and goofy grin painting his face, Ivan's father flung open the door and made his grand entrance. "Where's the chef?"

Jaden began to smile, but it faded as he came to stand just inches in front of her.

"Jaden, right?"

Nodding, she said, "Hello, Dr. —"

He cut her off before she could finish. "I have a joke for you."

"Oh boy, here we go," Ivan muttered, and Jaden shot him a nervous glance.

"What do you call two turtles having sex?"

Jaden could feel the blush heat her cheeks. There was no possible way Ivan's dad could know about their turtle-watching adventures. Right? This was just a coincidence?

"John!" Marie scolded.

Confused, stunned, and amused all at once, Jaden swallowed hard and looked him in the eyes. "Umm…I would have to say a slow poke?"

"What?" He wrapped his arm around Jaden's shoulder. "Did you tell her my joke?" Ivan's father demanded, looking at Ivan.

"Well, you have about fifty different ones, and they're all terrible, so no," Ivan replied with a grin.

John shot him a suspicious look and turned his attention back to Jaden. "You're all right. I don't care what my wife says. You're a keeper."

"John!" Marie scolded again.

Turning back to the table, a grin now plastered across her own face, Jaden reached over and took Ivan's hand.

Ivan's father momentarily disappeared, only to reappear with a bottle of his finest homemade wine of the year. He cracked it open for all to enjoy, and in the midst of the merriment and conversation, Marie served them some fantastic pasta. The night wore on, and several bottles of vino later, the group remained immersed in laughter and stories. Finally Ivan's mom excused herself from the table, which pretty much pulled the plug on everyone's party. One by one the rest of them said their good nights before retreating to the bedrooms. Jaden, now feeling like one of the family, gave each of them a farewell hug.

"Are you ready for me to show you to your room, madam?" Ivan asked with a yawn.

"*Si, señor,*" Jaden replied and followed him and her luggage down the hall to the guest room. As they crashed on the bed, Jaden asked, "So how did I do?"

"You mean minus the thing you have hanging from your nose? I'd say you handled yourself perfectly."

Fear shot through her. "What?"

Ivan restrained her as she moved to jump off the bed. "I'm kidding. Don't you know me by now?"

"You ass," Jaden retorted, settling into the curves of his chest. "I love your sister—she's hilarious. Your mom is *so* sweet, and your dad… Oh, God, I can see where you get your personality."

"You made my day, baby girl. Watching you with them was amazing."

Jaden smiled. "Where's your brother?" "He's working tonight, but he'll be here first thing in the morning for the festivities."

Feeling playful, Jaden couldn't help what she was about to do next. "So, this is my room right?"

"Yep, for tonight anyway."

Jaden reached down and grabbed his crotch, pulling her hand away just as quickly. "Too bad," she said wistfully. "I had plans for us tonight."

"God, you're a tease," Ivan groaned and placed Jaden's hand back on the growing bulge in his jeans. "Tomorrow we're gonna have our own place, and rest assured I'm going to get you back for this."

Ivan reached down and trailed his fingers up the inside of her leg. With the pad of his thumb, he stroked the fabric that concealed her sweet spot. Throwing her head back into the pillows, Jaden moaned as Ivan's fingers worked their magic. But just as abruptly as he'd began the sweet torment, he ended it, sliding off the side of the bed. "All right, baby girl, I'm gonna hit it. We both need some sleep. Busy day tomorrow."

"You're freaking kidding me, right? You are *not* going to leave me hanging like this!"

"Well, unless you want to wake up the whole house, there's no other choice."

"Fine," Jaden sighed. "But we're even."

"We're nowhere near even. Wait until tomorrow when I get my hands on you." Ivan offered her a mischievous grin. "Payback's a bitch!"

"Good night, Ivan," Jaden groaned as she buried her head under the pillow.

"Good night," he replied as he flicked off the lights and exited the room.

CHAPTER 23
"Ain't Nothing Like The Real Thing"

Jaden awoke to the aroma of bacon floating into the bedroom. No doubt Marie was whipping up some good home cookin'. Tossing back the thick green comforter and welcoming the cool air as it danced across her skin, Jaden slid out from beneath the covers and unzipped her bag, rummaging for clothes. After making a mess of her suitcase, she decided on a comfy pair of jeans and hand-knit sweater her grandma had given her. Jaden scooted down the hall to the bathroom and breathed in the second lovely scent of the morning: lavender. No wonder it was one of Ivan's favorites, it must remind him of home. She set her bag of toiletries on the counter, and after brushing her teeth and pulling her hair into a ponytail, she applied a quick bit of makeup in preparation for round two with the family.

Following the bacon smell, Jaden headed down the hall and was surprised to find Ivan's dad masterminding the entire breakfast. Feeling slightly dangerous after a good night's sleep, Jaden strolled into the kitchen to spark up a conversation.

"So, is your cooking as good as the wine we had last night?" Jaden asked, obviously startling the poor man who nearly fumbled the pan of hot grease.

"Good morning, Jaden. Did you sleep well?" His voice filled the kitchen, and with expert hands he steadied the pan and carried on as if nothing had happened.

"Yes, I did. Thank you." She sat at the kitchen table. "I love that bed. I may have to get one of those egg-crate mattress covers for myself."

"Loverboy's outside, if you're looking for him." John motioned to two male forms through the window, who appeared to be braving the cold to set up a deep fryer.

Ivan had pulled his hair into a ponytail that hung out the back of a well-worn baseball cap, and yesterday's five o'clock shadow had bloomed into a ten o'clock scruff. He looked different clothed in boots, gloves, dirty jeans, and a red-plaid hooded jacket — very sexy in a burly, rugged sort of way. She was sure the other man was Ivan's brother who must have arrived in the wee hours of the morning. Jaden watched contentedly through the window as they bantered back and forth.

"I can go get him," John offered.

"Thanks, but that's okay," Jaden said, bringing her focus back inside. "They look busy. Besides, I'm more interested in what you're doing."

"Well, it's no French omelet, but BLTs built this house." John laughed and stepped aside, displaying his frying bacon and the already toasted bread, complete with lettuce, mayonnaise, and tomato. "Would you care for one?"

"I'd love it," Jaden said. "I thought you'd never ask."

Putting three strips of bacon on a sandwich, he cut it in half and handed her the plate. "*Bon appetit!*"

Jaden dug right in. "Oh, my God, this is amazing," she said, taking another large bite. It had been months, if not longer, since she'd had bacon, and this was a little slice of heaven.

"You can't really mess up a BLT," he said with a smile and joined Jaden at the table. He soon started in on his own sandwich.

Bursting through the door with a wave of cold, Ivan and his brother made their entrance, grunting and groaning as they shook the snow from their boots. In their layers of heavy winter clothing, they looked as though they'd just come home from a hard day's work.

"Baby girl, you're awake." Ivan smiled and kissed her good morning.

"Ahem," a voice behind him cackled. "Aren't you forgetting something?"

"Oh, right. Sorry. PJ, this is Jaden. Jaden, this is my brother, PJ."

Emerging from behind Ivan was a smaller, more Italian-looking version of him. PJ was also dressed lumberjack style, just a much higher-end lumberjack than the ragged jeans and plaid jacket Ivan wore.

"So you're the infamous Jaden I've heard so much about." PJ stripped off his heavy jacket.

Jaden rose to properly greet Ivan's older brother. Now prepared for what was about to happen, she opened her arms and PJ engulfed her in what she was affectionately calling the "Rusilko Bear Hug."

"It's a pleasure to finally meet you," she replied, shivering at his hands against her back. Even through her sweater he felt noticeably cold.

"I hope you're ready for some bird." PJ motioned to the deep fryer outside. "You picked a good time to come. Holidays in this house are fantastic."

Jaden couldn't help but grin. "Yep, I can't wait!"

"Good, because—"

"First she has to pass the test," Ivan interrupted.

"What test?" Jaden asked nervously. Knowing Ivan, it was something completely off the wall.

She looked around, confused. All three Rusilko men glanced at each other and began to laugh.

"Oh yeah, the test. You got ammo downstairs?" John asked.

"Enough, I hope. She's a greenhorn." Ivan looked at her and winked. "But I'm sure she'll do just fine."

Finally catching the gist of their plan, Jaden's heart beat faster. She'd never fired a gun, let alone held one. Wiping her sweaty palms along the legs of her jeans, Jaden swallowed her fear, and with a new-found confidence, she replied, "Greenhorn, huh? I'll show you who's a greenhorn."

"That a girl," John boomed and wrapped his arm around her shoulder. Looking to his son, he said again, "I think this one's a keeper."

"Is that a challenge, Ms. Thorne?" Ivan asked with a grin.

"Of course it's a challenge. You don't really think I'm going to let you show me up in front of your family, do you?"

"You're on." A sly smirk crept across his face. "But you'll have to dress warmer than that. Follow me. I have some clothes that should fit you."

Jaden followed him through the house, detouring past her room and taking a set of stairs to the basement. He paused as they reached the bottom. Turning to look over his shoulder, a look of worry crossed his face. "I should've asked this before, but by any chance are you against hunting?"

"I'm not really against it," Jaden said. "I've just never considered trying it. But as you've taught me, there's a first time for everything."

Seeming satisfied, Ivan nodded and led her farther into the basement. As they turned the corner, she could see why he'd looked so worried only seconds before. The room they now stood in resembled a museum of natural history. Animals and fish of varying shapes, sizes, and species decorated the every inch of the walls that surrounded them. The glassy eyes of wild boars, bears, and buffalo stared back at her. Completing the ensemble of animals was a hammerhead shark that spanned the entire length of one wall.

Nervously, Ivan started to explain. "Some people don't like fishing and hunting, but they don't understand that hunters and fishers are huge supporters of conservation."

"Baby, you don't have to sell me on this. Hunting isn't a bad thing if done properly and responsibly. My dad has told me horror stories about poachers he's caught in the park, and it's people like that who give hunters a bad name."

Ivan smiled, his eyes full of relief. "Okay then. On to our wardrobe selection."

Ivan pulled open a huge armoire, and Jaden could see it was full of heavy cammo clothing. "Hmm, sexy."

"Baby girl, you could make a chastity belt look sexy," Ivan teased as he dug in the closet and fished out a jacket and pants for her.

Taking the items, she began to put them on. "What about the guns?"

"You worry about keeping your sexy little ass warm, and let me worry about the rest. I'll have you from greenhorn to markswoman in no time flat." Ivan grabbed another cammo outfit from the closet and slipped it on.

Jaden noticed Ivan staring at her with a sexy, mischievous glimmer in his eye as she pulled on the last of her ensemble. "Does this turn you on, Dr. Ivan?" she asked, swaying her hips. "Does seeing a girl in cammo gear make you hard?"

Jaden smiled as she watched a series of emotions flash across his face: lust, frustration, disappointment, and finally resigned amusement. With his family upstairs, he had no opportunity to rip her clothes off and take her hard and fast like he'd done the day before. She shivered just thinking about it.

"Now you're really gonna get it," Ivan said, grabbing Jaden by the ass and pulling her to him before crushing his lips to hers and biting them a little.

"I hope so," she said breathlessly as she pulled back and started toward the stairs, swaying her hips once again.

They returned to the kitchen where the entire family greeted her with a round of applause. Enjoying the moment, Jaden did a three-sixty, modeling the oversized brown-and-green outfit, and ended with a curtsy.

Noticing that only Ivan, John, and Elise had donned their camouflage, Jaden asked, "Are you two not coming with us?"

Leaning lazily against the counter, PJ looked as if he could fall asleep on the spot. "I'm still recovering from the drive this morning. I think I'd better sit this one out."

"I wasn't born with John's hunting enthusiasm," Marie added. "I'll stay behind and start supper."

"So are we all ready to go?" John asked, taking a goofball stance and squeezing Jaden's shoulder.

"Only if you are," Jaden replied with as much confidence as she could gather.

The four cammo warriors then bustled through the front door and into the cold, crisp November morning. Puffs of steam rose up through the air every time Jaden exhaled, but the cold against her exposed skin was a welcome reprieve from the overheated feeling the snowsuit created.

"Whew," Jaden breathed, catching Ivan's eye.

"You'll thank me later," he promised as he hurried past her with an armful of gear. Following closely on his heels, Gia pranced around happily as the men loaded the gear into the back of yet another Jeep.

Grabbing Jaden by the hand, Elise dragged her toward the Jeep. "Come with me. You and I can sit in the front and chat. The men can sit in the back with that idiot dog of theirs."

Stifling a laugh, she followed Elise into the car. Sure enough, after loading the remainder of the gear, Ivan and John, along with Gia, piled in the back. With the flick of the key, Elise started the Jeep and tore out of the driveway. House after house passed by in a blur, until eventually they reached the outskirts of town and miles of dense woods. Clad in cammo and carrying a small arsenal in the back of the Jeep, Jaden couldn't help but wonder if she'd seen this in a movie somewhere.

"So Jaden," Elise said, breaking the silence that had settled over them. "Why my brother? I mean, look at him. What would you want a scruffy bear like that for?"

"Elise…" Ivan groaned from the back.

Elise flashed him a smile in the rearview mirror, and Jaden turned to give him one of her own. Ivan's sister must've prepared a mental list of questions in advance, because no sooner did she answer one than another immediately followed. She did her best to answer with humor and wit, and she was rewarded with a broad grin and nod of approval from Ivan, who now leaned forward, listening intently to what she had to say.

When the inquisition finally came to an end, Elise slid a disc into the CD player. Neil Young blasted through the speakers, accompanying them along the final leg of their trip. Jaden could tell by the way the men carried on that John, much like Ivan, had a passion for music. Settling back in her seat, Jaden listened to Ivan, John — and Neil — belt out the lyrics to "Heart of Gold."

CHAPTER 24

"Country Roads"

As they entered the forest preserve and drew near their destination, Jaden looked around nervously, fighting the butterflies that had returned with a vengeance. This was it--there was no more fooling around. Remembering Ivan's words on the plane about being a good shot to impress his father, she knew this might be her only chance to truly fit in.

Elise pulled the Jeep up to the front of a small cabin, and two more chocolate labs emerged from the woods to bombard them with excitement as they piled out of the car.

"Okay, Jaden, this is where we're gonna do some shooting," John said in a serious tone. "This is a buddy's house, but just to warn you, this is real country living out here, so don't be offended by anything that's said."

Having known a few roughnecks back in Colorado, Jaden now gave John a reassuring shoulder squeeze. "No worries. I'm not offended *that* easily."

Ivan joined the ladies and escorted them up to the door as Gia and the other labs headed into the woods for some exercise. "I'll get everything from the car," he said. "Go get warm, and Elise, keep her safe."

He jogged off in the direction of the Jeep to help his father, and Jaden's curiosity got the best of her. "What does he mean keep me safe?" she asked. "What was he talking about?"

"Ignore my brother," Elise said, directing Jaden through the front door. "Van's the man."

"Who's Van?"

"My dad's friend. He's the real McCoy."

Entering the cabin, Jaden discovered even more animals mounted on the wall, but she also noticed beautifully handcrafted wood furnishings. Apparently Van was a carpenter of sorts. A noise behind her alerted Jaden to the presence of another person, and she turned to find a short man with a full beard and grayish black hair as long as Ivan's. He sported a Pittsburgh Steelers shirt and a pair of worn blue jeans.

"You son of a bitch, comin' out here and harassing my dogs," he yelled as Ivan's dad burst through the front door carrying a load of gear.

"Now behave, gnome," John warned. "We have company today."

Van turned to look at Jaden and did a double take. "I thought you were Ivan with long hair. He's turned into a stone dweller since moving to Miami." He extended his hand. "The name's Van. It's a pleasure to meet you."

"The pleasure's all mine," Jaden said, shaking his hand. "I love your home, and the wood furniture is beautiful."

"Ah, it's a hobby." Van shrugged off the compliment. "Are you a stone dweller too?"

"Oh, hell, no," Jaden quickly clarified. "I'm from Colorado originally, so I've spent more than my fair share of time in the woods. I only recently moved to Miami."

"So you're a concrete cowgirl then, eh? But the *big* question is, can you shoot?"

Not knowing what to say next, Jaden returned his shrug. "I guess we'll find out soon enough."

"I got a fire started out back, and everything's set up. Heaven forbid if the stone dweller had to set it up. Speaking of, where is Ivan?"

"He's getting the rest of the stuff from the car," Elise answered.

Van motioned for them to follow. Heading downstairs, they entered a room full of machines and carbides brimming with fermenting beer and wine. Recognizing the bottles from the Rusilkos' house, Jaden realized this must be where the wine-making magic happened. They stepped through a set of doors and into the freezing cold of Van's snow-covered backyard. A bonfire roared, and to the left of it sat an old cooler and a wooden bench. To the right was Ivan, fumbling around with some contraption that resembled a catapult and cursing quietly to himself.

"You okay over there, city boy?" Van called.

"Better than you, old man." Ivan finished whatever he was doing and jogged over to the fire to shake Van's hand and thank him for allowing them to be there.

"Who's shooting?" Ivan asked. "Besides Jaden, of course." With an arm around her waist, he led her to the catapult.

"Today's for the young'uns," Van announced. "We're just gonna sit back and watch, right, John?"

Ivan and Elise gave each other a knowing look as Van and their dad took up residence on the bench beside the fire. "'Sit back and watch' is code for 'open the cooler and pass me a drink,'" Elise half-whispered as she passed.

Ivan presented Jaden with a shotgun and proceeded to give her a crash course on shooting, while Elise readied the bright orange clay pigeons.

"Okay, baby girl, here's what you do, I'll load it, and you push it into your shoulder like this." Standing behind her, Ivan showed her how the gun should feel in her hands.

With his body pressed close to hers, Jaden let her mind momentarily drift to images of Ivan and what she wished he were doing back there, but when said something about taking off the safety, she regained her focus.

"When you're ready, click this lever forward and say 'Pull!' Elise will pull the string, and that orange disk over there will go flying. Aim in front of it and shoot. The disk will fly into the path of the pellets. Remember, shotguns shoot a spray, so as long as you're close, you'll nail it."

Feeling the pressure, Jaden frowned and whispered, "Pray for me."

"No matter how you shoot, baby girl, you look fantastic in that horrible outfit," Ivan said with a sultry grin.

"Here we go," came the announcement from the bench. John sat up and hoisted a glass of wine into the air. "To Jaden!"

"To Jaden," Van and the others chimed in.

She tried to mentally prepare herself. Gripping the gun, she jammed it into her right shoulder, shut her left eye, and yelled pull. Elise yanked the string, sending the orange disk soaring through the sky and across the backyard. Jaden's heart raced, time stood still, and she pulled the trigger, creating an explosion of noise and fire and a burning odor as the gun kicked back mercilessly into her shoulder.

Everyone watched as the disk's flight was interrupted by the spray of pellets, and it exploded in midair. *Oh, my freaking God,* Jaden half thought and half whispered to herself, surprised by the rush of shooting the gun. *Holy shit, I can't believe I did it!* Turning to face the group, which sat with looks of amazement on their faces, she dropped the gun to her side and played the Dirty Harry role to a tee. "Is that all you got?"

Not one of them had a snappy comeback, so Jaden screeched, "Oh, my God!"

Ivan rushed to her side for what she thought would be a congratulatory hug, but instead, he snagged the gun and put on the safety.

"Don't want you to go two for two on killing things just yet," he said. Setting the gun back on the ground, he swept her into his arms. "That was amazing, baby girl. You couldn't get any more perfect."

"Not bad for a city dweller, eh?" Jaden asked, pausing to admire his neon orange knit hat.

"City dweller? I thought you were from Colorado," Ivan teased. He turned to address the peanut gallery on the bench. "It's your turn to shoot, Mr. Backwoods Mountain Man."

"I can't, already had a drink." Van lifted the glass high for Ivan to see and looked more than a little relieved.

"What about you, doc?" Jaden scoffed. "You're all talk, but I don't see you stepping up to take a shot or two."

"Or two, eh? I'll show you how it's done. Load two," he said, turning to Elise.

"Big man, showing off in front of the ladies," his father jeered. "Fifty bucks says that pretty little girlfriend of yours is a better shot."

"Yeah, yeah," Ivan said, smiling at his dad with a gleam in his eye.

Jaden looked from Ivan back to the men on the bench and smiled a wobbly smile. Hearing John use the word *girlfriend* warmed her, and seeing how they'd all unquestioningly welcomed her into their life was enough to bring tears. She fought hard to hold them back and returned her gaze to Ivan, who now planted his feet in the snow and steadied himself. Putting the gun to his shoulder, he aimed and yelled the magic word.

"Pull!"

Two large cracks echoed in the air around them, and Ivan fired off two shots. The bright orange disks continued to fly through the air, landing in one piece fifty yards away in the snow. Ivan stood motionless, likely knowing this was something he was *never* going to live down. Not only would this traumatic event haunt him for the rest of the weekend, but the tale of this disaster could quite possibly follow him back to Miami. Jaden shook her head, almost feeling sorry for the guy as he slowly turned around. He faced the silent crowd, and then it began.

"You should be embarrassed, stone dweller. Boo! Even Gia can shoot better than that," Van offered.

Ivan kept his head down and headed straight for Jaden. She opened her arms to comfort him. "It's okay, baby. I still think you're sexy — effeminate, but sexy." Not able to hold off any longer, she let him have it with a side-splitting laugh.

Bowing his head in defeat, Ivan took the harassment with good nature, as usual. "Okay, Elise, grab me the Midnight Rider."

Elise bolted to the car and returned with what looked to be a wartime weapon. Ivan took the gun from her and loaded it.

"Okay, baby girl, since you already passed round one, this is the grand finale." Ivan handed Jaden the assault rifle and gave her another quick lesson. He pointed to an orange and black target that hung from a tree. "It's the same rules as last time, only we'll be aiming for that target instead of the disks. Just point and click, but don't stop pulling the trigger until you're out of ammo. You have a round of twenty shots."

"Seriously?" Jaden asked as she placed the earmuffs Ivan offered over her ears, blocking out the sounds of the jeering men and muffling his voice.

"Yes," he assured her. "This is the fun part."

Feeling all eyes on her, Jaden lifted the gun to her shoulder and took a deep breath. "Here we go."

She took aim like the last time, and Jaden looked down the barrel of the gun at the target flapping in the breeze. Expecting the same reaction, she tensed up and pulled the trigger. But with an ear-stabbing screech and no kick, the first bullet set sail, startling Jaden with its volume despite her ear protection. She could see Ivan motioning for her to keep firing. Letting her inhibitions go, she focused on the sensation of shooting the semiautomatic. Excitement coursed through her as round after round flew through the air.

As the gun went dry, Jaden continued firing, not even realizing there were no bullets left. Coming down from her ten-second high, she cried, "That was fucking amazing!"

Immediately mortified that she'd let the F-bomb slip in front of Ivan's family, Jaden turned to him with a look of horror in her eyes. But then she heard John and Van cheering her on.

"Now that's what I call a backwoods chick," Ivan's dad announced.

"Let's see how she did first," Ivan teased. He grabbed Jaden's hand and pulled her across the tundra to the target on the tree.

"Not one hit? You've got to be kidding me," Jaden said as they drew close enough to see the target. Her shoulders slumped.

"Trust me, no one ever hits the first time," Ivan assured her. Then he smiled. "Ten hits!" he announced to the faraway crowd.

Still shaking from the excitement, Jaden laughed as Ivan tore down the target and crumpled it up, destroying the evidence.

"I think it's time for a drink!" He slung his arm around her shoulder.

"I agree. I need one after that."

Ivan rummaged in the cooler once they rejoined the group, but Elise said, "I'm cold! I'll take my drink inside."

"Don't you want a chance to shoot?" Jaden asked. "I'm sure Ivan could handle pulling the string for you."

"Nah, it's better to let his embarrassing performance with the gun linger," Elise said with a laugh. She darted out of the way as Ivan tried to slug her shoulder, and everyone returned to the makeshift winery. The glasses of homemade wine flowed freely, as did the stories and crude jokes, most of which came from John and Van—and would have gotten them into trouble in a public setting. But here, in the middle of the woods, there were no holds barred. After a few glasses of the wine, Jaden found herself sharing a racy joke or two. Why not? She was in the presence of friends and family, and she was having fun.

Realizing that the time for dinner was fast approaching and Ivan still had to deep fry a bird, they said their goodbyes, and Van stocked them up with Jaden's favorite blend for the evening, strawberry rhubarb wine. Gathering Gia and their equipment, they piled into the Jeep and headed home, where Jaden knew there'd be more food, wine, and family fun in store.

CHAPTER 25

"Drift Away"

Elise pulled the Jeep up in front of the house, and the gang rolled out. "Aw yeah!" Ivan cheered.

"Really?" Jaden asked, a bit skeptical as she look over to where PJ had already started the oil heating in the deep fryer.

"Done in forty-five minutes and delicious," Ivan assured her. "But don't worry, mom's got one in the oven as well."

Ivan and his dad took care of putting the guns away and unpacking the gear while the ladies went ahead into the house. Inside, Jaden was engulfed by the smells of sweet potatoes, pumpkin pie, and the *piece de resistance* completing its final hour in the oven. She felt the unsettling feeling of homesickness wash over her. It was her family's tradition to prepare the same type of Thanksgiving feast.

"I'm glad you girls are back," Marie exclaimed. "Hurry up and get changed for dinner, and Jaden, would you please meet me in the living room when you're done?"

"Of course," Jaden replied, wondering why Marie wore the all-too-familiar mischievous smile she'd seen on Ivan's face so many times.

Jaden shook the snow from her boots, kicked them off, and waddled to her room to discard the fifty-pound snowsuit that was now causing her to sweat like a fiend. Selecting a comfy pair of khakis and a white sweater, she quickly changed and ran a brush through her hair, leaving it down in a style she knew Ivan loved. She emerged from her room and joined Marie in the living room, where a table full of beautifully crafted earrings, bracelets, rings, and rosaries sat before her. "Ohhh," she sighed as she sat down next to Marie.

Marie handed her a bracelet. "I'd like you to pick out a few pieces," she said.

"Marie, I can't do that." Jaden turned the bracelet over in her hand, admiring its details.

"Honey, please," Marie urged. "It's the least I can do for the girl who's made my son a new man. I've never seen him so happy before—not even when he was traveling the world for modeling. His smile now is by far the brightest I've ever seen, and I have you to thank for that."

At a loss for words and overcome with emotion, Jaden wiped a tear. "At least let me pay you for them."

Marie placed a hand on Jaden's shoulder. "I could never take your money. What you've given my son is worth more than any piece of jewelry."

"You guys have been so amazing. I don't even know how to begin to say thank you." Jaden leaned over and swept the tiny woman into her arms, giving her a bear hug of her own. "Thank you so much for everything."

"So please, dear, pick a few." Marie smiled.

Looking at the jewelry before her, Jaden was at a loss. She didn't want to choose something too expensive… She fingered a few pieces and finally settled on a pair of black teardrop earrings set in gold, a turquoise bracelet, and the piece that had first caught her eye when she sat down—a tiger-eye rosary.

Marie began to laugh. "When Ivan was in high school, he got mono during the summer before his senior year and couldn't go out or do anything for two weeks, so I taught him how to make jewelry. Like most of his other hobbies, he went overboard and turned out more pieces that I knew what to do with, but eventually I sold them all, except for one. It was his favorite, and he told me to sell it for a hundred dollars or not to sell it at all. The materials were only eight dollars, so of course no one would buy it. Many people looked at it, but no one would ever agree to such a steep price. You just picked it as one of yours."

"No way," Jaden gasped. "Which piece is it?"

"I'll let him tell you." Marie smiled and began packing up the jewelry that remained on the table.

"Thank you so much, Mrs. — I mean, Marie. These are beautiful, and I'll cherish them."

"You're welcome. Well, did you shoot okay? Did you pass their test?" Marie asked, packing away the last piece with a twinkle in her eye. "You must be starving after being out in that cold all day."

"Umm, I'm pretty sure I passed their test, but I'll let Ivan tell you that story, and yes, I'm famished."

"Let's get to it then. Ivan should be about ready to start his bird."

Jaden rested her hand affectionately on Marie's arm. "Thank you again, for everything."

"Anytime. Just promise me you'll come back soon and visit us."

"I'd like that." Jaden stood and followed Marie back into the kitchen.

She removed the small diamond studs she was wearing and tucked them safely into the pocket of her jeans, replacing them with the new earrings Marie had given her. With the bracelet and the rosary weighing down her other pocket, she couldn't help but wonder what Ivan had made. She knew he loved turquoise from the rings that he wore. Fishing the bracelet out of her pocket, she slid it over her wrist, wondering how long it would take him to notice it.

Jaden looked out the kitchen window to see the Rusilko men standing around a bubbling cauldron of oil. A gigantic raw turkey sat on the table in front of them, and next to that sat six glasses of wine, begging to be consumed. PJ walked over to where an odd-looking fire pit occupied one corner of the patio and began to stoke a fire. Catching her looking through the window, he motioned for her to join them outside.

Jaden tossed on a jacket and went out, with Marie and Elise following closely behind.

"Are we ready to kick off Turkey Day?" Ivan asked as he pulled on a pair of heavy-duty gloves.

Hanging the bird from a hook, he slowly lowered it into the pot of bubbling oil. A sizzling sound filled the air as the water still left on the turkey's skin met the oil. With a look of deep concentration, Ivan finished easing the bird into the deep fryer. Small, champagne-like bubbles surfaced, along with a truly drool-worthy aroma.

Dispensing the glasses of wine, John said, "Let the girl who impressed us today with her fine shooting and dirty jokes give us a toast."

Damn it, Jaden thought. Clearing her throat, she raised her glass. "Here's to finding the only family, besides my own, who could make me feel at home on Thanksgiving. Thank you all for welcoming me. Oh, and let's not give Ivan too much grief over his embarrassing display of marksmanship today. It must be tough getting your butt whipped by a girl."

"Cheers. *Salud. Nostrovia!*" Everyone toasted in unison, each in their own way, except Ivan. His eyes full of what very much looked like love to Jaden, he simply smiled and raised his glass to her.

After drinking down the last of their wine, the women disappeared back into the kitchen, leaving the men and dogs to stand guard over the fryer. Once the door closed behind them, PJ and John jumped right in.

"Okay, how the hell did you get so lucky?" PJ demanded. "First Irena, then the Australians, then that string of models, and now Jaden—a girl who has looks *and* the personality to match?"

Ivan shrugged. "I finally took a chance, and it worked."

"You took a chance and it worked? That's bullshit. You'd better thank me for those Rusilko genes." John puffed out his chest, reminding them he'd once been a bodybuilder in his own right.

"Listen, I don't know what you did to land a girl like Jaden, but she's great, and you seem truly happy. I have to admit, I was a bit concerned after the last one."

"You have no idea how happy I am." Ivan smiled and raised his glass. "To family, a collection of people you never would have otherwise met, but are so damn lucky you did. I love you guys."

"To family," the others echoed.

Inside, the women were gabbing like teenage girls at a sleepover. Jaden showed Marie a few tricks of the trade while Elise flipped through the pages of *OD* and asked Jaden more random questions about her past and her family.

A series of annoying beeps altered them that both birds were now done, and it would soon be time to eat.

"I'm glad Ivan brought you home," Elise said, tossing the magazine on the counter.

"Oh, why is that?" Jaden asked, balancing the roasting pan on the stove as she shut the oven door.

"Because I've always wanted a sister," Elise said, smiling as she rose to call in the men.

Fighting back tears, Jaden kept a tight grip on the roasting pan and took a moment to regain her composure. A cold draft blasted her from behind as the door opened and the men entered the kitchen. Ivan carried his turkey and placed it on the counter beside the stove.

He turned to her with a proud look on his face, which immediately crumbled into concern. As he pulled her into the living room, Jaden realized he had mistaken the joy on her face for distress. "Baby girl, what's wrong?" he asked. He raised his hand to her cheek.

"Nothing wrong, it's just that…" Jaden fought back a sniffle. "Elise called me her sister."

"And that makes you sad?"

"No, of course not."

"Then why are you crying?" Ivan asked, holding her close.

"I don't know," Jaden admitted and buried her head in his chest. "Your family is amazing, and it sucks that we have to leave so soon."

Placing a finger under Jaden's chin, he lifted her head. "Listen, you have all the time in the world to get to know them. We can come back as often as you want. Heck, Christmas is only a month away. That's the best time to be here."

Using the sleeve of her sweater, Jaden wiped her eyes. "You must think I'm stupid."

"You are not stupid——" Ivan began, but was cut short by his mother's voice.

"Dinner's done," Marie called.

Ivan shook his head. "Care to carve with me, baby girl?" he asked, leading Jaden back to the kitchen counter.

"In front of everyone, baby? That's brassy!" She grabbed a knife, and they began to cut chunks of succulent flesh from the bones, arranging them neatly on two trays.

With the birds carved and the table overflowing with food, dinner was ready. John and Marie sat at their respective places at the ends of the table. Elise and PJ sat to their father's left, and Ivan and Jaden to his right. "Just like old times," Ivan said. "We've been sitting like this since I was a kid."

Marie poured each of them a glass of wine and looked around the table, her eyes coming to rest on Jaden. "It seems that this year we have even more to be thankful for. Who would like to say grace?"

"I would," Jaden replied, her voice cracking. Ivan's hand squeezed her leg beneath the table, and she was sure he was grinning ear to ear, but she was too nervous to look up.

"That'd be lovely, dear."

Closing her eyes, Jaden crossed herself from forehead to chest and from shoulder to shoulder. "In the name of the Father, and of the Son, and of the Holy Spirit. Bless us, oh Father, for these thy gifts which we are about to receive from thy bounty, through Christ, our Lord. Amen."

"Amen," everyone replied, their glasses clinking in cheer as the holiday feast began.

Jaden eyed the big bowl of mashed potatoes Marie handed her, trying to calculate how many miles she'd have to run to burn off that many carbs. She'd spent the past three weeks exercising like crazy and didn't want to throw it all away in one meal, but they looked *so damn good!* After a moment of hesitation, she threw caution to the wind. It was Thanksgiving, a time for indulgence.

Everyone took turns passing dishes around the table, Elise occasionally going right instead of left, resulting in heckling from the hungry crowd. But finally every plate overflowed with turkey, cranberries, stuffing, and corn, all mixed together and swimming in a pool of homemade gravy. Laughter filled the air, along with jokes, stories, and the delicious smells of a traditional Thanksgiving meal.

Eventually plates began to empty and glasses ran dry as everyone had their fill. A collective groan rose contentedly when Marie reminded them to save room for dessert.

Elise and PJ began to clear away the dishes, and Marie reappeared with a freshly cooled apple pie in one hand and a pumpkin pie in the other. Digging in the fridge, Elise gathered the vanilla ice cream and a can of whipped cream and brought them to the table. All this was topped off with coffee, heavily laced with sweet liqueurs and cream. Jaden couldn't even begin to count the calories, but today there were no diets. She felt a bit giddy — about pie, for God's sake, but she and Ivan hardly ever ate dessert in Miami. Digging in, they indulged in the extravagance before them, eating enough to satisfy her sweet tooth for the next year.

"Have you showed Jaden the trophy room yet?" Marie asked, breaking Jaden's focus from the last bit of delicate crust before her.

"No," Ivan quickly replied, seeming embarrassed. "I don't know why you guys hang on to all that stuff."

"Don't be modest, son," John added. "I'm sure Jaden would love to see it."

"Yes, I'm sure she'd love to see it," Jaden replied, shooting Ivan a crooked smile.

"Here, take your coffees and go. We'll tidy up here," Marie said, handing them two more cups in exchange for their now empty dessert plates.

"Thanks, Mom," Ivan said as he stood and motioned for Jaden to join him.

Elise and PJ belted out catcalls as Ivan led her from the kitchen. She caught him shooting them his middle finger as they rounded the corner out of sight.

CHAPTER 26

"Midnight Rider"

"Is this really necessary?" Ivan asked as they went downstairs to where Jaden now knew the animal museum was located.

"Oh, come on, don't be a spoil sport. Are you embarrassed?" She poked him on the shoulder as they descended the last few steps. "Well, would you look at that? The great Dr. Ivan is humble."

"All right, you made your point," he shot back and threw his arms up in defeat. "Well, here it is."

He opened a door, and Jaden immediately began walking the circumference of the room. Instead of mounted hunting prizes, these trophies and certificates were John and Marie's children's achievements. PA Hockey Player of the Month was etched on several of the plaques, some containing Ivan's name and others PJ's. A three-foot trophy topped with a miniature muscle man and the words "Iron City Bodybuilding Champion" stood off to one side. Numerous hockey trophies sat on shelves, and state championship medals hung from nails on the wall. All of this was very impressive, but what caught her attention was a scrapbook labeled *Mr. USA 2008/2010.*

She grabbed the book from the shelf. Ivan tried to snatch it away, but she pulled it out of his grasp. Inside she found articles and interviews from international newspapers and magazines. Other pages displayed pictures of Ivan posing with beautiful women, skydiving, flying planes, racing cars, and feeding kangaroos. Sighing anxiously, he tried to grab the book again, but once more Jaden pulled it away. As she reached the back, she discovered why he was so concerned. The last few pages were covered in pictures of Ivan and Irena, as well as a few of the articles that had been written about them.

Jaden realized that if she'd found this book a few months ago, when they first started dating, she would've been jealous and intimidated by what she saw. But now, in Ivan's home and with his family, she felt secure. Regardless of what had happened in his past, *she* was his future. Placing the book back on the shelf, Jaden sat on a sofa and motioned for Ivan to sit down as well.

The sofa sank beneath his weight as he took his place beside her. "So, what do you think?" he asked, looking at his hands.

Jaden took a long sip of her coffee. "Why did you and Irena break up? She's beautiful, she seems to be cultured, and she must have been a nice person because I've never heard you speak a bad word against her. What happened?"

"Do you want the long or the short version?" Ivan laughed and set his coffee down on the table. "In all truth, time and distance are the two factors that will make or break a relationship. Too much or too little of either results in disaster. She was a fantastic girl, and we tried so hard to maintain a long-distance relationship. We did for a while," he added, his eyes far away. "I did everything imaginable to make things work, but in the end, we both realized we were clipping each other's wings. I couldn't live with myself knowing she gave up on a dream, and she felt the same way." Ivan sighed. "The sad thing is, the harder we tried, the more it wore on us, and we eventually ended with a less-than-friendly parting of ways."

"How so?" Jaden inquired.

"Well, let's just say I caught her with her hand in the cookie jar," he said with a wry smile. "I was heartbroken—not because I'd lost a lover, but because I lost a friend. It was then that I swore I'd never again attempt a long-distance relationship. They're doomed from the start. I promised myself I'd never lose a friend that way again. I'd rather sacrifice a relationship to keep a friendship."

Jaden lifted his arm and placed it around her shoulder. Resting her head against his chest, she let the sound of his beating heart soothe her. She felt a peace with his answer, but she wasn't certain he felt the same way. Taking his hand in hers, she squeezed it reassuringly.

"Ivan, we've both had our fair share of dents and burns. Some are just worse than others. I've come to realize that no matter how past relationships have ended, they always leave a mark on your heart. We'll always carry around a piece of that person with us, because part of them is what helped mold us into the people we are today. Whether it was a lesson learned or a lesson taught, there's a reason they were in our lives, and we should be thankful for what they gave us." Jaden smiled as she tilted her head and brought her lips to meet his. In her heart, she kissed Ivan not as her boyfriend, but as her lover, her partner, and her soul mate. "Thank you for telling me that. It means a lot."

"How did I get so lucky?" he asked and silenced her with another kiss, this one more heated and full of need.

Jaden broke the kiss and sat back on the sofa. Still reeling with passion, she now looked at the mounted animals that hung from the walls with all the accolades. She felt a little creeped out as dozens of glassy eyes stared back at her. "I can't help but shake the feeling we're being watched," she said with a smile.

"You too?" Ivan asked. "We have to get going anyway. I have a surprise for you tonight, so go upstairs and pack your bags."

"Yes, doctor." Jaden always liked the response that elicited. As soon as she stood, she felt the stinging pleasure and pain of Ivan's hand as it came down across her ass.

"You're in for it tonight, mister," she yelled over her shoulder as she took the stairs two at a time.

"Promise?" Ivan caught up with her, cupping her ass and urging her to go faster.

Throwing her stuff into her bag, Jaden double and triple checked to make sure she wasn't forgetting anything. With her bag slung over her shoulder, she turned off the light and closed the door to the guest room, hoping it wouldn't be too long until she returned. When she rounded the corner, Ivan stood at the entrance to the kitchen with his family close by, waiting to say their goodbyes.

"You guys better get moving if you want to make it by dark," Marie said.

Jaden followed her gaze out the kitchen window to the darkening sky beyond and the faintly glowing, opalescent snow.

"Come here, dear." Marie gave Jaden one last hug and bid her adieu.

Each member of Ivan's family wished her well, hugged and kissed her, and reminded her she was always welcome back. At the end of the line stood Elise, arms wide open. "I'm gonna miss you, girl. I wish we had more time."

"I'm gonna miss you too," Jaden said and launched herself into Elise's hug. "I'll be back soon though."

"Promise?" Elise asked.

"I promise." Jaden smiled, afraid of the tears if she said anything else. She turned to find Ivan close behind her, saying his farewells. He seemed to be having a hard time saying goodbye too.

"Make sure you come back," John bellowed as they walked out the front door. "And I'm talking to Jaden, of course."

"Ha, ha… Very funny, old man," Ivan replied as he shut the door behind them and led Jaden to the waiting car. He opened her door and helped her into the car before loading their luggage into the back.

Just as the Jeep roared to life, the front door of the house opened and Marie poked her head out. "Leave the car at the airport," she yelled. "I'll pick it up when I drop your sister off tomorrow."

Shooting his mom a thumbs-up and blowing her a kiss, Ivan revved the engine and put the Jeep in reverse.

"What an amazing time," Jaden said, taking one last look at the family as they all waved from the window.

"The night's still young, baby girl."

Jaden had no clue where they were going, but she was happy to be topping off the perfect weekend with what was sure to be an unforgettable night. Sitting back in the plush leather seat, she listened to the Counting Crows sing about oysters with no pearls and long Decembers. But Jaden *had* found a pearl, and December was shaping up to be one of the best months ever.

Ivan stroked the back of her hand, speaking volumes without uttering a single word. Not far into the trip, he turned down a small dirt road. Lush evergreens and bare maple trees lined the sides of a snowy and slushy road. As they progressed further into the forest, the trees grew denser, and the dirt road seemed worse for the wear.

Jaden sat up in the seat, paying more attention to her surroundings. They pulled up to a gate that blocked the way to a snowy, tree-filled corridor. Ivan hopped out and unlocked it, pulling it aside and granting them entry to the smaller road that lay just beyond.

"I'm not even going to ask," she said when he returned to the car, shivering from the cold.

Farther down the snow-strewn path, Jaden said goodbye to civilization and hello once again to the backwoods of northwestern Pennsylvania. Off in the distance she could see a small wooden cabin nestled in a clump of barren trees, complete with a stack of freshly cut firewood neatly arranged on the porch. She realized this was what Ivan meant when he said they'd have their own place.

"Oh, my God, this is beautiful."

"It's no Ritz, but it'll serve as our home away from home for the night." Ivan turned off the car and opened the door into a blast of frigid air.

"I love it," Jaden mused as she slid out of the car.

"Don't speak too soon," he warned. "There's no electricity or running water. I hope you don't mind roughing it for the night."

"Even better," she assured him, turning to face him in the fading light. She felt certain he could keep her warm.

"You never cease to amaze me, baby girl." Ivan walked to the back of the Jeep and retrieved not only their luggage, but a few other items someone had placed there prior to their departure.

With the luggage in one hand and a flashlight in the other, Ivan helped Jaden pick her way up the icy path that led to the cabin. Placing the bags on the ground, he unlocked the front door, and before she could protest, he swept her into his arms. She blushed and buried her face in his chest.

"A palace for my princess," Ivan whispered as he kicked open the door and carried Jaden over the threshold.

CHAPTER 27

"Love Of My Life"

The cabin was black inside, completely devoid of light. Setting Jaden back on her feet, Ivan fumbled around in search of a lantern. He knew it usually sat on the dresser, so he felt his way across the room until his hands found the cold metal casing. He pulled a small plastic lighter from his pocket, first using it to *see* the lantern, and then using it to light the wick and illuminate the cabin where he'd spent so many summers with his aunt.

For reasons unbeknownst to him, Ivan felt nervous, like a teenage boy about to kiss his girlfriend for the first time. There was something different about tonight, something he couldn't quite put his finger on. When he spoke, his words came out jumbled together. "Do you want me to light a fire?"

"I was promised one, so now you'd better deliver, doc," Jaden demanded, her voice confident as she sat down on the bed, letting her legs fall open in such a way that he instantly grew hard.

He went right to work at building a fire, both to impress his girl and to banish the numbness that had taken over his extremities—well, except for one of them. But Ivan had a feeling he and Jaden would be generating heat of their own soon enough. Kicking open the door to the woodstove, he made quick work of arranging the dry logs his dad had already stacked in a dummy-proof way. A small flame was all that was needed to ignite the bundle of kindling beneath the wood, and within minutes a fire roared to life, bringing light and warmth to the cabin and its occupants.

Braving the cold once more, Ivan went back outside and returned a minute later with their bags. He set them down on the floor beside the bed, drawn in by Jaden's capricious smile, which again caused his cock to rise to full attention.

Jaden shifted, and the bed creaked as she leaned back and rested on her elbows. Ivan watched as her eyes roved over the cabin. "So, are we breaking and entering?" she asked with a naughty look.

Laughing, Ivan filled her in. "This place belongs to my aunt. She moved to the city when the winters got too hard for her to handle, but I spent a lot of time with her here when I was a kid, chasing fireflies, hunting for insects, and learning to draw." Ivan pointed to one of the drawings on the wall: a man holding an umbrella and being blown away, rendered in black and white. "We used to pick a song and draw pictures that represented it. This one here is 'Dust in the Wind,' as imagined by an eight-year-old."

Jaden smiled and shook her head. "You're truly a man of many talents! And I think it's finally warm in here." As she stripped away her outer layers, Ivan began removing some of his clothing as well.

"I love it. It's so cozy," she said. "But no running water?"

"Don't worry about that. The toilet flushes. We just have to use bottled water." Pulling back a cloth on the counter, Ivan revealed the several now-frozen gallons of water his mom had dropped off earlier in the day. He moved the containers over next to the fire to thaw. "Mom is a doll."

"Baby, I feel like I'm in a romance novel or something," Jaden said. "Now all we need is for you to fight off a pack of wolves and make love to me all night." She began to remove some not-so-outer layers of her clothing.

"Well, I can't promise the wolves…" Ivan said seductively. Then in an instant, he pounced. Tackling her back into the bed, he rubbed his hardness along her naked thigh. "But maybe we can make that romance novel an erotic one, eh?"

Just as Jaden began to respond, Ivan sprang from the bed and gathered a large box from the counter. He pulled out a plastic container, two wine glasses, and two bottles of strawberry-rhubarb special from Van's house.

"It wouldn't be a romance novel, and I wouldn't be a gentleman, if I didn't at least wine and dine you first." Ivan uncorked one of the bottles and poured two glasses.

"What else is in the box?" Jaden asked, sitting up on the bed and cloaking herself in the sheet.

"Patience, baby girl. First you have to close your eyes and open your mouth." Ivan couldn't stop the laugh that escaped him as Jaden's gaze drifted between his legs. "Don't let your mind wander *there* just yet. I have something else for you."

Obediently, and seemingly without any hesitation, Jaden closed her eyes and opened her mouth. Ivan carefully placed a treat on her tongue. Eyes still closed, her eyebrows furrowed for a moment as she sought to solve the mystery. Then she smiled and bit down. "Mmm…chocolate-covered strawberries. To hell with wolves, this is so much better!"

Ivan sat down, popping a strawberry in his own mouth, and Jaden crawled over to straddle his legs, her eyes never leaving his as they locked in a sexy stare down. She reached for the button on his pants, but he stopped her.

Grasping her shoulders, Ivan flipped Jaden on to her back, and using the weight of his body, he pinned her to the mattress. He marveled as the fire's glow danced across her chest, her nipples hard and erect.

"That's not fair," Jaden teased, tugging at the waistband of his jeans. "You're still dressed, and I'm almost naked."

"Almost, but not quite," Ivan croaked. He hooked a finger around the edge of her panties and pulled them down, adding them to the pile of clothes on the floor. "*Now* you're naked."

Jaden rested her head against the down pillows and closed her eyes.

Ivan's fingers hugged the soft contours of her body as they greedily explored every inch. He already knew every freckle, every mole, and every scar that marked her porcelain skin, but he'd never grow tired of the way she felt beneath his hands. Moving to lay beside her on the bed, his smile widened when Jaden sighed her approval. With unhurried movements, he continued to trail his fingers across her skin and up the inside of her leg, stopping when he reached her smooth pussy. Her breast felt warm against his lips as he pressed them to her skin, and he whispered softly as he drew her into his mouth. "Let me in."

Jaden uttered a low moan and whispered, "What's the magic word?"

But he could tell her mind was already made up when she spread her legs a little farther without waiting for his response. Her soft folds felt like satin to the touch, warm, slick, and smooth. His fingers teased over her until he found what he was looking for and slid a finger deep within. Jaden moaned and arched into him, and Ivan grew impossibly harder. Sliding another finger in, Ivan stroked Jaden as if he were playing a guitar, but the music she made was much sweeter.

"Do you have any idea how beautiful you are?" Ivan murmured as his fingers continued to caress her, readying her body to take him. Just feet away the fire roared, casting flickering light on her skin and streaking her ebony hair with hues of gold. Never in his life had Ivan witnessed such a breathtaking sight. Jaden's body quivered as his fingers found the sweet spot buried deep within, each of his movements bringing her closer to climax.

"Oh, God," Jaden cried, her body moving in sync to the strumming of his hand. He brushed his thumb lightly against her clit with each thrust.

"Ivan, please…" she begged. "Make me come."

"Is this what you want, baby girl?" he asked. Circling her swollen bud with his thumb, Ivan stroked deeper into Jaden's body, and he could feel her muscles grip his fingers as she inched closer to release. "Yes," she breathed as he took her taut breast into his mouth, rolling her rigid nipple between his teeth.

And then he felt her release. Jaden cried out and spasmed as her body drenched Ivan's hand.

Ivan slowed his movements as he eased Jaden down from her high. When the trembling subsided and her breathing returned to normal, she finally opened her eyes. The color of pristine emeralds shone brightly in the glow of the roaring fire, and Ivan felt his heart stop for a moment. This goddess who had stolen his heart was a vision to behold. He could look at her for the rest of his life.

Ivan brushed the arc of her cheekbone as he kissed her mouth. Jaden parted her lips, welcoming him. Her tongue felt warm against his, and she tasted of strawberries and wine. There was nothing rushed or rough to this kiss; it was tender and soft. It was the delicate kiss of two souls.

But the moment of tenderness passed quickly, as Jaden sprang into action and worked to rid him of his pants. She lowered the zipper, and Ivan pulled his jeans down and over his ankles before ripping off his shirt, leaving him naked as the day he was born.

Jaden climbed on top of him and hovered just inches above his dick while working a condom down his length. Then with a naughty smirk, she thrust herself over him. The feel of her velvety softness enveloping him drove all rational thought from his mind. With slow, deliberate strokes, he thrust into her again and again as she rode his cock hard and long. Jaden worked him as if he was a sex toy. Switching her movements between erotic bounces and harsh grinds, she gave herself to him, whipping her hair back and forth.

Ivan rolled her onto her back and brought both her legs to rest on his shoulders, allowing for maximum penetration. Jaden's eyes widened, never leaving his as their bodies worked in unison. She bucked her hips, urging him faster, but instead Ivan slowed his pace. Once more she tried to urge him on, and again he refused.

Smiling down at her, Ivan whispered through gasps of air. "Trust me, it'll be well worth the wait."

The tension began to mount as their bodies struggled for release through a haze of pleasure. Finally his pace quickened, and he drove deeper and harder into the very core of her body, each thrust bringing them closer to a monumental, earth-shattering climax.

Jaden clutched his wrists, and he could feel her nails digging into his skin as she struggled for a grip. He was sure he'd see the marks of her efforts later. A cold breeze passed across his bare skin, a sharp contrast to the blaring heat of the fire, and Ivan shivered. Their bodies moved in sync as he relentlessly propelled himself forward, and in a moment where time stood still, they cried out their ecstasy in unison, screaming as their bodies exploded in pure, unadulterated bliss.

What seemed like an eternity later, Ivan rolled on to his side and faced Jaden. The emotions that had been building inside him for the past few months had finally crested, and it was time he bared his soul to this woman who'd claimed not only his heart but his entire being. No longer able to hold back the feeling that had been planted the moment she walked into his life, nurtured through every second they'd spent together, strengthened through challenge, and bloomed in the presence of his family, Ivan spoke.

"Jaden," he whispered, trailing a finger across the glistening skin of her stomach and coming to rest at the apex of her nipple. He continued to trace a circular pattern around her breast, but his mind was elsewhere. The look of pure contentment on Jaden's face was enough to give him the strength to continue. "Love is a word that gets tossed around way too much."

Jaden immediately propped herself up on her elbow and began to speak. "Ivan, I—"

"Wait, let me finish," he interrupted, silencing her by gently pressing the tip of his finger to her lips. "I think love is a bullshit word. How can four letters strung together represent what happens when two beings who were destined to be together find each other and take their places alongside one another? That, in my mind, isn't love. It's a miracle."

Ivan looked into Jaden's eyes, and she stared back at him with such love and adoration that he could scarcely continue. "Jaden, with you, I think I've finally found my miracle, my once in a lifetime. I love you more with each breath you take and with every smile that graces your face. I know I'm in love with you, because you make every day I'm with you the best day of my life."

"Ivan…" Jaden began again. She trailed off, seeming to search for words. "I've wasted so many years and heartbeats and tears on what I believed to be true love," she finally said. "Since I met you, my life has gone from mundane to extraordinary, but…"

She fell silent again, and Ivan could feel his heart beating a million miles an hour. After everything that had happened between them, was she really going to reject him?

"Jaden, I never meant—"

"Shh," she breathed. She pressed her lips to his and silenced him with a kiss. "Let me talk now, baby."

A mixture of emotions engulfed him all at once—fear, panic, affection, and adoration, all mingling to form the greatest of feelings, love.

"Never in my life have I met anyone like you," she said. "You've given me more joy in the past few months than most people know in a lifetime. I don't know what I did to deserve you, but here you are, offering me what I've been searching for my entire life. The words 'I love you' don't even come close to what I feel for you, Ivan. I could say I love you a million times over, and it still wouldn't be enough. I do love you, Ivan. I love you more than life itself. I will always love you, and I will *never, ever* let you go. That I promise."

They lay together on the bed and listened as outside the cabin a symphony unfolded. Trees cracking in the cold provided a natural beat as the wind strummed the branches. A solitary bird chirped somewhere in the distance. At this exact moment, around a small cabin in the woods of western Pennsylvania, a masterpiece was created just for them, a masterpiece that could only be crafted by the hands of a divine being, capable of sweet perfection.

Kissing Jaden as if it were the first time, Ivan joined her in celebrating their love again and again until the fire dwindled. Then, and only then, did they close their eyes and drift into a peaceful sleep.

Chapter 28

"Change The World"

Only partially covered by the blanket, Jaden awoke to a breeze chilling her exposed skin. There wasn't much left of the fire, but as she stretched in the morning light she could feel the warmth radiating from Ivan, still sleeping beside her. She pulled back the covers and tried to stand, but his arm wrapped around her waist and pulled her closer.

"Good morning, baby girl," he moaned, still groggy with sleep.

Jaden sighed contentedly and relaxed into him. "Morning, baby."

Today felt different from the other times she'd awakened in Ivan's arms. Yesterday she'd been his girlfriend, but today, in the comfort of his warm embrace, she was his lover, his soul mate. She shivered and pulled the blankets back up around her neck.

Ivan held her tighter and raised up to place a gentle kiss to her lips. "Are you cold?"

"A little," Jaden admitted, returning his kiss with twice the passion.

Wordlessly, Ivan got up, grabbed the extra blanket at the foot of the bed, and wrapped it securely around his body. He placed two more logs on the grate and a handful of kindling on the still-smoldering embers. Within seconds the tinder caught fire and warmth began to fill the cabin. In two long strides, he returned to the bed.

Jaden admired his naked form as his blanket dropped to the floor. She'd gotten used to seeing him fully aroused first thing in the morning, but the sight of him still brought a smile to her face. Her mind flooded with memories of the night before—the love they'd shared until both were too spent to move. As Ivan climbed back in bed, Jaden grasped his cock and began stroking with long, leisurely movements, eliciting a guttural moan that stemmed from somewhere deep within his body.

"Baby girl, we have to get ready soon," he protested, but his actions spoke louder than words. With each stroke of her hand, his hips thrust forward to welcome the warmth and pleasure her touch brought him. Sinking farther beneath the covers, they once more loved one another.

As they lay naked and satisfied in each other's arms, Ivan looked down the length of the bed and asked, "Why do you always sleep with your feet out of the covers?"

"I don't know," Jaden replied, wiggling her toes. "Why do you always cross your right leg over your left, but never the other way around?"

Ivan laughed. "I can't."

"What do you mean, you can't?"

"It's a weird idiosyncrasy of mine. Just feels wrong the other way." Ivan pulled back the blankets and sat up on the side of the bed, but Jaden's hand stopped him from going any further.

"Where are you going?" she asked, trying to hide her growing sadness. This magical trip was coming to an end far too soon.

"We have to get ready to go. The fun and the sun await our return," he said, smiling half-heartedly.

Jaden pulled Ivan back into bed and into her arms. "I have a better idea. Why don't we stay here? We can be cabin folk. You can hunt, and I can cook."

"I wouldn't mind that," Ivan replied. "But unfortunately, real life beckons. What will Bianca do without you?"

Jaden could see goose bumps rise on his backside as Ivan began to gather their clothes from the heap on the floor. "Aren't you cold?"

"I'm freezing." Ivan slid into his jeans and pulled a shirt over his head before bringing Jaden her clothes. "Jaden, I want you to know I meant every word I said. I love you more than anything."

"I love you too," she whispered softly. "I'll love you until the end of time." She smiled broadly, suddenly full of warmth. They loved each other, and this was only the beginning of the future they were destined to share together.

"We'd better hit it," Ivan said, ever practical and probably determined not to run through the airport this time. "We slept in a bit late."

"Umm…I wouldn't call that sleeping." Wiggling into her wrinkled clothes, she joined him as he brushed his teeth with bottled water at the sink. "This is like camping," she laughed. "I'm going to miss this place."

"Really? No running water or electricity?" Ivan draped his arm over her shoulder and pulled her to his side.

"I'm going to miss all of it." She raised her arms and motioned to everything at once. "The cabin, your family—heck, I'm even gonna miss shooting guns."

"I told you, baby girl, we can come back whenever you want," Ivan assured her. Picking up their bags, he headed out to the Jeep.

Jaden stepped through the door and into the cold mid-morning air. Joining him at the car, she slid into the front seat and watched as he locked up the cabin. This small cabin in the middle of nowhere would forever be part of her now. Smiling, Jaden wiped a stray tear from her cheek. The Jeep roared to life and began its return trip down the long dirt road and back to civilization, but Jaden kept her eyes fixed on the cabin, the place where they'd committed their hearts to one another, until it faded from view in the trees.

As they slowly transitioned from woods to rural to urban on the way to the airport, Jaden stole glances at Ivan and caught him peeking back at her several times. There was something different about the way he looked at her now, the way he held her hand, and the way his smile lit up his face—but it was a good different. Occasionally they spoke of their plans for the month or something funny that had happened with his family, but it all seemed trivial. They were in love. They could say nothing and say everything all at once.

The airport swarmed with holiday travelers, making it nearly impossible to navigate the overcrowded parking garage. After finally securing a spot, they unloaded the Jeep and headed for the check-in counter, hand in hand. After the lengthy line through security, they found two seats together at their gate and a few moments to sit and relax as they waited for the boarding call.

"All in all a pretty great trip, eh?" Ivan asked.

Lowering her magazine, Jaden looked at him and smiled. "The best three days of my life."

"You made my mom's day when you accepted these," he told her.

He brushed aside her hair, and she could feel him touching the black earring that dangled from her ear. Jaden twisted the bracelet on her wrist, remembering what Marie had said about Ivan's days crafting jewelry. "Did you make them?"

He shook his head. "I haven't made jewelry in years. I specialized in my mom's favorite, rosaries, but it's been forever since I made one." He captured Jaden's wrist in his hand, noticing the other piece she'd received. "It all looks beautiful on you."

Jaden smiled. He'd made the rosary! It was safely tucked away in her luggage. Maybe she'd reveal its presence later on, but for now it was her little secret. Hugging his arm, she nestled into his shoulder, exhausted from the whirlwind trip but perfectly content with life and head over heels in love with the man of her dreams.

"We would now like to offer boarding for our first class passengers," the gatekeeper screeched.

Ivan stood and took Jaden's hand, leading her toward the jet bridge. "I didn't even check my email," he announced proudly. "My inbox is probably loaded."

"Mine too," Jaden laughed, realizing her messages had gone un-checked as well. After three days off the grid, who knew what she'd missed.

Chapter 29

"9 Crimes"

Jaden stifled a yawn as she stretched, waking refreshed and reenergized in the comfort of her own bed but missing the feel of Ivan next to her. Slinking out from her beneath the comforter, she went to the kitchen in search of something to eat—not at all sure what she'd find. Jaden opened the fridge and was pleasantly surprised to discover leftovers brought back from Tasha's Thanksgiving dinner with Michael and his family.

She hurried to fix herself a turkey sandwich, then looked for a spot to eat it. She moved into the living room and her eyes fell on the computer. *Oh, God, my email,* she thought with dread. But there was no time like the present—she was working tonight. Jaden sat, took a hefty bite of her sandwich, and waited for the computer to power on. A few clicks later she'd signed in to her email account.

"Thirty-eight new messages," she mumbled around the turkey. "Not too bad."

Quickly sorting through them, she deleted half as spam, but one message caught her attention. It was from Jessie—casting Jessie—and the subject line read: *meeting ASAP?* Jaden's head began to spin as she opened the message:

> Jaden, please call me as soon as possible. We need to talk
> right away. I'll come and meet you wherever and whenever.

What the hell was this all about? *She'll come to me?* Rather than overanalyze, Jaden picked up the phone. She tried to dial the number Jessie had given her, but her fingers were very uncooperative and refused to stop shaking. Jaden took a deep breath and tried to gather her thoughts. Looking down at the number pad on the phone, she slowly dialed and raised the receiver to her ear.

"Jaden!" A familiar, high-pitched voice rang through the phone. "How are you doing?"

"I'm good, and you?" Jaden responded uncertainly.

"I'm doing fantastic!" Skipping additional pleasantries, Jessie jumped right in. "Are you free for lunch today?"

"Yes, I am, but…" Jaden stuttered.

"Great, meet me at Segafredo's in an hour. I'll fill you in on all the details then."

"Okay, but is there something going on I should know about?" Jaden needed more information. *Now.*

"I have to run, but I'll explain everything when we meet."

"Okay, I—" Jaden began, but her words were abruptly cut off as Jessie hung up the phone. Her mind reeled with excitement and uncertainty. *It's just a small part*, she reminded herself. But it could also be the break she needed—the part that would boost her career beyond Miami.

Her mind immediately jumped to Ivan. She started to dial but then remembered she hadn't told him about the audition. Might be a bit awkward to bring it up now, so Jaden decided she'd talk to Jessie first. After all, she *was* the Queen of Unrealistic Expectations, and this lunch meeting could easily be nothing.

Jaden hurried into her room and threw together an outfit. Who knew a black skirt would work so well with a red tank top, but it did. Grabbing her phone and keys, she set off for Segafredo's—and whatever lay ahead.

When she arrived at the restaurant Jaden was surprised to find Jessie already seated at a table outside, looking as anxious as Jaden felt. "Hi, Jessie," she said politely.

The woman jumped out of her seat and returned the greeting as if they were lifelong friends. "Jaden, you look stunning as usual. Have a seat. Are you hungry?"

"I'm fine, thanks." Never mind that she'd left most of her turkey sandwich still sitting in front of the computer. She sat and the waitress handed them each a menu, but Jaden set hers aside. Ordering food would only prolong the buildup to what Jessie had to tell her. Instead she gathered her courage and asked, "So, what's up?"

"Congratulations, you got the part," Jessie said with a broad smile. "You're the new Culinary Queen of Bravo." She completed her announcement with a screech, as if *she'd* just been offered the part.

"Wait…what?" Jaden asked, still not quite sure what was going on.

"You got the part. They're giving you your own show and want you in LA to start shooting in two weeks. They're planning to feature your stunning good looks, personality, *and* culinary skills. They want to promote you as the whole package! How amazing is that? Zero to sixty all at once. LA and celebrity chef stardom, here you come!"

"I'm not sure I understand," Jaden said, still not giving in to the excitement. "What do you mean they're giving me my own show? I thought this was a one-shot deal—I was going to be a competitor."

"Yes, that's the part that you auditioned for, but the executives at the network were also looking for someone for a new show airing this fall. As soon as I saw your profile, I knew you'd be perfect."

Not knowing whether to cry, scream, or faint, Jaden settled for a hearty laugh. "Oh, my God. I'm going to Hollywood?"

"Yes," Jessie shrieked, drawing the attention of more than a few diners around them. "Here's all the information you need and the contracts." Jessie passed Jaden a large manila envelope. "I suggest you have someone look them over before signing, but I think you'll find that everything's in order. All I can say is you must've made quite an impression. I've never had a director contact me and ask to get a particular person to casting before."

The brown manila envelope was heavy in Jaden's hands. Setting it on the table, she turned her attention back to Jessie. "I don't understand."

"You need to sign the papers so I can have a courier take them back to LA. We're on a tight—"

Jaden cut her off midsentence. "No, I understand that part. What do you mean by contact you directly? Who did?"

"The director of the network did, and he asked that I contact you about the casting. You're one lucky girl to have friends in high places."

Jaden wracked her brain. Who the hell did she know who could have facilitated a casting call from Bravo? Maybe it was the food critic? Or maybe someone had stumbled across Dirk D's blog. Whoever it was, she owed them a huge debt of gratitude. But Jaden's wonder was short lived as the reality of the situation began to sink in. "So I have to move to LA?"

"Yes, they'll help you find a place and cover whatever moving costs you incur."

"God, this is so much, so fast…"

Jessie reached across the table and gave her hand a squeeze. "Jaden, I hope you realize how big this is. People wait half their lives for a chance like this, and most never get it. You must have an angel watching out for you, because this is the opportunity of a lifetime."

"I know. I'm just a bit stunned but really excited," Jaden assured her.

"Good. I'm glad, and I'm glad that I could tell you in person."

What about Bianca? What about Tasha? Jaden thought. *And what about…Ivan?* A looming dark cloud threatened to rain on her parade. Leaving Miami would mean leaving Ivan — he'd made that perfectly clear — and she didn't know if that was something she was prepared to do. How could she possibly break the news to her best friend and the man she loved when she hadn't even told them she'd auditioned for the part? They were the cornerstones of her life, and they were about to crumble.

Geoff would be the easiest to tell. Her boss would be happy for her and grateful for her time at the restaurant. He'd be able to claim a celebrity chef made her debut at Bianca. No doubt his business would *increase* after she left. And after the initial shock, Tasha would be happy for her. She knew of Jaden's star-studded dreams. Plus, she'd now have a place to stay in LA. The thought almost made Jaden laugh out loud.

What about Ivan, the man who not two days ago had professed his love for her, and she for him? Would he embrace her decision? Would he fear it? Would this be the end of everything they'd built together? A thousand scenarios raced through her mind, but every one led back to their Thanksgiving trophy room conversation. Never again would he risk a friendship for a long-distance relationship, he'd told her. A sickening feeling swelled in the pit of her stomach.

Why on the day that one dream came true did another have to be snatched away?

Jaden thanked Jessie once again and retrieved the large manila envelope, tucking it safely under her arm as they shook hands and said their goodbyes. Arriving back home, she paid the cab fare and shuffled up to the apartment, each footstep feeling like she'd walked a hundred miles. As she opened the door, Jaden found Tasha sitting in front of the computer.

"Hey, girl," Tasha's happy voice rang through the condo. "How was Pennsylvania? I want to know everything. Is Ivan as burly as I think he is? Did you guys get it on in the woods? How was his family? Did you like his sister? Is his brother cute?"

"It was," Jaden said, "the best three days of my life."

"Then why the hell do you have that look on your face? Why are you just standing there? You're acting all weird — and why was there a half-eaten turkey sandwich sitting in front of the computer when I got up? I know how much you hate wasting —"

"Tasha," Jaden said, interrupting the barrage of questions. "If you had to choose between a lifelong dream and a surprise miracle, what would you do?"

Tasha opened her mouth, then closed it. She studied Jaden for a moment and said, "Well, a lifelong dream is something you've worked and worked for, hoping to achieve. A miracle is a random coincidence that works in your favor. If I had to choose between the two, I'd pick the dream, because a dream can only come true once. Miracles happen every day."

Jaden sat on the sofa and clenched her fists, trying to hide the trembling that was slowly taking control of her body. "Tasha, they just selected me to become the chef on a new show on Bravo, and they want to me to move to LA. I have to be there in two weeks to start filming," she said. "This is what I've always wanted — it's my dream come true."

"Oh, my God! Jaden! That's — wait, so why are you so sad? Hell, I'd be doing back flips. We should celebrate!"

"Because I don't think Ivan will be coming along for the ride," Jaden said, shaking her head.

"Oh? Why do you think that?" Tasha asked, her voice full of compassion. "I'm sure the two of you will figure something out."

"I don't know…I just don't know." Jaden sighed and sniffed, wiping a tear from her eye. "While we were in Pennsylvania we talked about his past relationships and why they didn't work out. Ivan said he'd never risk a friendship for a long-distance relationship ever again—and I can't blame him. Up until now I felt the same way. What's worse is that I can't even ask him to consider it—or consider making a move when he's worked so hard to build a life for himself in Miami. He's got the new stuff debuting at the spa, all his patients are here, and he knows everyone in town from politicians to socialites to business owners. I can't ask him to leave that for *my* dream. Ivan has his own dreams to follow."

Tasha joined Jaden on the couch and smothered her in a hug. "Jaden, it is what it is. You and I both know that things happen for a reason. If the two of you are meant to be, you'll find a way to stay together, but you have to let fate sort it out. I'm sure Ivan will be so happy for you, and he'll want to see your dreams come true. I know he'll want you to embrace this, not pass it up because of him."

Jaden burst into tears and was relieved when Tasha just sat with her for a while. They rocked gently together on the couch. "I know you're right," Jaden finally managed after her tears had subsided. She did feel some measure of comfort in Tasha's words, but her heart still felt ripped in two. Wiping the last of her tears with the back of her hand, she looked up at her longtime friend. "You'd better come to LA and help me get through all this crap."

"Just try and stop me," Tasha laughed. "But first we need to have a going-away party."

CHAPTER 30

"The Scientist"

The phone in Ivan's pocket beeped, alerting him to an incoming text message and diverting his attention from a long, stressful but successful day at the spa. Pushing his white coat aside, he retrieved his phone and scrolled to the new message. Finally! It was Jaden asking him to come over for dinner. He excused himself from the patient waiting in the exam room for a moment.

Ivan read the message again. He'd made several attempts over the past few days to make plans or even just talk with Jaden, but she'd been busy—and a quieter than usual—since their return. He hadn't seen her since he'd dropped her at home on the way back into town, and their rapid-fire text messages, both dirty and sweet, had dwindled to sporadic one-liners. Work had demanded her attention before, but this time she seemed distant, not just stressed. Maybe he'd scared her off by moving too quickly. They'd only been together three months…but they'd shared so much, it just seemed natural. He sighed. Whatever this was, he couldn't put his finger on it, and it worried him.

Thinking positively, Ivan smiled as he envisioned the chance to catch up and get Jaden back into his arms. He quickly typed his response:

I'll be there as soon I'm done working, baby girl.

Turning his attention back to his patient, a Russian VIP who'd flown in just to see him about weight loss, Ivan smiled and felt a renewed enthusiasm. "All right, Mr. Abramov, how can I be of service?"

A few hours later when he'd finished with the last of his patients, Ivan wasted no time with paperwork or tidying up his office. He hopped on his bike and motored home as fast as he could. Reaching his condo, he jumped in for a quick shower. Not even bothering with a towel, he air-dried a bit, then tossed on a pair of jeans and his favorite red shirt.

He'd had wanted to do something extra special for Jaden, so as a tribute to her recent accomplishments he'd had her magazine cover framed in magnificent mahogany, complete with professional gift-wrapping. Now seemed like the perfect time to give it to her, and he grabbed the package and returned downstairs. Knowing he was only minutes away from seeing Jaden, the birds seemed to chirp louder, the air tasted saltier, and his step felt lighter as he strolled to catch a cab.

He slid into the backseat and exchanged pleasantries with the driver, but the cabbie seemed in no mood for a love-drunk fool. Ivan contented himself with watching the scenery outside the window, and within minutes they pulled up at Jaden's condo building. With a smile and a cordial thank you, he generously tipped the driver for the sub-par conversation he'd provided and hurried into the lobby, anxious to see his love for the first time in almost a week.

Ivan waited anxiously as the concierge called up, and after getting the go ahead, he practically skipped to the elevator. When he exited, the door to her apartment loomed in the distance, and with purposeful strides, he closed the gap between them. In his eagerness to see her, he knocked heavily on the door.

After what seemed like an eternity, especially since he could hear her pacing around in there — *what was she doing?* — the door swung open, and she was revealed.

"Baby girl, it feels like it's been an eternity! Look at you, stunning as usual." He darted in for a kiss before handing her the gift.

"What's this?" Jaden asked, only half-heartedly returning his kiss.

"It's nothing special, just a little something I had made." An alarm sounded somewhere deep within him.

"Ivan, you really shouldn't have." Jaden fingered the corner of the meticulously wrapped gift. She looked up at him and smiled before tearing at a corner of the paper. Her eyes grew teary the moment she saw what it was. "Thank you. I love it," she said, her voice thick with emotion.

Ivan pulled her into his arms. "It's not *that* nice, baby girl."

"No, it's not that." She rested her head against his chest and said nothing more.

"Hey, are you okay?" he asked as he brushed aside her inky hair. He had the sinking feeling that whatever was weighing on her mind would soon be weighing on his as well.

"Yeah, just tired," she lied. "It's been a long week. Why don't you have a seat on the balcony, and I'll get us something to drink."

"All right," Ivan said as he reluctantly released his hold on her. Ignoring the knot tightening in his chest, he slid open the doors and stepped outside, positioning himself for an optimal view of the ocean.

Jaden appeared a moment later carrying two glasses of red wine. Something was wrong. He knew it. She wasn't acting like herself. Ivan hoped it was exactly what she'd said it was — tiredness — but he knew there was something else. Every instinct in his body told him it wasn't good. In fact, his mind screamed that this was bad, very bad.

Whatever she needed to tell him was wearing on her. Not wanting her to bear the burden any longer, Ivan took charge of the conversation. "Jaden, I know you well enough by now to tell when something isn't right. The only other time I've seen you like this was in the restaurant when I came to see you for the first time." Taking a sip of his wine, he braced himself for the unknown and continued. "You should know I'm the easiest person to talk to. I've only been truly mad twice in my life — perturbed many times, but mad twice. There's nothing you can say that will make me angry or make me love you any less. You don't need to ease me into something, just be honest and straightforward."

Jaden looked into his eyes for a moment and took a deep breath. "Ivan, before we left for Pennsylvania, I was contacted by an agent and asked to audition for a national TV show."

Ohhh! Ivan already knew this story, because he'd been one to help facilitate that very thing happening. But why was this her reaction? "Uh-huh," he managed.

"When I got back, I found out I not only got the part, I've been selected to host my own show." Her eyes shone with tears, but she couldn't stop herself from smiling a little. "But accepting means I have to move to LA…in a week."

Just as life flashes before your eyes in the moments before death, the love life Ivan had created with Jaden now played like a movie across his mind—and she drove the car that threatened to run down his hopes and dreams for their life together. His gaze drifted, not away, but through her as she continued with a story he already knew by heart. Ivan could feel his miracle slowly shattering like a piece of untempered glass, and he only occasionally picked up bits and pieces of what she was saying. The details were trivial, because it all boiled down to whether he would break his commitment to never pursue another long-distance relationship.

As Jaden tried to compare their relationship to her lifelong dreams and find some sort of balance, it was as if she were reading his love life's biography. He'd had this conversation before, and it had resulted in him not only losing a girl he almost asked to marry him but a best friend as well.

"I know what you said about long-distance relationships, but—" Jaden choked back a sob. "I promise it'll be different this time. I don't want to lose you, and I've wanted to tell you ever since I found about all of this, but I didn't know how."

Jaden's five-minute story had passed by in what seemed to be months for Ivan. He looked out at the ocean as his heart cracked into pieces with the crashing of the waves. He was beyond happy that Jaden's dreams were coming true. She so desperately wanted this, which was why he wanted it for her as well. Would he have changed a thing from the second he laid eyes on her at the Winemaker's Dinner to this moment when she was stepping on his heart? No. He wouldn't have passed up the chance to know this amazing woman who shot guns, drank wine, seared tuna, and embodied his definition of love.

He knew Jaden had put hours of thought into the words she'd said to him, but Ivan needed only a heartbeat to formulate his response. He cared too much for the woman who stood across from him with emerald-glass eyes, pleading for him to risk their friendship for their love in a three-thousand-mile relationship. He his heart told him his decision was the right one, even though it was the hardest thing he'd ever had to say.

"Jaden, that is absolutely fantastic. I'm so happy for you and so proud of everything you've accomplished. You deserve the world, and this looks like your chance at it. This show is going to be a huge success, because people won't be able to help falling in love with you. I know I couldn't," Ivan said, trying for a smile. He stopped to compose himself, running a hand through his hair and fumbling with the silver hoop in his ear. "I want you to know that what we had was special, something that would make God himself envious. Our love will forever be tattooed on my heart."

Jaden uttered a strangled cry and brought her hands to her mouth. Ivan forced himself to continue speaking and willed his hands not to reach for her. "Like I told you before, risking our friendship on the chance of a long-distance relationship is something I just…I just can't do. But even though you're losing a boyfriend, you're keeping a best friend. *That* I can promise you, and I'll always support you and help in any way I can."

"Ivan, I love you more than you could ever imagine," Jaden immediately responded. "Losing you will totally break me."

"Baby girl, you have such an amazing time ahead of you, and I love you too. It's funny how once you're in the midst of a relationship you change as a person. Sometimes for better and sometimes for worse, but with you…I've never been better. You'll always have a fan in Miami—well, two since Tasha is here," he added, trying to fight the sadness that consumed him. Letting Jaden see how torn apart he was would only make things worse. "I can't ask you to stay, and I won't. This is your dream and what you've always wanted. Unfortunately, I can't go share it with you either. I have commitments here—patients, friends, work—all the things *I've* worked for. Please know I love you, Jaden, and I always will. Promise me you'll *never* forget our moments together."

With that, Jaden threw herself into his arms, sobbing hysterically. "I'm so sorry, so sorry," she wailed.

"Please, baby girl, never apologize for succeeding. You make me so proud."

As Jaden cried in his arms, Ivan Rusilko, a man of success and prestige, officially fractured into a broken heart. Everything else fell away as he stood at the edge of reason, overwhelmed by emotion. But he remained convinced he'd made the right decision. With Jaden pressed against his chest, they stood together on the balcony for what seemed like hours without saying a word. The Miami sun slowly sank beneath the horizon, and a cool breeze took its place.

Jaden cried into his shirt as his sure, strong hands stroked her hair, sharing this last moment as a couple. Ivan knew the second they parted, it would have to be over.

Jaden found his lips for a soft kiss, which was abruptly cut short as Ivan pulled away. He wanted nothing more than to take Jaden by the hand and lead her into the bedroom, to make love to her one last time, but he knew better. Making love again would only make things more difficult for both of them.

Instead, Jaden took a deep, cleansing breath, and hand in hand they walked inside.

As the awkward moment of departure became inevitable, Ivan fought back the beast. "Can I ask you one thing before you go?"

"Of course, anything," Jaden responded.

"Can I take you to the airport?"

"Oohhhhh," she uttered as a long sigh. But then she smiled. "Yes, I'd love that."

Taking her hand in his, Ivan kissed it softly and whispered, "Jaden, I always knew you'd be a star. Thank you for everything you've given me."

And with that, Ivan made his exit, a love-crippled man.

CHAPTER 31

"Going To California"

The next week wasn't easy. Ivan busied himself with work and exercise, but neither could heal the gaping hole in his chest, or the turmoil in his mind. He'd promised to be her friend, so he and Jaden had been texting each other very casually, and each message made the situation worse. He longed to send her the spicy little messages they'd once shared and to inevitably end up in her arms, no matter how long it took to find an open window in their schedules. He found himself second-guessing the decision he'd made, but he always arrived at the same conclusion. Too big a risk.

He'd even thought through the process of just packing up and moving, but that wasn't really a possibility. His new diet program was generating tons of buzz for the spa, so this would be a horrible time to leave, assuming his contract would even make it possible. And starting over in another city? Major career setback, maybe a career ender. His patients came to *this* facility to find him, and his network—both personal and professional—was here. Just too big a risk. Every scenario he played out ended in heartache. It was a lose-lose situation.

The sun didn't shine as brightly, the ocean seemed a dingy blue, and the feeling of walking on air had been replaced with a fifty-pound weight that hung heavily around his shoulders. Ivan also realized he'd broken one of his rules during their relationship: Never listen to your favorite music during emotional times. The songs that used to spark excitement deep within him, that had helped relax and energize him, now conjured up emotions and memories that consumed him.

Since no one yet knew about their breakup, his phone continued to vibrate with messages of congratulations on Jaden's success, as well as the usual inquiries from colleagues and friends about work, plans, and the upcoming weekend. He wasn't interested in any of them, but Ivan couldn't help but pause at a message from Tasha. He opened it and read through several times:

> Hi, Ivan. I know it's short notice, but we're having a going-away party for Jaden tonight at the restaurant. Starts at 8. I hope you can make it.

Tomorrow he'd taxi Jaden to the airport, and it would be hard enough saying goodbye to her then. No way could he cope with doing it twice and witnessing the heartfelt goodbyes between her and her friends tonight. He texted Tasha his reply:

> Sorry, but I have work commitments I can't get out of.
> Thanks for asking, though.

Unsure how much more congratulating he could take, and not wanting to talk to anyone, Ivan decided to take a vacation from all of it for a few days. He turned off his phone and stuffed it back into his pocket. He turned his focus to medicine and to getting himself back into his now-elusive groove.

A large banner that read *Congratulations, Chef Thorne!* hung across the main entrance of Bianca, and Geoff had closed an hour early to accommodate all the people planning to attend the soiree. A sea of familiar faces swam before Jaden's eyes as she made her way out into the restaurant, followed closely by Michael and Tasha. Teary eyed, Susan stood front and center with a large bouquet of flowers from the kitchen staff, and a white tissue stuck out of her shirt pocket. Nearby stood Geoff, looking even more somber than usual, and behind him stood Bert, Jaden's hand-picked *sous* chef, already wiping away the tears that gathered in the corners of his eyes. Even the food critic from the Miami *Herald* had made a surprise appearance. Jaden scanned the crowd for the one person she'd hoped would show up, but Ivan was nowhere to be seen.

Shrugging off the somber mood that threatened to descend upon her, Jaden forced a smile and joined in the festivities. Halfway through the party, her phone buzzed with an incoming text from Ivan.

Have a blast at the party, Jaden. See you in the morning! J

He called her Jaden…She'd become so accustomed to baby girl, and she suddenly realized how much she'd be missing it. *But life moves forward,* she told herself. Mustering her courage, she texted back:

Ivan, thanks, and I wish you were here for this. See you tomorrow early.

After a long string of well wishes and more than a few tears, Jaden, Tasha, and Michael excused themselves only to be stopped at the door by a very drunk and very upset waitress.

"I'm gonna miss you," Susan bawled as she grabbed Jaden in a hug and cried on her shoulder. "It's not going to be the same without you here."

"Susan," Jaden said soothingly, patting her friend on the back, partly to console her and partly to prevent the poor girl from going into hysterics. "It's okay, sweetie. You can come and visit whenever you'd like. As soon as I get set up out there, I'll email you my address and phone number. We won't lose touch, I promise."

"Really, you mean I can come and visit you in LA?"

"Of course you can. Besides, it's not like I'm never coming back to Miami. Tasha still lives here, so I'm sure I'll be back to visit everyone." *Yeah, everyone but Ivan,* Jaden thought. Would they ever get past this? What if she came back and he was with someone else-- would she be able to handle that? Jaden forced the thought from her mind. That problem wasn't going to be solved tonight.

With Susan under control, the three hailed a taxi and headed for home. Tasha and Michael seemed tipsy, but Jaden was stone sober. She'd had a few drinks to be sociable, but they'd had absolutely no effect. She unlocked the door of the apartment, and Michael and Tasha stumbled by her, giggling off to bed. Jaden looked at her watch. She had just enough time to catch a quick nap before her eight a.m. flight.

Still in her pajamas, Jaden stood in the doorway of the living room giving the apartment the once-over. She told herself she was making sure she hadn't forgotten to pack anything, but mostly she was just going to miss this place. A cold hand touched her shoulder and she jumped. Turning around, she came face to face with a teary Tasha. Michael stood at her side with his arm around her waist.

"Well, Chef, I guess this is it," he said.

"I'll be back to visit."

"You better be," Michael teased. "Tasha won't let you live it down if you don't." Untwining his arm from Tasha, Michael gave her a long hug.

"I'm going to miss you," Jaden whispered, her own eyes clogging with tears as she hugged him back. In the few short months they'd known each other, they'd grown to be good friends, and Jaden appreciated all he'd done for Tasha.

"I'll give the two of you some privacy." And with that, Michael disappeared down the hall, leaving Jaden and Tasha to say their goodbyes.

As they took a seat on the sofa, Tasha grabbed Jaden in a hug and cried, "What am I going to do without you?"

"The same thing you did before I moved to Miami," Jaden replied in the most reassuring tone she could muster. "Only this time, you won't be here alone. You'll have Micky."

"I know," Tasha cried. "But it won't be the same without you."

"I'll come back as often as I can, and we'll talk every day on the phone. It'll be like I'm still here. Maybe I'll come and spend a few weeks when the show is on hiatus. I'm sure they're not going to film year round."

"Do you promise?"

"I promise," Jaden said, somewhat reluctantly. Lately it seemed she'd made many promises, most of which she'd broken. If she were a woman of her word, she and Ivan would still be together. Jaden had promised him forever, and failed.

Wiping the tears from her eyes, Tasha stood up. "Call me as soon as you get there."

"I will."

"You're gonna be amazing. Ivan was right—you're a rock star." With one last hug, and a parting kiss, Tasha said her final farewell and went back to her bedroom.

Even though she knew Michael and Tasha were still in the other room, the apartment felt cold and empty, and Jaden felt helplessly alone. She knew she should be double checking her luggage and maybe sneaking a few moments of rest before Ivan picked her up, but she also knew sleep would elude her. In a sorrowful stupor, she trudged across the living room and sat down in front of the computer. Maybe checking her emails would help the time pass.

Opening her inbox, she found a new message from a Stacey Anderson with a subject line reading: *Welcome to the big leagues!* Jaden clicked on it and began to read.

> Hello, Jaden.
>
> Congratulations on becoming our new superstar. I hope you're ready for a whirlwind of publicity and excitement. Kevin Gibbs, owner of the network, and myself would like to meet with you on Tuesday. I know that's only a few days away, but in this business time is money. Looking forward to seeing you again.
>
> Stacey Anderson
>
> Casting Director, Bravo
>
> 555-818-3298
>
> stacey.anderson@thefc.com

Wait, "seeing you again"? What does that mean? Jaden wracked her brain trying to remember a time she'd been introduced to someone named Stacey Anderson. Maybe at one of the parties Ivan had taken her to? But surely she'd remember meeting someone *that* important. At a loss, Jaden turned off the computer, and within moments her phone beeped to alert her to an incoming text message. It was Ivan making sure she was up.

> I hope you're awake, beautiful. It's time to fly!

For a split second, Jaden let a smile creep onto her face. This was the first time Ivan had shown any humor or real cheer since their breakup—*was that what it was?* But her smile quickly faded. It was also the longest they'd gone without actually talking since they met. Then sadness washed over her, sending Jaden into an all-out panic attack. If this was the right thing to do, why was it so hard? Shouldn't she be happy now, not feeling uncertain? What if she were making the wrong choice by leaving? What if she were meant to stay in Miami and live out her happily ever after with Ivan? No, she told herself firmly. This was her dream, and she needed to take hold of it.

Jaden's fingers trembled as she tried to formulate an equally pleasant response.

Up and ready. Thank you, handsome.

She took her time dressing. She'd laid out comfy yoga pants and a top as the perfect ensemble for the six-hour flight to LA. With any luck she'd be able to get some much-needed sleep and arrive ready to jump right into the thick of things. Saying goodbye once had been hard enough, so instead of telling Tasha she was off, she scribbled out a note and left it on the kitchen table.

The morning breeze chilled her as she stood in front of her former building, but soon the black beast that had picked her up for their first date rounded the corner. The Jeep, with its top down, pulled to a stop in front, and Ivan slid out the driver's side door wearing flip flops, camouflage shorts, and a white tank top. Just one look at him and memories of the passionate nights they'd shared overcame her, but they were safely and promptly tucked away.

"Hey, girl," he said as he pecked her on the cheek and started to grab the luggage that sat on the curb.

"Hi." Jaden had been half hoping for a kiss on the lips. But what did she expect? He wasn't her boyfriend any more, merely her friend bringing a greeting.

Cramming the last suitcase into the back of the Jeep, Ivan returned to the passenger side and opened the door, ushering her inside.

"Always the gentleman," Jaden said as she took Ivan's hand and let him help her in.

The sun was still low on the horizon as Ivan pulled away from the curb and sped off in the direction of Miami International Airport. The greenish lights on the stereo clock cast an eerie glow inside the

Jeep, and they drove in silence, only occasionally glancing in each other's direction. She wanted to speak, but what was there to say? Nothing would change Ivan's mind. Or at least she was pretty sure…

"Are you okay with everything, Ivan?" she asked, breaking their silence.

Slowly turning to face her, Ivan offered a forced half smile. "Do you want the truth or the sugar-coated answer?"

"The truth," Jaden answered.

"I'm stuck between a rock and a hard place. Three years ago I would've packed up and followed you, or I would've asked you to stay. Or I might've even taken the chance on the whole long-distance-relationship thing."

Stopped at a red light, Ivan turned and faced her head on. "I won't lie, it sucks right now. But it's something I'll deal with, and in time get over — maybe not all the way over, but I'll get through it. I'm happy for you, Jaden, happy that your dreams are coming true. That's all I ever wanted for you, even if I'm not there to share it."

"Ivan…" She struggled for the right thing to say, but nothing would mend a broken heart, hers or his.

"It is what it is. We all have a cross to bear, and this just happens to be mine at the moment. But this too shall pass." Then he abruptly shifted the gears of the conversation before she could even formulate a response. "You excited, young lady? Ready for stardom?"

"Yeah, I think so," Jaden said after a moment. She'd been correct. There was nothing she could say to change his mind. "I'm scared shitless but excited."

"Don't be. They'll treat you great," he replied with a wink.

As the Jeep pulled to a stop in front of the departures area, Jaden leaned across and placed a tender kiss on his cheek, letting his addictive aroma fill her senses one last time. Damn, she was going to miss that smell. "Thank you for everything, Ivan."

He nodded sadly but said nothing.

Jaden watched as Ivan retrieved her luggage from the back of the car and placed it at the curbside check-in. He offered her a final look, and Jaden crumbled and rushed into his arms, giving him the patented Rusilko Bear Hug.

"Don't forget me," Jaden cried, clinging harder.

"How could I forget the best thing that's ever happened to me?" Ivan whispered low in her ear. Pulling back, he looked Jaden square in the face and smiled. "I stumbled across a quote last night, and it made me think of you," he said. "Life is short: Forgive quickly, kiss slowly, love truly, laugh uncontrollably, and never regret anything that made you smile. Jaden, you made my soul smile, and I'll never forget that."

Jaden nodded and watched as Ivan returned to his Jeep. With a final wave goodbye he drove away. "Don't cry because it's over," she said softly to herself. "Smile because it happened."

Jaden traversed the airport feeling isolated and put off. Less than two weeks ago she'd taken this exact route with Ivan as they made the trek to visit his family in Pennsylvania. She reached the gate with time to spare, which meant more time to mull over everything that had happened in the past few days. They hadn't been separated for an hour, and already Jaden found herself remembering the silly little things that had made their relationship so great: his random childish voices, the way they both loved cheesy, scary movies, the way she could get him hard with just a look, and the way he could get her wet by licking the base of her neck…or licking other things… They'd known each other so well after only a few months.

That's over now, Jaden scolded herself. *It's time to grow up and make grown-up decisions. I'm going to get on this plane, sit in my seat, fly across the country, and realize my dreams. I have to.*

The attendant at the counter announced the boarding call for first class passengers. Grabbing her personal items, Jaden prepared to board her flight — the flight that would lead to a dream but had taken away her miracle.

The wheels of the 747 touched down with a bone-rattling bump as Jaden and the other one hundred fifty passengers celebrated the end of the six-hour flight. She was in LA, which meant her new life as a celebrity chef had officially begun.

LAX was a mob scene compared to the laid back feeling of MIA. As she pushed her way through the throngs of people and followed the signs to the baggage claim, she kept a lookout for the driver the network was supposed to have sent to take her to her new apartment.

Well, her temporary, network-owned apartment that was hers to use until she could find a place of her own. The escalator carried her down toward the baggage claim, and Jaden noticed a Hispanic man with a bushy moustache holding a sign labeled *Thorne*.

Jaden couldn't help but be impressed. They'd actually sent someone. The network had really pulled out all the stops in their rush to get her to LA. "Hello," she said, approaching the man. "I'm Jaden Thorne."

"Good afternoon, Ms. Thorne," he said with a thick Spanish accent. "My name is Adam, and I'll be your chauffeur."

Adam? How un-Spanish, she thought as the pair waited to collect her bags. It was nice to have someone do all the heavy lifting for her, although it reminded her that Ivan was not here, grabbing her bags as usual. Of course schlepping her bags herself would probably have reminded her of that too. After gathering all of her belongings, Jaden followed Adam outside, then waited as he'd instructed while he went to pull the around.

As she waited, Jaden turned on her phone and sifted through her messages. There were several from various friends and family wishing her well, but there was nothing from Ivan. Disappointed and a little perturbed that he hadn't even texted her, she answered the important messages, letting Tasha and the network know she'd arrived, and then slid the phone back into her pocket.

Jaden took careful note of her surroundings as she slid silently into the backseat of the car. Sleek black leather covered the interior, black tint darkened the windows, and refrigerated air blew from the vents that encircled her. "This sure isn't a Jeep."

"No, ma'am, it's a Lincoln," Adam replied stiffly, not getting the joke. How could he?

They wove into the dense LA traffic and onto the freeway. Jaden noticed how different the landscape was. LA was brown and hilly, whereas Miami was colorful and vibrant. And the traffic was horrendous. Jeez, she didn't want to deal with *that* every day. Traveling twelve miles in just under two hours, they finally arrived at her new apartment.

A quaint, white, one-bedroom townhouse in a secluded community would serve as her abode for the next few months. It even came equipped with a garage, which her car could live in once it had been shipped across the country. Jaden unlocked the front door and stepped inside. Semi-new furnishings decorated the interior in a tasteful but rather bland style. It might not be the best, but heck, it was free, Jaden reminded herself. Following closely behind, Adam entered the living room and set the bags down in the middle of the floor.

"Thank you," Jaden said as she fished in her pocket for a tip.

Adam nodded, accepted the folded bills, and retreated from the townhouse, shutting the door behind him as he left. The sound of the door was very final, and Jaden was hit with the sudden realization that she was alone. But this was something she needed to do — or at least that's what she kept telling herself.

She poked her way through the townhouse, familiarizing herself with each of the rooms and where everything was located. Her bags still sat in the middle of the living room floor, but they'd have to wait until later. Tomorrow was a huge day. She had to meet this Stacey and the network owner, and she'd begin her new life as a celebrity chef, but for now all Jaden wanted to do was sleep. Digging in her biggest suitcase, she searched feverishly for her toiletry bag only to find an out-of-place envelope she didn't remember packing. She flopped on her bed in a heap and opened it, immediately recognizing the atrocious handwriting.

> Jaden,
>
> There will always be a taste of you in my mouth, the sound of your heart in my ear, and the feel of your skin etched in my mind. You deserve the world, so never settle for anything less. I will always cherish the time we spent as lovers and look forward to the memories we'll make in the years to come as friends.
>
> Your fellow turtle watcher,
>
> Ivan

How on earth had Ivan had the time to sneak this into her suitcase? She'd been standing beside him practically the entire time. *That's why he didn't call. He was waiting for me to find this.* Smiling, Jaden suddenly felt better about everything. She tucked the note back in the envelope and placed it on her dresser. Then, grabbing her phone, she texted the author of this sweet gesture:

I got the card, Ivan…Thank you for creating my first smile in Los Angeles.

CHAPTER 32

"Under Pressure"

Today was the big day. Jet lag slowed Jaden to a crawl as she opened the first of her suitcases and began to unpack. It was a dreaded chore, but if she wanted something clean to wear—or anything to wear, actually—it was a necessary one. She settled on high heels and her favorite blue sundress, one that could flaunt her curves yet look semiprofessional at the same time.

With the sundress in hand, she gathered her makeup case and headed for the first floor bathroom. She dumped the entirety of her makeup collection on the counter and set to work, somehow achieving the desired results in record time, even without Tasha's help. She then sifted through her jewelry case for accessories and found the tiger-eye rosary. She slipped it on as a necklace. Something so special could only bring her luck. With one last appraising look in the mirror, Jaden picked up her cell phone and dialed Adam, only to learn he was already waiting with the car out front.

It was early December, but LA hadn't seemed to notice. The breezy day taking shape, with temperatures to reach the mid-seventies, was but one in a string of so many days just the same. Perfect, Jaden supposed, but as she stepped out the door of the townhouse she rather missed the wall of humid heat that often greeted her in Miami. Nothing about this city was familiar. Even the air was different. Eager to focus on the upcoming meeting, not what she'd left behind, she raced down the front steps to where Adam stood with the car door open.

"I hope you know where you're going," Jaden teased as she slid into the car.

"Of course, Ms. Thorne. It's only five minutes away," Adam responded in the same no-nonsense tone of voice he'd used at the airport.

"Super." Jaden chuckled to herself. Either the man had no sense of humor whatsoever, his English was worse than she thought, or he was perpetually morose. In any case, he was a far cry from the free-spirited and fun-loving Miami Beachers she'd grown accustomed to.

As they made the five-minute drive to the meeting, Jaden's thoughts drifted back to her friends in Miami. So much for focus. The restaurant was just opening for dinner. Tasha was probably at the gym or watching TV, and Ivan was no doubt still elbows-deep in high-end Miami medicine at the spa. With her thoughts stuck on Ivan, Jaden didn't realize they'd arrived at Bravo's LA offices, or even that the car had stopped, until Adam opened the door.

"Right in there, Ms. Thorne." He motioned to the main entrance of the building. "Take the elevator up to the forty-fifth floor, and the receptionist will show you in."

"Thanks," she said, stepping back into the LA sunlight. As she crossed the mezzanine of the modern high-rise, she could see the rolling landscape of the Hollywood hills.

Jaden entered the elevator and pressed the button for the forty-fifth floor. The doors slid shut, revealing her reflection in their mirrored surface. Staring intently at herself, she realized her dream was about to come true. She was about to become a TV chef. You didn't get much more part of the scene than that. Jaden absently twirled the rosary in her fingers as the elevator began to rise, and her stomach began to flutter. Soft music floated through the air, only to be replaced by a chime as the elevator reached its destination. She expected to exit into a hallway, but instead, the doors opened directly into the waiting room of the network's offices. A middle-aged woman with brown, curly hair sat behind a grand desk that sported the all-too-familiar logo.

Looking up from behind a stack of papers, the woman smiled. "Good morning, Chef Thorne."

Stunned that the woman knew her name, Jaden managed to smile back and return the greeting. "Good morning."

With the press of a button, the receptionist announced her arrival. "Jaden Thorne is here to see you, sir."

"Excellent, send her in," a masculine voice answered.

"Please follow me," the woman instructed and led Jaden to a large pair of doors to the right of the waiting room. "Mr. Gibbs and Ms. Anderson are waiting for you."

The double doors opened revealing a long hallway. As the two women made the trek to the opposite end of the corridor, Jaden took in the posters that hung on either side. Each frame contained a picture of one of her predecessors — names and faces Bravo had helped make famous, or more famous. As they neared the end of the hallway, a plaque on a large wooden door came into view: *Mr. Kevin Gibbs, President and CEO.* The receptionist knocked on the door and a lump formed in the back of Jaden's throat. This was it, her time in the spotlight, her time to be the rock star everyone seemed to think she was.

The doors swung open and Jaden walked in, head held high. Spectacular floor-to-ceiling windows overlooking the Hollywood hills dominated one wall. To her left was small sitting area decorated with black leather and mahogany furnishings, and to her right sat two plush armchairs that faced an overly tanned, well-dressed, silver-haired gentleman whose face was largely obscured by a bushy beard.

He stood and greeted her with enthusiasm. "Ms. Thorne, what a pleasure to see you again, and under such different circumstances."

What? Was he making reference to some joke she was supposed to get? If so, it was totally lost on her. She had no clue who this guy was, other than the head of the network, of course. Searching her memory, Jaden shook his outstretched hand. "Yes, it's been a while."

He returned to his spot behind the large mahogany desk, and Jaden took a seat in one of the armchairs across from him. Where had she met him before? She'd met the CEO of Bravo and not even realized it? Impossible! She tried desperately to connect the dots but came up short. She prayed something would trigger a memory and she'd recall who this guy was before making an ass out of herself.

"You've had quite a ride the past few months, haven't you?" His gaze drifted to another large wooden door opposite the one Jaden had entered. "Stacey will join us in a minute. She had to step out to make a phone call."

Just who the hell are these people, and where do I know them from? Jaden was even more confused now. Stacey's email made it clear that the two of them had met before, and now Kevin Gibbs, the CEO of the network, was carrying on like they were old friends. Just then Jaden heard the door open.

"Ah, Stacey, there you are." Mr. Gibbs stood to greet the latecomer.

Jaden slowly turned and her eyes came to rest on a tall, slender figure approaching her: dirty-blonde hair, mid-thirties, perfect tits, perfect ass, and a smile from ear to ear—the mystery woman! *What the fuck?* Jaden could scarcely wrap her head around what she saw. Stacey was the blonde from the Winemaker's Dinner who'd draped herself on Ivan's arm, the woman she'd met at the party and at the restaurant not once, but twice—all without catching her name. *This* was the person responsible for the job offer that changed her life? No, it couldn't be! No wonder she'd seemed so personable, and yet so secretive, every time they'd talked. She was sizing her up, playing some Hollywood entertainment mind game.

Walking right up to Jaden, Stacey leaned down and gave her a big hug. "So great to see you again, girl! Is everything going okay? The house suitable?" she asked with great interest.

"Yeah, it's great. Thank you," Jaden responded in a confused tone.

"I am *so* glad Jessie was able to get you to that casting," Stacey proclaimed. "I told her it was of the utmost importance!"

Then it all hit Jaden like a ton of bricks as the pieces fell together. So many of the people she'd met in the last few months had been instrumental in the series of events leading to this exact moment. And Jaden suddenly realized who the puppetmaster pulling the strings for her was: Ivan. It had all started the day he'd tracked her down and made a romantic ass out of himself at the restaurant. He'd brought everyone to Bianca for a reason.

Jaden shook her head. How could all of this have happened without her clueing in? Had Ivan been intentionally light on the details in his introductions? And then it hit her. Patty, the birthday boy, had been a co-owner of a TV network. Was it Bravo? Jaden looked again at Kevin Gibbs and glimpsed a familiarity that hadn't revealed itself to her even moments ago. If she replaced the suit with a pair of jeans and designer shirt, removed the beard, and added an extreme tan he would look identical to… Jaden gasped. "Mr. Gibbs, you're Dr. Shaunnessey's partner. We met at his birthday party!"

"I was wondering how long it would take you to recognize me. I could tell by the look on your face that you didn't have a clue who I was." He laughed. "It must be the beard," he added, running a hand across his wooly face. "And please call me Kevin." Looking past her, he waved in an assistant who stood in the doorway.

Jaden sat silently, trying to process all of this new information as thankfully, the others busied themselves with some shop talk. Stacey, her assumed arch nemesis, the thorn in her side, the woman whose hair she'd fantasized about ripping out, turned out to be the casting director for a major cable channel. She had been the one who contacted Laura and set up the audition. As it turned out, Stacey was not the enemy, she was a true ally.

This overwhelming realization screeched to a halt when a familiar scent flooded her senses and stirred her soul. It sent a rush of warmth through her, followed by an array of feelings and memories: sand at her back, a trail of kisses that tattooed her neck, the chill of Pennsylvania air against her skin, wine teasing her lips, and the hum of Frank Sinatra on a momentous Sarasota night.

Then, clear as a bell, the voice she'd come to love and cherish called to her, "Baby girl."

It's him…he's here! Jaden whirled to find the man she adored and tell him she was wrong. He was her miracle and she wanted him no matter what the cost. But her excitement quickly faded to despair when she found a five-foot-four desk clerk with a bad haircut and acne standing before her, not the tall, long haired, muscled man she'd come to love. The smell—Ivan's smell had tricked her. The wrong man was wearing the cologne she'd come to associate with pure passion.

"What did you say to me?" she demanded, both disappointed and confused.

"Coffee, ma'am?" the assistant repeated, looking at her strangely.

"Oh. Ahhhhh, no. Thank you." Jaden looked at her lap and exhaled deeply. *What the hell was that,* she thought to herself. Then she remembered her realization.

Ivan. He was the catalyst of her ascension to stardom. He'd selflessly helped promote her career through his connections, and in what turned out to be his final act of devotion, he'd made the ultimate sacrifice for her: love suicide.

Jaden felt a knot tighten in her stomach. Ivan had given her everything, and in return she'd kissed him goodbye at the airport. *What the hell have I done?*

"Okay, so, I think we're about ready to get started, Ms. Thorne. Thank you for your patience," Kevin said, interrupting Jaden's swirling thoughts.

Jaden smiled weakly. She could feel two pairs of eyes boring into her. "Ahhh…" she said, completely unable to focus on what was happening in the office. Her thoughts lingered on the last time she'd seen Ivan: driving away from the airport, heartbroken and dejected. How could she not have seen all this? Jaden tried to rein in her emotions, but it was no use. Her heart filled with regret, even as she sat in the meeting that would change her life. She knew what she had to do.

"How many days until the first rehearsal?" she asked, her voice loud in the quiet room.

Stacey paused to glance at Kevin. "It'll be in five days," she answered slowly.

"I have some things to take care of first," Jaden announced, rising from her chair. Her body moved boldly, but inside she pleaded silently for them to understand.

Kevin studied her for a moment, and then he rose as well. "Okay, then. I guess that about covers it for now," he said, answering her silent plea. "We can reschedule a time to talk again."

"Thank you," Jaden practically shouted over her shoulder as she rushed from the room.

"Good luck!" she heard Stacey yell after her.

Everything passed by in a distorted rush as Jaden sprinted to Adam and the waiting town car. Dreams happened every night, but she knew now that Ivan — her miracle — was once in a lifetime.

CHAPTER 33

"The Letter"

"Back home, ma'am?" Adam was standing next to the town car as if he'd somehow expected her when Jaden came sprinting out of the building.

"LAX. How fast can we get there?" she yelled. Pushing past him, she opened her own door, jumped into the backseat, and motioned for him to pick up the pace.

A look of alarm on his face, Adam raced to the driver's side, hopped in, and sped off. "Is there anything I can do to help?" he asked, eyeing her through the rearview mirror.

"Do you know what time the next direct flight leaves for Miami?"

"There are several that leave this afternoon," he replied. "But the next one departs in an hour."

"Can we make it?"

"I'm not sure, but we'll sure as hell try." Evidently infected with Jaden's anxious excitement, Adam floored the town car, swerving in and out of traffic in his rush to make it to LAX.

Jaden jumped out of the car as it screeched up to the ticketing area. It was a good thing she hadn't unpacked everything, because her passport and all her other identifications still rested safely in the side pocket of her purse. Jaden ran through the airport at full steam, skipping to the front of the line and drawing nasty glares from the people behind her. A string of cuss words aimed at her echoed through the air, but she ignored them, tossing her credit card onto the desk and tapping her foot impatiently as the ticketing agent gave her a look.

"I need the next flight to Miami, please."

The stout, bearded man behind the counter guffawed as if he was privy to some sort of inside joke. "All we have is first class tickets, and it's fifteen hundred dollars."

"I don't care. I'll take it."

Ten minutes later Jaden was weaving her way through security and toward the terminal. She barely saw anything around her, because the only thing she could focus on was six hours away. She reached the gate and barely broke stride, heading right into first class boarding. Finding her seat, she slammed back a glass of cheap white wine and prepared to tempt fate one last time. The plane rumbled down the tarmac and took off, and Jaden closed her eyes, racing toward the man who'd sacrificed his heart for her dreams.

As the plane started to lose altitude, Jaden began to lose her nerve. What the hell was she doing? What if Ivan refused to see her? After all, she'd essentially told him she'd rather be famous than be with him. Imagining the situation reversed, Jaden cringed. The outcome looked bleak. Her unease continued to build as the plane made its final approach to Miami. Had she thrown it all away?

The wheels of the plane touched down, and the chipper voice of the flight attendant on the intercom reminded everyone to gather their personal belongings. Jaden laughed. Aside from her phone and her purse, everything else she owned was still sitting in the middle of the living room floor of her temporary townhouse back in LA. Jaden was glad to not be burdened by luggage. The sooner she could get out of the airport and back to Ivan, the better. As the exited the plane, the harsh artificial airport light contrasted with the darkness outside, and Jaden had to laugh again. After a six-hour flight and a four-hour time change, her body truly had no idea what time it was.

In her haste to get out of the airport and catch a taxi, Jaden almost didn't notice the man with a mane of brown hair standing at a nearby gate as she deplaned. Nor did she at first notice the well-worn jeans that covered his muscular legs. It wasn't until her eyes found the leather carry-on bag that sat on the floor beside him that Jaden began to sense something familiar. Her mind must've been playing tricks on her, because for a moment she thought of Ivan and the way he always wore the same jeans and carried the same bag when he traveled. Thoughts of Ivan triggered by her senses had fooled her once already today. This time she was determined to stay focused.

Still, her pace slowed to a crawl as she passed the man, who was turned away from her. The way he stood, his hair falling down around his neck and his right leg crossed over his left, perhaps because it felt wrong to do it the other way, was eerily familiar. Skirting around the waiting area, Jaden tried to get a better look. *Get a grip*, she told herself. Everything and everyone reminded her of Ivan. Her thoughts had been consumed with him for months.

Just as she was about to leave and find a taxi, the man turned — just enough for her to catch a glimpse of his profile. It *was* Ivan. He stood at the gate, listening to music on his phone and reading a sports magazine while he waited to board the redeye to…LA?

He must have sensed he was being watched because he slowly raised his eyes and looked around. And then he saw her. Jaden stood, unable to speak and barely able to see him through her tears. He dropped the magazine, grabbed the back of a nearby chair for a moment, and then he began to run.

With their eyes fixed on each other, they drew together like magnets, and their bodies locked as they met in the middle of the terminal. Jaden threw her arms around Ivan, weeping tears of joy, and Ivan buried his face in her neck. Her heart raced as she felt another miracle beginning to unfold.

"Baby girl, I'm so sorry," Ivan whispered against her neck. He hugged her tighter, as if she might disappear.

"No, Ivan. I'm the one who's sorry," Jaden said, her heart rejoicing to hear him call her baby girl again. "I know now what you did and what you sacrificed for me. I should have realized it a long time ago. I would pass on all the TV shows in the world if it meant keeping you. I should never have gone to LA."

Ivan looked deeply into her eyes. "Of course you should have."

"I should've what?" Jaden choked out.

"Jaden, as much as I love you and want you by my side, I would never want you to pass up an opportunity like that. Going to LA is the right thing to do. It's a chance of a lifetime. I know I said I'd never have a long-distance relationship again, but I can't imagine my life without you. These last few days—only hours, really—have been an eternity. No matter what I envision for my future, you're a huge part of it."

Jaden tried to pull back so she could look at him, but Ivan pulled her closer.

"I love you so much, and I was coming to LA to tell you I'll do whatever it takes to be with you. If it's a long-distance relationship, so be it. We've been given something most people only dream of, and I have no intention of ever letting you go again. Three months ago I wanted to help by introducing you to the right people, but everything spiraled out of control so fast, and before I knew it, my good intentions had cost me the thing I treasure most."

Before she could stop them, the words left her mouth. "Would you have done it if you'd known where it would lead? I mean, would you still have introduced me to those people?"

"If that's what you wanted," Ivan replied. "I would give you anything your heart desires, even if it means your happiness over my own."

He paused, and Jaden could feel his eyes lock on hers once again. "Why didn't you tell me when they called you in for the audition? You know I would've supported you."

Not having the courage to look into his face, Jaden turned away. She studied the floor as she spoke. "It was like a dream come true when I got that call, but I've come to realize my dreams mean nothing if you're not part of them."

Ivan cupped Jaden's cheek and turned her face to meet his. "I can see the love in your eyes," he told her. "Welcome home. Not to Miami, but to me."

He crushed his lips to hers, parting them gently. They shared a kiss that slowed the janitors in their work. There wasn't usually much to look at in the airport at this time of night, but theirs was quite a show. Breaking their embrace for just a second, Jaden stared up at Ivan. With a content and hopeful heart, she asked, "What now?"

"Tomorrow we can figure things out, but for now I'm going to take you home and have my way with you, baby girl." Ivan smiled, but Jaden could detect an unmistakably serious look in his eye, and a bolt of fire raced through her.

Ivan reached down to pick up his bag and slung it over his shoulder. Jaden joined her hand with his, and they walked back through the terminal toward the exit.

"I don't care what happens as long as it involves you, me, and the rest of our lives," Jaden declared with wild abandon. She suddenly felt free, so free.

"Well, Chef, this was only the appetizer. Just wait until you taste the entrée."

Acknowledgments
Dr. Ivan Rusilko

What is love?

Is it a lightning bolt that instantaneously unites two souls in utter infatuation and admiration through the meeting of a simple innocent stare? Or is it a lustful seed that is sown in a dark, dingy bar one sweaty summer's night, only to be nurtured with romantic rendezvous as it matures into a beautiful flower?

Is it a river springing forth, creating lifelong bonds through experiences, heartaches, and missed opportunities? Or is it a thunderstorm that slowly rolls in, climaxing with an awesome display of unbridled passion, only to succumb to its inevitable fade into the distance?

I define love as education…

It teaches us to learn from our mistakes, capitalize on our opportunities, and make the stupidest of decisions for the rightest of reasons. It gives us a hint of what "it" should be and feel like, but then encourages us to think outside the box and develop our own understanding of what "it" could be.

Those that choose to embrace and learn from love's educational peaks and valleys are the ones that will eventually find true love, that one in a million. Those that don't are destined to be consumed with the inevitable ring around the rosy of fake I love yous and failed relationships.

I have been lucky enough to have some of the most amazing teachers throughout my romantic evolution, and it is to them that I dedicate this book. The lessons in life, passion, and love they taught me have helped shape who I am today and who I will be tomorrow.

To the love that stains my heart, but defines my soul…I thank you.

ACKNOWLEDGMENTS

Everly Drummond

What started off as a whimsical idea has spiraled into something more than I could have ever hoped for. If it wasn't for the playful and charismatic nature of Ivan Rusilko, this book might have forever been nothing more than an errant thought. Your stories, humor, openness, honesty, and good nature brought this story to life, and it has been a pleasure collaborating with you. I can say with absolute certainty that is has been one of the most exciting, albeit intense, years of my life. Thank you.

Thank you to the awesome team at Omnific Publishing: Elizabeth Harper, Micha Stone, Traci Olsen, Lisa O'Hara, CJ Creel, and our amazing editor, Jessica Royer Ocken — the gurus behind this insane idea. You saw the potential in this little endeavor of ours when no one else would.

And thank you to all of my readers for all of your kind words and well wishes. You encourage and inspire me to continue telling my story.

A huge thank you goes out to Katie Byrne, the winner of our "Name That Character" contest. What started as a simple online conversation has grown into a friendship of epic proportions. Your friendship and advice have become a constant in my life, one that I hope to have for many years to come.

And what kind of person would I be if I didn't send out a special thank you to my peanut gallery: Maggie Smith, Chris Gilpin, and Wendy Shores. You put up with my craziness without question. Thank you can't even begin to describe my gratitude for all that you have done. I love you guys so much.

And last but not least, a heartfelt thank you to all of my family and friends. I am truly blessed to have been surrounded by so many amazing people. I love you all with every fiber of my being. If it wasn't for the love and support of Ed Wilkinson, Loretta Drummond, Lynn Wilkinson, and the rest of the Wilkinson and Drummond clans, I can say with certainty that I wouldn't be where I am today. Thank you.

About the Author

Dr. Ivan Rusilko, DO, CSN, PT, is an accomplished weight loss, wellness, physical enhancement and sexual health physician affiliated with the prestigious MIAMI Institute in Miami, Florida. A certified sports nutritionist, champion bodybuilder, international male fitness model, and former Mr. USA 2008 and 2010, Dr. Ivan graduated from the Lake Erie College of Osteopathic Medicine in 2010 and sits as the national media and public relations expert and spokesperson on diet, exercise and sports nutrition for the American Osteopathic Association (AOA).

Dr. Ivan has been a feature health writer and lifestyle coach for numerous magazines and online publications including *The Washington Times* and *Quarter Life Health*.

With his debut novel, *The Winemaker's Dinner: Appetizers*, co-authored by Everly Drummond, Dr. Rusilko is excited to offer a male voice in a predominantly female authored genre. Always one with a story to tell, he hopes to continue writing, exploring new genres and projects.

He is proud to bring two of his passions, his medical wellness and sexual health background and writing together in this unique project. He hopes that The Winemaker's Feast Trilogy will help spark an enthusiasm and ignite liberation among women, inspiring them to celebrate their sensuality and focus on their sexual health in order to achieve a better quality of life.

About the Author

As a student of the Centennial College Social Service Worker program, and the Trent University Biology program, Everly Drummond had a previous life in administration and transportation before launching her career as a writer. Everly's other writing projects include City of the Damned, a paranormal romance series, and *Blood of the Ancients*, a YA paranormal romance. All four novellas in the City of the Damned series have appeared on the Amazon.com bestseller list. Everly resides in Toronto, Ontario, where she is currently working on the second installment to *The Winemaker's Dinner* with co-author, Ivan Rusilko.

Romantic Suspense

Whirlwind by Robin DeJarnett

The CONduct Series: With Good Behavior and *Bad Behavior* by Jennifer Lane

Young Adult

Shades of Atlantis and *Ember* by Carol Oates
Breaking Point by Jess Bowen
Life, Liberty, and Pursuit by Susan Kaye Quinn
Embrace by Cherie Colyer
Destiny's Fire by Trisha Wolfe
Streamline by Jennifer Lane

Anthologies

A Valentine Anthology including short stories by Alice Clayton, Jennifer DeLucy, Nicki Elson, Jessica McQuinn, Victoria Michaels, and Alison Oburia

Erotic Romance

Becoming sage by Kasi Alexander
Saving sunni by Kasi & Reggie Alexander
The Winemaker's Dinner: Appetizers by Dr. Ivan Rusilko & Everly Drummond